What the critics are saying...

ಐ

"Sylvia Day is a terrific writer. One of few who understand the fine art of crafting top shelf romantic erotica." ~ *WNBC.com*

"...wickedly entertaining..." ~ *Booklist*

MISLED

"Whew! Talk about an intense, suspenseful passionate novel! Misled is an amazingly fascinating book. From the beginning, Sylvia Day captured my attention and had me setting on the edge of my seat until the very last word was read. This is a keeper." ~ *Erotic-Escapades*

"Misled is an engrossing, well crafted story of vampires and love. The plot moves quickly, with sizzling hot love scenes that will have you eagerly turning the pages. Sylvia Day has written an erotic explosion of secrets, love, and vampires that will leave you begging for more." ~ *Romance Divas*

"Misled is dark and erotic with suspenseful twists, just like the main characters. The sex scenes require availing yourself of something ice cold while following these alphas from one sector to another, chasing both bad guys and each other in their attempts to find out just who is being Misled." ~ *Romance Reviews Today*

"Sylvia Day will definitely be on my must buy list in the future. From dodging bullets, hiding from one another, to hunting a traitor, and white hot seduction, Misled is not a book to be missed." ~ *The Road to Romance*

KISS OF THE NIGHT

"Ms. Day did an astonishing job of depicting a great emotional connection between Briana and Alexei, which I found to be highly arousing. I also applaud Ms. Day on a wonderful job of hiding the identity of Briana's would-be killer - I was totally shocked. This is definitely another keeper to add to my collection." ~ *Erotic-Escapades*

"This romance has your dark-Knight in shining armor and a damsel who, although in distress, handles the situation with finesse. With a strong heroine, a romantic hero, and great storytelling, this is a trip of a life time!" ~ *Romance Divas*

"Kiss of the Night is an intriguing tale that readers will come back to again and again. The love scenes are sensual and steamy and the plot is action packed. Sylvia Day has penned a wonderful vampire story that is sure to keep readers coming back for more." ~ *Romance Junkies*

"Kiss of the Night is one of the sexiest, most uninhibited love stories I have ever read. The action plot is very intriguing, and even I did not know who was trying to kill Briana until the last chapter. Sylvia Day knows how to write an erotic vamp story that will please paranormal lovers to the very end."~ *Fallen Angels Reviews*

Sylvia DAY

DECLASSIFIED: *Dangerous* Dark Kisses

ELLORA'S CAVE
ROMANTICA PUBLISHING

An Ellora's Cave Romantica Publication

www.ellorascave.com

Declassified: Dark Kisses

ISBN 1419955284
ALL RIGHTS RESERVED.
Misled Copyright© 2005 Sylvia Day
Kiss of the Night Copyright© 2005 Sylvia Day
Edited by Briana St. James
Cover art by Syneca

Trade paperback Publication September 2006

Excerpt from *Ellora's Cavemen: Dreams of the Oasis II*

With the exception of quotes used in reviews, this book may not be reproduced or used in whole or in part by any means existing without written permission from the publisher, Ellora's Cave Publishing, Inc.® 1056 Home Avenue, Akron OH 44310-3502.

This book is a work of fiction and any resemblance to persons, living or dead, or places, events or locales is purely coincidental. The characters are productions of the authors' imagination and used fictitiously.

Warning:

The following material contains graphic sexual content meant for mature readers. This story has been rated E–rotic by a minimum of three independent reviewers.

Ellora's Cave Publishing offers three levels of Romantica™ reading entertainment: S (S-ensuous), E (E-rotic), and X (X-treme).

S-*ensuous* love scenes are explicit and leave nothing to the imagination.

E-*rotic* love scenes are explicit, leave nothing to the imagination, and are high in volume per the overall word count. In addition, some E-rated titles might contain fantasy material that some readers find objectionable, such as bondage, submission, same sex encounters, forced seductions, and so forth. E-rated titles are the most graphic titles we carry; it is common, for instance, for an author to use words such as "fucking", "cock", "pussy", and such within their work of literature.

X-*treme* titles differ from E-rated titles only in plot

remise and storyline execution. Unlike E-rated titles, stories designated with the letter X tend to contain controversial subject matter not for the faint of heart.

Contents

Misled

~11~

Kiss of the Night

~129~

Also by Author

❧

Ellora's Cavemen: Dreams of the Oasis II *(Anthology)*
Wish List

About the Author

❧

Sylvia Day is the bestselling author of erotic romantic fiction set in most sub-genres. A wife and mother of two from Southern California, she is a former Russian linguist for the U.S. Army Military Intelligence. Called "up-and-coming" by Romantic Times and "wickedly entertaining" by Booklist, Sylvia is quickly building a name for writing emotional erotic works for the preeminent publishers of erotic romance.

When she's not working on her next book, you can find her chatting with visitors on her weblog, message board and chat loop. Stop by http://www.SylviaDay.com to say hi and meet all her bad boy heroes.

MISLED

Dedication

This story is dedicated to two fabulous women — Tawny Taylor and Jordan Summers. Tawny for holding the "Some Like it Hot" contest where it became a finalist, and Jordan for reading the contest entry, getting in touch with me and becoming a dear friend. Both women gave me a much-needed dose of confidence at the start of my career.

Thank you both.

Prologue

Sable Taylor was going to jail for sure this time.

And Derek watched the events leading up to her arrest with a slight smile.

Leaning back, he rested a broad shoulder against the wall and crossed his arms. Sable was no more than a blur to the humans who milled around Windemere Court's Palladian-style City Hall, but his vampire sight caught her movements without any trouble at all. The bounty hunter raced along the white stone walls, her lithe body moving with little strain as she chased the murderer they were both pursuing.

He could help her, he supposed, but Sable wouldn't appreciate it. Despite his job as a Special Task Force agent, he was the enemy to her, direct competition in the capture of wanted criminals. He did it for justice, she did it for money, but he didn't think less of her. She'd earned his respect, in addition to more carnal interest. An interest she returned, but refuted at every oportunity.

When they'd first met he'd been a rookie and he'd learned a lot by watching her in action. He'd see her in a flash, a brief moment of sharp recognition, before one of them, usually him, made off with their quarry. Every time he saw her she was more beautiful than he remembered. Sable honed her body with hard training and a diet of blood. Her hair was jet black, deeper in color than his own raven locks and completely straight, a long curtain of silk. Her skin was as pale as starlight and just as luminous. And her eyes—he dreamed about her eyes. They were a rich blue so startling the sight of them always caught him off guard.

He'd lusted after her since the moment he'd first seen her. He had smelled her lush scent and heard the barely-there beat of her heart, and he'd known she was one of his kind. The last two years of watching Sable work—admiring her skill, her daring and her bravery—had only made him want her more. Their work, by nature, was a lonely existence. Always in pursuit, hunters never stayed in any one place long enough to become attached to anything. Or anyone. Sable knew what his life was like, because she lived one similar to it. That affinity gave their inevitable pairing a common thread he looked forward to exploring.

But first they had to get through this capture.

They were hunting Jared Ione, one of their kind who'd crossed the line between drinking to live and drinking to kill. Jared was a vampire in his physical prime but he was barely staying ahead of Sable, whose physical stamina made Derek's jaw ache and his fangs descend. Imagining all that energy in his bed was enough to make his cock hard. Just once he'd like a lover that gave as good as she got—an equal, his match.

He expected it would take another minute at most before the authorities in City Hall put an end to the chase. Windemere had a law against vamps using their superhuman abilities in public buildings. It was considered too dangerous to humans to be in the path of vampires running at full speed. A straight-on collision was often deadly. But Sable was known for ignoring any laws that got in her way. With her uncommon beauty and blatant, innate sex appeal, she could usually talk her way out of any scrape. But this time, Derek was going to step in and apprehend her before she had the chance to do any sweet-talking. He was tired of waiting for her to come around to his way of thinking, which included a couple of weeks and his four-poster bed. Two years, damn it. He'd spent two years lusting for her.

Today he was going to get what he wanted.

As he'd predicted, two Windemere officers stepped into view and one of them took aim with a net gun. The built-in tracking device locked onto the racing vamps and the officer fired, encasing the two straining bodies in a single net. With a stunning crash they fell to the floor, both of them growling in near-deafening frustration. Startled humans scattered with piercing screams. Derek pushed off the wall and strolled to the rescue, flashing his badge with a smile.

"Hello, officers," he greeted.

"Damn you, Atkinson!" Sable yelled, fighting futilely against both the entrapment and the vamp locked with her. With a low snarl, she reached for her blaster and neutralized Ione.

It took a few minutes to untangle her, then another minute more to cuff the unconscious vamp and hand him over to the waiting officers.

"He's my catch!" Sable complained, setting her hands on shapely hips and glaring at him. Dressed in a black sleeveless bio-suit, every ripe curve was displayed to his view.

Derek licked his fangs which had descended, as they did whenever a vamp was hunting...or lusting. It was part of the mutation brought on by the virus. *Damn, she was hot.* Long legs and curvy in all the right places, with full breasts and a lot of attitude. He really liked the attitude. She was one hundred percent pure alpha female. "Turn around."

"What?" She stood her ground.

"I've got to cuff you."

"*What?*"

He stepped closer and breathed her in, his body instantly waking to full arousal. It took everything he had to fight off a hard-on. Her scent called to him on the cellular level, stirring his blood and then sending it straight to his cock.

"What the hell are you doing, Atkinson?"

He reached around her waist and set the cuffs against her wrists. They measured the circumference automatically and secured with a soft click. "Saving you from a month in jail."

With her breasts pressing into his chest, Derek didn't want to move. But he had to get her out of Windemere before the authorities changed their minds and decided to keep her. Since he had no intention of letting her out of his grasp, that wouldn't be good. For a variety of reasons, he didn't need to attract trouble from headquarters. But he'd do it for Sable.

He wanted her bad enough.

Derek set his hand on the curve of her ass and prodded her down the main hallway, then off to the transport bays. They weaved through the fluted columns, skirting the crowd that had gathered to watch the arrest.

"They can't see us now," she said in a furious whisper. "Let me go!"

He laughed. "That's all the gratitude I get for saving that sweet ass of yours?" He gave a firm squeeze and then pushed her up the ramp of his waiting Starwing, following directly behind.

His gaze dropped to her seductively swaying hips and he was lost. Totally and completely consumed by lust. He hit the lock and the ramp lifted behind him. The sudden vacuum of the ship amplified her appeal. Finally, they were enclosed together, tucked away from the rest of the universe. Free to catch their breath and get to know one another. In every way possible.

Two damn years. He should have lost interest, but he liked her too much. She was unique. In all of his centuries, he'd never met a woman like her.

Sable's eyes narrowed as he unzipped his bio-suit. Her fangs descended as she hissed at him. "I'm grateful, but I'm not *that* grateful. You just cost me one hundred and fifty thousand credits, that's payment enough."

Her frame was stiff, her glare unwelcoming but the scent of her arousal permeated the air. Sweet and ripe like cherries, it was intoxicating. The hard-on he'd avoided before swelled with a vengeance, his cock hardening instantly and painfully.

"If you'd shown a little patience, Ione would have left City Hall eventually."

"I can't afford to have patience, Atkinson, when you're hunting the same bounty as I am."

Derek let his suit drop past his hips to pool on the deck. He watched with satisfaction as her eyes darkened at the sight of his rampant erection.

"Stay away," she said in a choked voice.

"Come on now, baby. Be honest. Staying away is the last thing you want me to do."

Sable backed up warily. "You may be thinking about your dick, but I'm thinking about my accounts. And right now they're in need of a credit infusion." She tried to race past him to the cargo bay door, but he'd anticipated the move and easily blocked her exit.

"Since you took Ione right out from under me, I need to capture Castle," she snapped. "He's worth almost as much. I don't have time for this if I want to pay my bills."

Derek reached out and slowly lowered the zipper of her suit, giving her the opportunity to wrench away, if that's what she truly wanted. He growled his approval when she didn't move and then shuddered as the lush valley of her cleavage was revealed to him.

"We'll get our man, baby," he assured her in a voice made husky with desire. "I have it on good authority that Castle will be at Deep Space 12 in two days. We'll catch him then. In the meantime, we have some time to spend together."

His fingertip drifted across the soft swell of her breast. "I know you feel it, too," he breathed, "this need between us. We've got two days, we're going in the same direction, why shouldn't we have a little R&R and burn this thing out. I don't know about you, but it's starting to affect my job. I can't think about work when I'm thinking about you."

"My ship—"

"I'm towing it," he said quickly, jumping on that telltale bit of capitulation.

"You planned this!" she accused.

"Now how could I know you'd break the law in Windemere?" he pointed out innocently. "Don't blame me for taking advantage of an opportunity you presented me with."

As he studied the creamy beauty of her exposed skin, his voice lowered further. "Can I help it if watching you work makes me hot?"

She swallowed hard, her blue eyes wide. "It does?"

"Hell, yes. All that power and stamina. You think fast and act faster. It turns me on."

"I've known men who are threatened by my work."

"You've known idiots."

He stepped closer, suppressing a smile as she continued to hold her ground. Sable was staying put because she wanted to, not because he was making her. He'd tried in the past to use his sensual call on her, a vampire survival mechanism that helped them subdue prey so they could feed. He was much older than she was and therefore more powerful, but she was always able to throw off his calling with ease. He didn't mind, it meant she was seduced by *him* and not the vampire within him.

He, in turn, was seduced by everything about her.

Sable was too much of a novice in the ways of vampires to know how to use her calling, but she had it just the same. Swirling around her like a thick fog, she radiated sex and desire. As he stepped closer, he was pulled into her sensual spell, pulled into her until he could think of nothing else. Wanted nothing else.

His hands reached out and tangled in the long silk of her hair. Clenching his fists, Derek pulled her head back, exposing the ivory column of her throat. He could hear her blood flowing and could see it pulsing the large vein under the nearly translucent skin. He leaned over her and stroked it with his tongue in a slow, deliberate back-and-forth glide. Sable moaned softly, her pose almost one of supplication, if not for the predator's fangs that betrayed her true nature.

It was her very nature that most appealed to him and in celebration of that, his mouth moved upward over her jaw. He licked her lips and then her fangs, growling when her tongue reached out and brushed against his.

With a quick tap on the cuffs, they released and fell to the deck. He reached between the open flaps of her suit, slipping his hands over her shoulders and pushing the bio-suit down her arms. The touch of her skin burned his palms and he knew she would scorch him alive when he fucked her. The mere thought of it made sweat mist upon his skin.

"Tell me to stop now," he groaned. "If that's what you want."

She bit her lower lip, her fangs causing tiny droplets of crimson to appear. The scent of her blood drove him to madness. The rest of her suit came off in shreds as his mouth lowered to hers.

Consumed by his frenzy, Sable gripped his shoulders and returned his kiss with equal passion. Her nipples, hard and peaked tight, stabbed into his chest. He pulled her closer until she spread her legs and rubbed the slick heat of her sex along the length of his cock. The warmth of her body, the sultry scent of her arousal, the sweetness of her blood, all combined to make restraint impossible. But he didn't need restraint. This was Sable, a vampire with the heart of a warrior and a body to back it up. He didn't have to coddle her. She wouldn't let him even if he wanted to.

"Touch me," she said into his mouth, and Derek realized he stood frozen and achingly aroused. Sable undulated against him, her thighs a firm cradle for his erection. He was covered in her cream and about to come from the sheer wonder of her cunt stroking back and forth across his cock.

Almost afraid to touch her and lose control, he placed his hands at her waist, his fingers gliding over her soft skin. Her tongue was fucking his mouth in the most erotic dance and Derek shuddered, loving how she took what she needed without hesitation. This wasn't just for him or just for her. They were in the moment together, something he'd anticipated but still found wonderfully unexpected.

Sable placed her hands over his and directed them to her breasts, pressing the hard, tight tips deep into his palms.

"Sable..." He groaned, his eyes closing as he kneaded the breasts he'd dreamed of for years, awed by how full they were despite how lean she was. Bending over, he lowered his head and took her in his mouth.

She gasped and arched into him. "Suck harder."

Derek trapped a ripe nipple against the roof of his mouth and suckled her, his cheeks hollowing on every drawing pull. Sable begin to quiver and then progressed to outright shaking until her legs gave way and he held her suspended in his arms, arched over his forearms, his mouth working her toward orgasm.

"Don't."

He lifted his head. "Don't what?"

"Don't make me come like this." Arching her hips, she ground her pussy into the root of his shaft, her short nails digging into his biceps. "Give me your cock."

Tightening his grip on her torso, Derek leapt, pinning her against the bulkhead, their feet dangling as he plunged into her creamy pussy and sank his fangs deep into her throat.

"Derek!" she screamed in surprised pleasure and pain, bucking against him in a way that made rational thought impossible.

Her tight cunt clung to his aching shaft, warm and welcoming. Her legs encircled his hips, pulling him inside with the physical strength he so admired. She melted around him, his cock clenched in a slick fist and bathed in the juices of her arousal. And she tasted liked heaven.

Sable had never called him by his first name before and somehow the simple familiarity touched him in a way he hadn't experienced in centuries. Raw, carnal need burned through his veins as her blood gushed down his throat, settling heavy and insistent between his legs. He slid out of her, his cock drenched with her cream, and she whimpered, a soft sound of protest that urged him to fuck her with slow, deep plunges. Her moan reverberated through the metal confines of his ship.

Derek gripped her thigh, opening her so he could fuck her pussy with steady, rhythmic pumps of his cock. *Damn you*, he thought, awash in pleasure he knew would be addicting. The feel of her cunt as he circled his hips and screwed deep into her was dizzying. He felt drunk on her, intoxicated by her taste and scent.

Her left cheek rested against the cool bulkhead, giving him access to her lovely throat and the elixir that flowed in the veins just beneath the surface. Her eyes were closed, her mouth parted. "Derek," she said softly, her voice slurred. "You feel so good…"

He was glad they had two days, because it would take at least that long before he had his fill.

He tore his mouth from her throat with a curse. "I need to fuck you. Hard."

"*Yes.*"

His jaw clenched tight, Derek abandoned his leisurely pace and fucked her like the animal he was, pounding into her tight, hot pussy with such force he shoved Sable up the bulkhead and onto the ceiling. The sensations were too much, coming on too fast—her full breasts pressed to his chest, her cunt milking his cock rhythmically, her breath gusting across his ear as she moaned his name in a primal chant of mindless pleasure.

"Take me," he growled, offering his throat to her. His eyes slid shut as her fangs pierced his skin, flooding him with heat and burning desire. He was going to come, he couldn't hold it back. His balls drew up tight, heavy with the semen he was about to empty inside her.

He reached out with his calling, establishing a mental connection. Normally he kept his thoughts to himself when his orgasm was upon him. He considered it a personal moment, not something he shared beyond his outward appearance of pleasure. Sometimes he eavesdropped on his partner's thoughts, just to make certain he was pleasuring her as much as possible, but his release was his own.

But this joining was different. He was so profoundly satiated by the act of fucking Sable that he felt almost...*grateful*. And he hated that he was so aroused, his balls rock-hard, his swollen cock aching, that he wasn't going to sate her in return.

In seven centuries, he'd never finished before his partner. Never. So he decided to share his pleasure with her, hoping she would find some satisfaction simply from giving so much of it to him. He also wanted to know her, to see into her thoughts and ascertain the pureness of her motives, because suddenly he didn't want to be just another fuck to her.

She was writhing over him, pinned between him and the ceiling, purring like a wildcat as she fed. He gripped her thighs and spread them wide, pumping his cock deep inside her.

The lushness of her body completely overwhelmed him. Sex wasn't meant to be like this, making a man mindless with need and out of control. This was deadly, ensnaring. He'd never get free.

Her silken pussy gripped his shaft in decadent ripples and he came, howling in rapture so intense it was painful. Derek poured the excess of sensation into her mind, showing her the dazzling blindness of his orgasm until Sable stiffened against him and burst into her own release, an orgasm so powerful she gripped his cock like a vise, holding him inside her as if she never wanted to let him go.

He didn't want to let her go either.

Misled

He had two days to convince her to give him a chance. After two years of waiting, Derek didn't hold out much hope, but he'd try his best. Thankfully his best was pretty damn good.

Firm in his intent, he lowered them to the floor and carried Sable to his bed.

Chapter One

Sable had found her prey. She could smell the fear pouring from him in misty waves, even over the odors of stale beer and cigarettes.

He knew she was hunting him.

Her mouth curved in smile so feral the men who watched her with lusty eyes looked away, their interest doused instantly. Stepping further into the dimly lit bar in the Deep Space 12 concourse, her hand dipped automatically to the lasersword held in the holster on her thigh. It was illegal to use weapons in the concourse, it was illegal even to carry a weapon but she had docked in the waste removal bay, affording her the opportunity to slip past security.

Scowling, she sniffed the air to check on her fugitive, Butch Castle, but also to search for another scent—one so masculine and virile it drove her to madness. In fact she could still smell it on her skin and it was keeping her hot and horny, distracting her when she needed to be the most focused. She forced herself to concentrate, tuning out the background music in the small bar and the paging of flight information echoing in the terminal behind her. Her focus narrowed, a huntress closing in for the kill.

Her shoulders relaxed when she confirmed she was the only vampire in the room. Still, Sable knew she didn't have long before Derek caught up with her. The handcuffs she'd used to shackle him to the bed would hold, but the bedposts wouldn't. She'd be damned if she'd let him steal another fugitive from her, even if he was the best fuck she'd had in over a century.

She stepped further into the bar…

"You know," purred a deep velvety voice behind her. "A guy could take it personally when his woman fucks him senseless and then leaves without a kiss goodbye."

Heat pooled instantly at the top of her spine and spiraled downward. Shocked, Sable spun around. "What the hell?"

Derek Atkinson stood barely an inch away, his strong hands gripping his narrow hips as he eyed her with his silver stare—a stare still molten with desire for her. "I wasn't done with you yet. I was just taking a power nap before we started again."

A shiver went through her body at his words. His raking glance stripped her of her clothing and left her naked to his view. *He'd wanted more of her? After two days straight of mind-blowing sex?* The man was an animal.

Her nostrils flared. Standing this close to him she could finally smell his delicious scent buried under the overwhelming smell of herself. No wonder she hadn't detected him sooner.

His eyes danced with devilish amusement. "I thought I was in pretty good shape, but I guess not if I'm falling asleep and you still have the energy to get up and chase my fugitive."

That arrogant comment penetrated her astonishment. "He's not *your* fugitive!"

He cupped her cheek with a warm hand. Instantly her skin grew hot, her pussy wet, her nipples hard. Even after two days straight of Derek's addicting carnal attentions she was still ready fuck him again. Immediately. Her fangs slid downward in anticipation.

"Sable, sweet." He smiled, his sensual lips curling upward to reveal pearly white fangs even longer and more deadly than her own.

Her mouth dried instantly.

His voice lowered and she knew he smelled her arousal. "You're a talented hunter, baby, no doubt about that. But your operation is small and you're often ill-equipped. If you just let me—"

Out of the corner of her eye, she saw Butch Castle edging toward the exit to the main concourse. Faster than the human eye could see her, she leapt over the tables between her and her prey. She tucked the man, easily twice her body weight, under her arm and left Derek without looking back. She heard him shout after her as she crawled along the wall to the traffic-free ceiling and ran to her ship. And then she couldn't hear anything with Butch screaming in terror as they flew through the concourse upside down, his human eyes unable to see more than a blur.

Sable could sense Derek swiftly gaining ground and cursed under her breath. She was no match for him physically, as he'd proven on several occasions in the past, and she was weighted down with the screaming human. She saw her turn coming up but maintained her lightning speed, feinting to the left at the last possible moment. Derek blazed past them. The ruse bought her only a few seconds but it was long enough for her to enter her transport and shut the cargo bay. Just as the portal locked with a hiss of air, she felt a thud as Derek slammed into the door. He'd probably dented the damn thing.

Sable shoved Butch Castle into the brig. "Take a shower," she ordered. "Wash the stench of fear off you. I'm hungry, so after we take off, I'll be back to feed." She saw his eyes widen in dismay and smiled. "Don't worry, you'll enjoy it. Humans always do."

Moving to the deck, she sat in her captain's chair and secured the five-point harness. Then she activated the exterior communication link. "Move away, Derek. I'm about to take off."

"Damn it, Sable," he growled. "You bitch! Didn't the last two days mean anything to you?"

She swallowed hard. Mean *anything*? They'd meant *everything*.

What an idiot she'd been to give in to her longing to have him. *Burn this thing out*, he'd said, and she'd leapt at the excuse to have him even though she'd known deep inside that it would only get worse.

Misled

Glancing up, she saw him standing in the loading bay, one hand plunging through his thick raven hair in frustration. He was undeniably gorgeous. Tall, broad-shouldered and thickly muscled, he took up her entire view screen from the chest up. Her heart pounded against her rib cage and her chest grew tight. "Don't play me, Derek," she said in a voice that betrayed her with its hoarseness.

He glanced up sharply and bore his metallic gaze into hers through the video screen. He couldn't see her, but his gaze still searched for answers. "It seems to me that I'm the one being played. Was I just a convenient fuck for you, baby? A couple dozen orgasms and I've outlived my usefulness?"

"Go to hell," she bit out, even as she shivered at the memory. "You were going to do the same to me, I just beat you to the punch. Now back off!"

He backed away a few steps, affording her a clear view of the massive bulge of his cock straining his suit. His handsome face was set in harsh lines, his gaze piercing in his fury. "If you believe that, Sable, after all the time I spent inside you, you don't know anything about me at all."

Sable closed her eyes for a moment, willing away the burning behind her lids that would prevent her from seeing her way out of the narrow docking bay. *If only things could be different.*

"Goodbye, Derek," she said softly as she terminated the audio. When she opened her eyes and looked at the screen he was gone.

And with a skilled tug on the controls, so was she.

* * * * *

Derek sat on the deck of his ship *The Viper* and watched Sable's sleek new model Starwing burst into lightspeed and disappear. The ship suited her perfectly. She liked new toys—the faster and more powerful the better—which was probably why she was so hot for him.

His lips twisted wryly. The last forty-eight hours had been the most pleasurable of his life. Considering how old he was, that was saying something. He'd never experienced anything as powerful as being with Sable; his cock had been painfully hard almost the entire two days.

He waited until it was clear for him to follow, set the navigation for the jump and went to take a shower. As he stepped under the spray of water, the unmistakable scent of hard sex rose from his skin to dissipate in the steam. Derek closed his eyes and rested his forehead against the cool metal of the shower stall. It wasn't hard to picture Sable as she'd been only a few hours ago, imprinting her smell on him in a way that he knew would never leave him. She was the fuck of the century, several centuries actually. He groaned a low tortured sound. It would probably take several more before he burned her out of his blood.

Now that he'd actually had her...well, he wasn't sated yet. Not by half.

Derek sighed as he finished rinsing his hair and then stepped out of the shower, his mind weary and heart heavy simply because Sable was no longer with him. She'd become a complication in a way he should have seen coming.

Entering his cabin, he paused at the sight of his rumpled four-poster. Sable had been astonished and then delighted at the sight of the bed. It was a luxury he indulged in because he spent so much of his time in pursuit. He'd tied her to that bed, draped her over the edge of it, fucked her on the floor beside it, taken her standing against the posts at the foot of it. He knew he would never look at that bed again without thinking of her. And wishing she were in it.

That damned impossible woman. She was going to get herself killed. Sable was too reckless and too impatient to study the rules of the worlds she invaded in search of her prey. Derek had attempted to offer his assistance, but every time he'd brought it up, Sable had silenced him with her body until he was too exhausted to keep trying. Part of him was grateful to put off the conversation, feeling a strange desperation to enjoy what he could, while he could. Then he'd woken up this afternoon and found himself handcuffed to the bedposts, her ship no longer trailing behind his.

Apparently, she didn't know how powerful a Master as old as he was could become. He'd dissipated into mist and followed her easily. She'd looked so astonished to find him behind her in the concourse bar. Astonished and instantly aroused. Whatever her reasons were for leaving, it wasn't because she didn't want him anymore.

Derek knew she was headed back to the Gamma Sector to turn in Castle and collect her bounty. There were field headquarters in every sector, but she seemed to prefer the one in Gamma, which was his. She'd collect the updated list of fugitives, settle on the one worth the most credits and then immediately take flight again in the hopes of avoiding him when he docked for the same reason.

She was running from him, but he wasn't fool enough to take it personally. He hadn't missed the regret in her voice when she'd said goodbye or the emotion in her gaze the last time they'd made love. Despite her fierceness, Sable was a tender and giving lover and she'd worshiped his body in a way that had to mean something to her. It sure as hell had meant something to him.

But he knew she wouldn't let her personal feelings get in the way of her plans. She was very good at her job. He'd have to be better if he hoped to catch a hunter of her caliber.

So the hunt was on.

And Sable was his prey.

Chapter Two

Impatient, Sable tapped her boot in rapid staccato against the floor. Detained for almost an hour in the captain's office of the Interstellar Council's Special Task Force, her nerves were on edge. The Gamma Sector field office should feel like home considering the amount of time she spent there, but Captain Hoff didn't like vamps. He didn't trust them and he'd lobbied hard to get them removed from the Force. The field office was his bastion and because of his anti-vamp sentiments she didn't like being there.

Groaning with frustration, Sable looked at the framed picture on the desk for the thousandth time since she entered the room. She was sick of looking at the redheaded captain with his pretty brunette wife and two red-haired kids. She'd give him another minute or two to show up and then she was leaving, whether he liked it or not.

Suddenly, she stilled, wondering if Derek had comm'ed ahead and arranged this delay.

As quickly as the thought came to her, Sable wrote it off. She knew how deeply she'd pleasured him—how could she not when he filled her mind with it?—but Derek Atkinson wasn't just known for his skills as an agent. He was also known for his prowess in bed, a singular skill he had no trouble sharing freely. She refused to believe she meant any more to him than the thousands of other women he'd screwed over the last six or seven hundred years.

But, damn, he knew how to fuck well. Sharing his bed had been so good, she couldn't regret it. There was something to be said for a man with several centuries' worth of experience in seducing women.

Okay. Who was she kidding? There was a lot to be said.

She'd always admired Derek's dark good looks and amazing body, but he'd been no more than that, a gorgeous man to drool over. She hadn't known anything more personal about him than she could gather from gossip and a few lines of text in a thin personnel file. Now she knew him as a man, in every way possible.

Derek was beyond amazing as a lover, sometimes wild and animalistic, other times tender and reverent. His mind, which she knew as intimately as his body, was clever and intelligent. He had a deep sense of honor and a desire to give meaning to his endless life with the worthwhile pursuit of justice. In short, he was all the things she admired in the male half of her species.

Sable wished she could have found something wrong with him, any little thing that would have made him less appealing. But she hadn't and because he was everything she wanted, she'd fallen for him. Hard. When he'd looked into her eyes the last time he slid inside her, she couldn't make it impersonal, couldn't make it just sex. He'd built the mental connection between them and they'd made love. Just the remembrance of it made her ache for him.

But she couldn't have him.

The door opened behind her and she rose. "Captain," she greeted with relief, thankful it wasn't Derek and grateful for the respite from her thoughts.

Hoff's tall, lanky form dominated the doorway. "Have a seat, Special Agent Taylor."

Sable sank back into the chair as the captain took his place on the opposite side of the desk. Behind him was an expansive window with a view of space beyond. "Good work bringing Castle into custody."

"Thank you, sir."

"Were there other agents in pursuit when you caught him?"

"Only Agent Atkinson." Sable's cheeks heated just from saying Derek's name. She hoped the perceptive captain didn't notice.

"You seem to run into Atkinson quite a bit. Do you think he suspects you?"

"No way." She knew that for certain. Derek would never have fucked her if he'd known she worked undercover for Internal Affairs. Instead he'd have looked at her with disgust and considered her a rat for hunting fellow agents. Her chest tightened painfully at the thought. Losing his respect would be too much to bear.

"Have you discovered anything new since the last with you?" he asked.

She wrinkled her nose. "You know I can't share IAB information with you, Captain. Not while the investigation is still underway."

Hoff's pale blue eyes narrowed. "When you make your arrest I want to be the first to know. I can't believe one of my agents is selling information to the Federation. You've been undercover for two years now and you haven't turned up anything incriminating. Maybe IAB is wrong about the leak coming from this field office."

Sable kept her face impassive. She knew IAB wasn't wrong. Within the last two days, the informant from this office had sold false information that she'd planted in the database. While she hated to have missed the opportunity to apprehend the traitor, she was relieved to exonerate Derek without a doubt. He'd been in bed with her for the last two days. And the shower. And the dining table. And the...

Damn, best not to think about that.

In any case, he hadn't gone anywhere near the controls of his ship to access the main computers.

"IAB is rarely wrong," she said with confidence. "There's a leak. And I'll find it." She stood.

As she made her way toward the door, the captain called after her. "You're dismissed, Agent Taylor."

She rolled her eyes.

Stepping out into the hallway, she crashed into a rock wall. At least it felt like one.

"Watch it," she ground out, as the wall steadied her. She looked into fiery silver eyes and bit back a groan. "Dere—er, Agent Atkinson."

Derek wore his dark blue STF uniform and she could barely catch her breath at the sight of him. She'd always been a sucker for a man in uniform and Derek made it look especially yummy.

He slid his hands down her arms, burning her skin and causing heated ripples of awareness to pool in her core. "Hello, Sable." His voice was rich and warm and filled with sensual promise. "In trouble with the captain again? What did you do this time?"

She scowled and shrugged off his touch, digging deep for the strength she needed to walk away. "I entered the docking bay a little too fast," she lied. Circumventing him, she headed down the hall with a rapid stride.

He fell into step beside her. "Who are you tracking now?"

"None of your damn business," she snapped, trying not to look at his handsome face with its sexy smile and angry gaze. He was obviously still pissed about her leaving him at DS12 two days ago. In a way, she was glad. It showed that he cared, if only a little.

"Fine," he said smoothly, but she heard the frustration in his tone. "Is my cum still dripping down your thighs?"

She halted abruptly, her mouth agape. "*What?*"

He shrugged and tried to look innocent, which was impossible. "That would be my business, wouldn't it? I mean if *my* bodily fluids are in *your*—"

"Shut up." Arms akimbo, Sable was certain she'd never been as furious in her life, which was exactly what Derek had intended with his outrageous question. He was not a man who took well to being ignored and he fought back with no holds barred.

He mimicked her posture and raised a raven brow. Despite his fury, he looked like heaven, *her* heaven, but she couldn't do a damn thing about that as long as she was undercover in his field office.

Sable loved his smile and his body, his silky hair and piercing fangs. She admired his strength and his control. He was cool and levelheaded when she was hot and brash. He was pulled together and quick on his feet, when she was falling apart and frozen in place. He complemented her in every way that mattered.

Except she wanted him forever and he wanted her for right now.

She used to love her job, used to love knowing she kept the Task Force clean and free of dirty officers. Now she hated it. She'd hated it ever since she met Derek two years ago, because her job prevented her from having him for however long he'd give her his attention. She was enough of a glutton for punishment that she'd be willing to take what she could get when it came to Derek Atkinson.

Sable closed her eyes and released a long, slow breath. When she looked at him again, she was much calmer and not as angry. "Listen, Derek. The time we shared was great, I have no regrets—"

"That's something, I suppose," he muttered.

"But it can't happen again. It really shouldn't have happened to begin with."

He snorted and his full lips tightened with displeasure. "How can you say that? I know you felt something."

"Maybe I did. But we both know you're not a long-term relationship kind of vamp—"

"How the hell would we both know that?" he growled.

"How old are you?" She arched a brow. "Several centuries old at least. And yet you've never been married, never been engaged."

"Maybe I hadn't found what I was looking for," he argued.

"Maybe you never will."

"Maybe I have."

Sable shook her head, squelching the flutter in her stomach, and started down the hallway again. "Whatever, Derek." She dismissed his statement with a wave of her hand. "It was fun, but now it's over. Let's not ruin the memory by arguing."

"Are you finished?" he ground out.

"Definitely." She kept walking as he slowed.

"Good."

He gripped her elbow and dragged her into an interrogation room on the left. Before she realized what was happening, he had her pinned to the wall, his mouth on hers, his tongue thrusting through her parted lips.

His long fingers moved through her hair, cupping the back of her head to position her as he wanted. The man kissed the way he fucked, deep and possessive, with a skill that stole her ability to think or move. His hips pressed hers to the wall, his erection hot and heavy against her lower belly. All around him she could smell his desire, heady and overwhelming, pure and gratifying.

Sable melted into him as his tongue stroked the inside of her mouth and his hands caressed her body with centuries' worth of devastating knowledge. He tasted so unbelievably good, like sin on a stick, and she wanted more. Much more. Her job was so lonely, her work all-consuming. Only Derek understood the rigors. His body offered a solace she had found nowhere else. Touching him, holding him was a much-needed respite and an intimacy unlike anything she'd known before. It was wrong to want him and hopeless, but she couldn't help it.

Tearing her mouth from his, she tugged his head lower, bared her fangs and sank home in the powerful expanse of his neck, claiming him, because he'd claimed her. Instantly the rich, intoxicating taste of his blood, aged like a fine wine, poured down her throat. She felt him probing her mind, coaxing and encouraging until she didn't care where they were. All she cared about was Derek, his big body and talented hands, the sinewy length of his muscles beneath her appreciative fingertips and the potent strength of his blood flowing into her.

Sable fed for long moments, writhing against him in an agony of lust. His blood should soothe her, calm her. Instead it heated her from the inside, making her skin tingle and her nipples peak tight. He caressed the length of her spine, holding her close, rocking his rock-hard cock against her clit. She ground her hips into that bulge, wanting to come with near desperation. Feeding was, by nature, a sensual act, but with Derek it was so much more powerful than the physical need to orgasm. It was almost instinctual.

"You know," he breathed, his deep voice vibrating against her lips. "It's never been like this for me."

Was he talking about the lust? she wondered.

That too, but also the gifting. I've never really appreciated it before.

Reluctantly, Sable withdrew her fangs, lapping at the tiny punctures with her tongue to seal them. When she leaned back to look at him, Derek's silvery irises were swirling like molten metal.

Gifting—the exchange of blood between vamps. It wasn't for sustenance. It was a gift, an exchange of the precious fluid that was the center of their existence. To some vamps, it was no more intimate than a kiss. To others, it was a deeply personal act, more so than intercourse.

He lifted her and carried her, his sexual intent clear. The room was small, windowless and metallic. The only items inside it were the small table he set her down on, a single chair, and a very horny master vampire.

"Someone will come in here," she whispered, a token protest.

"I'll keep them away."

"How?" As soon as she asked, she knew, somehow, he could do as he said.

"Trust me, baby," he urged as he pulled her to the edge. "You're mine. I won't share even a glimpse of you with someone else."

Sable hiked up the short, flared skirt she wore and shimmied out of her thong while Derek hit the catch on his uniform and shrugged his torso out of it. He pushed the garment down to his thighs, releasing the magnificent cock that had driven her to insanity just two days before. It was long and impossibly thick, beautifully shaped with a thick roping of veins that pleasured her from the inside.

"I love your body," she groaned as he stepped between her spread thighs, his cock in hand and aimed for her creamy opening. His chest was broad and sculpted, well-formed muscles flexing as he stroked himself, making his shaft harder and thicker.

"It's all yours, Sable."

She bit her lip, trying to dull the possessiveness she had no right to feel. Derek leaned over and licked her lip.

"Watch me take you," he whispered, his free hand pressing her gently backward until she set her arms behind her to support her weight. He lifted her skirt to her waist, drawing her eyes to the glistening curls between her thighs and the ruddy cock that approached them.

Sable watched, mesmerized, as he entered her with exquisite slowness, the flared head breaching her, stretching her. Her eyelids grew heavy as Derek surged slowly inside, hot and hard, a silken instrument of sexual torment and ultimate relief.

She shivered and moaned as he slipped deeper, sliding through her cream, his impressive width and length like a warm inner massage. He buried himself to the hilt, his head falling back as a shudder shook the length of his body. He offered a soft smile, revealing wicked fangs and molten eyes made bright by the animal let loose inside him. He withdrew and then pressed forward again, his stomach rippling with muscle as he gave a long, deep plunge.

"So hot," he said hoarsely. "So tight and wet." He pulled out until only the tip remained inside her. "Look at all your cream on my cock. It's the most erotic thing I've ever seen."

She swallowed hard, her skin damp from the heat.

"Put your finger in my mouth," he urged.

Leaning to one side, she freed one hand and did as he asked. His cheeks hollowed as he sucked, drawing on her with a steady suction, the tempo of which was echoed in the clasps of her pussy on his cock. She gasped, so aroused she couldn't think.

"That's what you feel like to me. It makes me want to come, Sable. It makes my balls ache. Does it turn you on? Watching me fuck you? Feeling me stroke you?"

"Yes…" Sable stared, her nipples so hard they ached, as he pumped his cock into her cunt, his rhythm so slow, his hips swirling and then lunging.

Nothing had ever felt as good as this. She'd never have enough of it, never stop craving it. The sex got better every time.

And more personal.

With a growl, Derek claimed her throat with his fangs as his thrusts picked up speed, propelling himself deeply into her with soft blows of his hips to hers. His thoughts entered her head with a clarity she was learning to treasure. *I've missed this, baby. I missed you.*

Sable wrapped her legs around his waist, adding her strength to his, making his cock strike deep, so deep. Derek wasn't like other lovers she'd had. Everything he did, every move he made was planned for her pleasure. His greedy mouth tugged at her skin, building an ecstasy so intense she came, bathing him in a rush moisture. He slowed, savoring her orgasm, his touch gentle as if he knew her fears and longed to soothe them. She longed to let him.

"So good," she moaned, her body on fire, and Derek growled his agreement as he drank. She gripped his flexing buttocks, urging him deeper when there was no deeper to go.

Sable felt him everywhere. He permeated everything with a merciless penetration that brought her as much pain as pleasure. Belatedly, she fought off his invasion, trying to shield herself from the devastation his loss would bring.

He reached a hand between them and stroked her clit in time with the thrusting of his hips. *You can't hold back. Stop trying.*

As her body tightened with another orgasm, tears slipped free and dripped onto her cheek.

Don't, he begged. *Don't cry. It's okay. I'm here with you. You're not alone.*

"I'm always alone," she cried softly. "It's the nature of our beast."

And her job.

He hunched over her, caging her to table, thrusting hard until she came with a scream. He released her neck and arched his back, a guttural cry torn from his throat as he spurted his seed deep inside her.

* * * * *

Derek stirred slowly, reluctant to lift his head from the pillow of Sable's breast. He felt drained and yet omnipotent at the same time. His strength was steadily increasing as he spent more time inside her. Sable charged him in some way he hadn't known existed, hadn't known was possible.

Was that why he craved her?

No, that couldn't be the reason. He'd wanted her before. The rush he experienced being with her was just an added enticement. It must be the virus. Perhaps together, he and Sable created a synergy. Even if he didn't desire her so badly, that alone was worth exploring.

He turned his head and looked at the two-way mirror on the wall. He saw nothing but an empty room, their reflections absent from the silvered glass. Sable was right. It was the nature of their beast to be lonely, set apart from others not of their kind. But they'd found each other. Against the odds and all of the rules.

He should have been more circumspect before taking her to his ship and fucking her for days. He should have known the lust riding him so hard meant more than he was willing to admit. If he hadn't been so blind, he could have courted her, wooed her, instead of getting his way with his cock. But that was not the way it went down and despite his chagrin, Derek couldn't regret it. Sable was in his arms and he was deep inside her, soaked in their cream. They had the sexual part of a romantic relationship worked out to perfection. The rest would fall into place eventually.

He pulled himself upright, but remained a part of her. Sable couldn't deny their connection when they were so intimately joined. Reaching down, he brushed the silky stands of her hair away from her forehead. His touch was reverent and adoring, as was the stroking of her right hand against his hip. Closing her eyes, her breathing slowed to a soft pant.

"What are you doing to me?" she whispered brokenly.

His thumbs drifted along the impossibly long length of her lashes, brushing away the tears that clung there. "What are you afraid of, baby?"

"I'm not afraid." She sat up. To his surprise, she wrapped her arms around his waist and rested her head upon his chest. "But this can't keep happening. It has to stop."

"Why?" He pulled back to search her face. The sadness in her eyes arrested his gaze. He'd felt it during their mental connection and was frustrated by the wall she'd erected in her mind. She only let him see a tiny portion of who she was, keeping the greater part of herself tucked away.

What wasn't she sharing with him?

"There's more than lust going on here, Sable. I know you feel it too. You wouldn't be crying otherwise."

"There are things you don't know about me."

"I don't care what they are." He was startled to realize he spoke the truth. He was a curious man, which made him good at his job. "I can wait until you're ready to tell me. All I care about is us—you and me and the way I feel when I'm inside you. The way you make me feel when you look at me like you're doing right now."

Sable glanced away and he gripped her chin, pulling her gaze back to his.

"Don't turn away from me, baby."

"Don't push, Derek. Okay?"

Derek released her and ran a hand through his hair. "I've spent six hundred years looking for this. I'm not about to let it go now that I've found it."

"Do you love me?" she asked bluntly, her sapphire gaze probing, invasive.

He choked at her directness and the questions it made him ask of himself.

"I thought so," she murmured without inflection. She shoved him backward, forcing his semi-erect cock from the shelter of her pussy, leaving him feeling bereft and rejected. She smoothed her short skirt over her thighs and slid off the table, pausing a moment to retrieve her thong. The wall between them was a tangible thing and it frightened him. And pissed him off.

"Damn it!" Derek tugged on his uniform, glaring at her. "Give me a chance to think."

"Forget it." Sable flew to the door before he could move. She paused on the threshold, her mouth thinned with determination. "Stay out of my life, Atkinson. Find another way to pass the time."

* * * * *

Sable sat in the cockpit of her Starwing and reminded herself that she was a strong woman who could handle anything. Rubbing her eyes, she leaned back in the captain's chair and wished she had roots somewhere, something that was hers, a place to call home. She'd taken possession of the highly desired ship compliments of a smuggler who'd been caught by Interstellar Customs. Almost everything she owned was confiscated goods from the impounds of half a dozen different law enforcement agencies. She had to have the best of everything to maintain the appearance of a money-hungry bounty hunter. Unfortunately, it also meant that Sable Taylor had nothing of her own.

She looked out the cockpit window at the half dozen ships docked around her. They branched out on spokes from the slowly spinning center that was the Task Force field office for this part of the universe. Derek's ship was easy to spot. He drove a Starwing not much older than her own, but his ship was definitely more luxuriously outfitted.

Derek Atkinson had money—lots of it. Judicious investments made over several centuries would make anyone rich beyond measure. It was a testimony to Derek's character that he chose to work for the STF rather than spend his days idly, surrounded by willing women. His imperviousness to bribery made him the least likely of her suspects. She was certain that no amount of money could entice Derek to whore himself to the Federation.

So who was the traitor?

She'd pondered that question a hundred times over. Starting the engines, she glanced down at the readout on the console. Jeffrey Leroy was next on her list of agents to investigate. He was in the Delta Sector tracking down a smuggler, so that was her next destination. Disengaging from the docking bay, Sable pulled the required distance away from the field office before programming the jump to lightspeed. Then she stood, stretching muscles made deliciously languid from two fabulous orgasms.

Taking a quick shower, she tried not to think about what had happened at headquarters and failed miserably. How could she not think about it? She'd ignored every protocol of her job by getting involved with an agent. And she was definitely involved, no doubt about that. It would be so much easier to blame it on loneliness eased by physical pleasure, but that wouldn't be true and she had to be honest with herself. Otherwise, she'd do something stupid, like fuck him some more, which was exactly what had gotten her in this mess to begin with.

Sable shut off the spray and toweled her skin dry.

And what the hell had gotten into Derek? He'd almost made it sound like what they had was more than just sex for him too, but she knew better than that. His terrified expression when she'd said the word "love" had proven that point. Yeah, the sex was great, fabulous even, but it wasn't a good thing when one partner was coming undone and the other one just wanted to come.

With a weary sigh, she threw herself on her bed and glared at the ceiling.

She'd been a fool to fall for Derek Atkinson—a full Master vampire with a sensual call that turned every woman into a mewling sex slave. She would bet a million credits he'd never been in love in his life. He'd lived centuries as a bachelor and seemed to enjoy it immensely, if rumors held true. He left broken hearts in his wake.

Just like hers.

She closed her eyes and without even trying, she could smell him, the scent of his skin infinitely alluring. Her breasts grew taut and heavy as she pictured his hot gaze and luscious mouth. Reaching up, she squeezed the swollen flesh to ease the ache and wished she weren't alone.

"I miss you, Derek," she whispered into the still air.

I know.

Sable's fists clenched as Derek's voice sifted like smoke through her mind. "Get out of my head!" she growled to the room at large. With deep concentration, she shoved him firmly from her thoughts.

"You know, baby," he murmured. "We need to figure out how you throw off my call so easily."

Her wide-eyed gaze shot to the doorway, shocked to find Derek lounging there with casual arrogance. Her traitorous heart leapt, happy to see him.

"Damn you, Derek."

Chapter Three

ಐ

Derek watched with rapt attention as Sable rose naked from the small bed and moved to the wardrobe. With the long fall of her dark hair and gently swaying hips, she was temptation incarnate. It took everything he had to maintain his casual appearance when the animal inside him longed to leap the distance between them and fuck her senseless. He couldn't help but wonder if he'd ever get enough of her. He wanted her as badly as if he hadn't just come his last drop a short while ago.

Tugging a short, sleeveless wrap off a hanger, she covered her lithe form and he bit back a groan of disappointment. When she turned to face him, her lovely face was studiously impassive, belying the rapid pounding of her pulse and the moisture he could smell pooling between her thighs. She was happy to see him, although she was trying hard to hide that fact. He hid a smile. She'd said she missed him.

"What are you doing stowing away on my ship?" she asked, walking past him.

"You can't run from me, Sable."

"I wasn't running." She growled in frustration as she realized they'd already made the jump to lightspeed. "Shit. What the hell am I going to do with you now?"

"I have a few suggestions," he offered helpfully. "Clothing optional."

She shot him an exasperated glance.

He strolled over to the captain's chair and made himself at home. He'd checked out the rest of the Starwing while she'd been in the shower. The entire ship had been stripped of every comfort. Obviously luxury was something she could live without. Or was forced to live without.

"How much trouble are you in?" he asked quietly.

She shot him a startled glance. "What?"

Derek waved his hand around the sparse deck in an all-encompassing gesture. "You're obviously in financial trouble. How deep are you under?"

"Why do you care?" Sable ripped the towel off her head and headed back into the bedroom.

"Who said I cared? Maybe I'm just trying to lighten my bank account."

He heard her snort derisively and he laughed.

"I don't want your charity," she grumbled.

"And I don't want your bullshit. Sometimes we get what we don't want."

Sable came back to the doorway, a reluctant smile curving her lips. It was the first time Derek had seen anything close to a smile on her face and he was awed by how it transformed her features from beautiful to breathtaking.

"Really, Derek. I don't need your money."

He frowned. "You'd tell me if you did?"

She laughed then, an enchanting sound that made him swallow hard. "No. I wouldn't tell you."

Derek pushed out of the chair with a curse. "Why the hell not?"

"I didn't fuck you for your money."

His eyebrows rose at the blunt statement. "Glad to hear it." Really glad, but then he'd never thought that anyway. Sable was too independent. He paused a moment and then asked the obvious question, damning himself for caring about the answer. "Why did you then?"

"For that massive cock of yours, of course." Her sapphire eyes glittered with wicked amusement.

When he scowled, she threw her head back and laughed with delight. The laughter poured from her, light and musical and before he knew it he was chuckling too. He was about to reach for her and pull her into his arms, when the ship rocked hard to the side, throwing her into his embrace. Alarms sounded.

"What the hell?" she gasped as she steadied herself against him. Her eyes went wide as she looked at him and he knew she was wondering how he'd saved them from a puddle of tangled limbs. She glanced down, noticing they hovered just above the floor. Her gaze was accusatory. "Is there anything you're *not* prepared for?"

He gave her a swift, hard kiss before moving to the captain's chair. They'd been so wrapped up in talking to each other, they hadn't noticed when the ship had fallen out of lightspeed.

"Shit! Hang on." He grabbed the controls, shut off the autopilot and activated the shields, before tilting them hard right. A phaser shot barely missed them.

Sable took the copilot's chair. "It's a Federation ship," she said in surprise after a quick glance at the console. She'd barely secured her harness before he was forced to make another evasive roll.

With grim resignation, Derek kept his eyes on the control panel in front of him and noted the second Federation ship approaching. "Now would be a good time to tell me what kind of trouble you're in, Sable."

"*Me*? Why does this have to be about me?"

He risked a side-glance at her. "Cut the shit. We're on the far edges of the Delta Sector. Why did you decide to drop out of lightspeed here?"

Her eyes met his for an instant, then she flushed and looked away. "To avoid you. I figured you wouldn't think to look for me here."

She punched a few buttons on the armrest and a visor lowered from the ceiling. Within seconds, the chair spun silently around as she watched their enemy through the visor and returned fire.

Derek shook his head. Damned impossible woman. "We're going to discuss your relationship issues later. Right now I want to know how two Federation fighter ships ended up deep in Council space at the exact remote location you decided to use."

"I have no fucking idea. I reported my intention to travel to Rashier 6, but not the flight plan. No one knew I was coming out here."

Derek watched as the second Federation ship flew over them, followed by a rapid volley of phasers from Sable. She was good. The second ship was already badly damaged.

"Maybe we stumbled onto something by accident." She spun her chair to the left and fired on the first ship.

The Starwing shook with teeth-chattering force. "Yeah, a *big* accident. Shields are down to seventy-five percent."

Sable fired back with even more ferocity. "Can you get us out of here?"

"No. That first hit knocked out the hyperdrive and the comm link. Whoever these guys are, they don't like you at all."

"They'll have to take a number." Her next round of fire destroyed one of the Federation ships. "Turn around so I can get the other one."

He pulled up and over, coming in behind the remaining ship that continued to fire on them with enthusiasm. "Shields down to fifty percent and falling fast."

Sable spun around and cursed. The remaining Federation ship was gone. "They jumped."

"They timed that well," Derek noted. "They arrived and left before the border probe made its rounds."

She shook off the harness. The visor automatically rose out of her way. "Why didn't they finish us?"

"I don't know but I think they probably weren't expecting a fight and ran out of time."

She stood, her short robe twisted by the movement of the

chair and the five-point harness until he could almost see her pussy.

He got hard instantly.

Shit. He shouldn't be thinking about that now. Frustrated, he bolted out of his chair.

"We have to repair the ship and get out of here before they decide to come back," he growled, raking a hand through his hair.

She shot him a quizzical glance. "Grumpy, aren't we?"

"Horny," he corrected and choked off a laugh at the grimace she made. She beat a hasty retreat.

"I'm going down to fix the hyperdrive," she shouted as she went below deck. "You work on the shields."

He could smell the arousal coming from her satiny skin. One word from him and her body was eager for his. Instead, she ran away.

Damned impossible woman.

* * * * *

Sable pushed her hair out of her face, and crawled on her hands and knees back into the maintenance shaft of the hyperdrive. She was eternally grateful that the repairs were almost done. The shaft was not designed for occupation, so the space lacked environmental controls, making it hot and uncomfortable. Only the upper half of her torso fit in the small space, leaving her hips bent at an odd angle.

She briefly wondered how much headway Derek was making on the shields. She trusted him to work on her ship, which spoke volumes about how much she respected and believed in him. A control freak, she preferred to see to everything herself so she knew a task was done to her satisfaction. She wasn't worried about that with Derek. He never did anything in half measure. Sable was relieved he'd been with her today. Without him, things could have been much worse. In fact, she might even be dead.

Derek was right. Those ships had been lying in wait for her. They'd disabled her hyperdrive, crippling her, but in the end had left her alive. Perhaps they'd meant only to delay her? But why? No one knew she was tracking down Agent Leroy besides IAB and that database was so secure not even the President of the Interstellar Security Council had access to it.

So who could have known where she would drop out of lightspeed when she hadn't even known herself until she'd punched the coordinates? It didn't make sense. Why not kill her and get rid of the threat she presented all together?

Yes! Derek's triumphant voice filled her mind. *I fixed the shields. How are you doing down there?*

"Almost done," she muttered as she reattached the ground.

Need a hand?

"No, thanks. You're familiar with the layout of these ships. The maintenance shaft is tiny. I'm ass-up in here as it is and cramped as hell."

Okay, baby.

The voice in her mind fell silent and strangely she felt lonely without it. She was getting far too used to having him around and the realization pissed her off to no end. Her foolish heart was determined to be crushed into dust.

She finished and slowly started backing out of the maintenance shaft.

"Look what I found," came Derek's voice in a hot puff of breath against her inner thigh just before his tongue delved into her pussy.

Startled, Sable jumped, banging her head. "Oww, damn it! What the hell are you doing?"

"Isn't it obvious?" he growled softly. Parting her folds with gentle fingers, he continued to lick her with sinuous laps, stroking across her clit until it swelled and peeped out. "You said you were ass-up. I had to come and see for myself."

He plunged his hot tongue deep inside her cunt and groaned, keeping her hips still when she tried to move. "And what do I find? You, bent at the waist, waving a prized piece of heaven at me." He tongued her clit with rapid flicks. "How could I resist a little taste?"

Sable's entire body had begun to burn with the first swipe of his wicked tongue. Now she was on fire. "Derek…" she moaned, throwing her hips back at him, needed more than his teasing torment.

His answering chuckle was filled with masculine satisfaction as he buried his mouth between her thighs with flattering enthusiasm. A moment before she'd been grumpy and frustrated. Now she was achingly, breathlessly aroused, her cunt creamy with lust and softening in eager anticipation of another wondrous orgasm. Derek lapped up her desire with deep licks and then dipped inside her, fucking her with the slow, steady plunges he knew she adored.

Sable dropped her head onto her crossed arms, tilting her hips upward to give him greater access to her drenched cleft. The man was unbelievably talented with his tongue, knowing just where to lick and when to slip deep. He lifted her higher, holding her hips aloft with effortless vampire strength. Openmouthed, he surrounded her clit and stroked it slowly with his tongue, back and forth in a wet glide, making sexy little groaning noises.

I missed this too, the taste of you.

She felt the smooth edges of his fangs against her labia and knew he was fully erect. The thought of his cock and the way it felt inside her made her whimper and drench his mouth. And still his tongue worked its magic, drifting back and forth across her exposed clit. *Out and in.* He was so skilled and he already knew her so well. Her short nails clawed futilely at the smooth metal beneath her.

"Derek…please…"

She screamed when she came, her voice echoing in the small confines of the maintenance shaft.

There was no time to catch her breath before Derek pulled back and then plunged his pulsing erection inside her, stretching her impossibly tight in her bent over position. He stroked his cock quickly, riding out her orgasm, making it last as long as possible.

I love being inside you.

"Yes…"

I love it when you scream and come for me. Do it again.

"Derek," she gasped, her entire body quaking with the force of his thrusts. He lowered her knees to the floor and pumped deeper, the heavy weight of his balls slapping against her clit with every downward stroke. "You're going to kill me."

He reached around her waist and between her legs, finding the spot where she stretched wide to accommodate him. *Come for me*, he ordered.

Sable couldn't even whimper when she came again. Her throat closed like a fist, as did her cunt, which clamped down on the massive cock riding her in an endless convulsion of pleasure.

Sable! Derek's stunned cry filled her mind, as he came hard and furious, his hands at her waist shaking, his breath heaving in great bellows, his shaft jerking violently inside her.

He collapsed against her back and her legs slid out from under them, shaking too much to support their weight. He pulled her from the hyperdrive shaft and rolled, spooning behind her as they both struggled to breathe.

Sable could have fallen asleep there on the floor, if Derek hadn't picked her up and carried her to the shower. Sated and tired, she leaned her body against his as he soaped her down and washed her hair. As his large hands glided over her skin, kneading in a way meant to soothe rather than arouse, she admitted she could get used to this kind of pampering.

"Does a good fuck always put you in such a generous mood?" she asked, as he rinsed her hair.

His lips curved in a sexy grin, but it was the tenderness in his gaze that stopped her heart. "Just good?"

"Okay, great," she amended.

"Just great?" he teased, as he began to soap his muscled chest.

Damn. Damn. Damn. He was so hot with his soapy hands caressing those beautiful muscles and water dripping from his raven hair. She really wanted to keep him.

"Fantastic, stupendous, mind-blowing," she said through suddenly dry lips. It was ridiculous how badly she craved him.

"Best sex you've ever had?" His silvery gaze probed too deeply for the question to be frivolous.

She shifted uncomfortably under the piercing silver stare and tried for levity. "With your libidinous reputation, I wouldn't think your ego would need any more stroking."

Derek's hands stilled and he frowned. "I don't mind telling you how much I enjoy making love to you."

Making love. Sable looked down, fighting the pleasure that wanted to well up within her. "You know I enjoy it," she said softly.

"Enough to be with only me? No one else?"

Her gaze flew to his in surprise. *Was he serious?* Suddenly very nervous, she leaned her back against the cool shower wall trying to create some distance between them. "What exactly are you asking me?"

"I want to try and make this work, Sable." Derek stepped under the spray to rinse off. "You and me. No one else."

Her eyes slid shut. He *was* serious. She wanted to laugh and cry at the same time. She knew what she should say, what her job demanded that she say. But she just couldn't do it.

"I'd like that," she whispered. Then she cried out in surprise as Derek pulled her against his chest and rewarded her with a quick, hard kiss.

"Thank God," he muttered with touching relief.

"I'm not finished."

He stiffened and pulled back to eye her warily.

Reaching up, she brushed his wet hair off his forehead with an affectionate caress. He had such strong features with his aquiline nose, stubborn jaw and firm lips. She felt safe with him, knowing how prepared he was for everything. Her life had always been chaotic and she often faced ramifications for her rash choices long after they were made. "I don't want anyone else, Derek. But I can't become involved with you right now. There are some things I have to take care of first."

"Like what?" His hands stroked the wet length of her spine possessively.

She tried to explain. "There are things you don't know…"

"Then tell me."

"I'm not supposed—"

"I don't care."

"You won't like it."

"I'll get over it."

She gave a rueful laugh at his dogged persistence. "Derek, can't you just—"

"No." His full lips thinned with determination. "Damn it. Do you want to be with me or not?"

"Yes, but—"

He shook his head. "No waiting. It's been too fucking long as it is. Two years, Sable. What's holding you back? A husband you have stashed somewhere? A lover? Do you owe someone money?"

"No. Nothing like that."

He shrugged. "Whatever it is, we'll take care of it. Together."

Sable reached behind him and shut off the water. "All right," she conceded with a sigh. "I'm—"

An insistent beeping sound came from the cockpit. Derek growled in frustration at the interruption. "Ignore it."

"The hyperdrive is recharged," she said with a smile she

knew didn't hide her relief. She wasn't ready to tell him yet. She didn't want to take the chance of ruining whatever it was they had. There was no doubt in her mind that she'd be better off with a hidden husband, than admitting she worked for IAB. It was the unspoken code. Agents didn't rat on agents. They protected their own. They didn't hunt them down.

"It can wait," he said obstinately. "Tell me."

Sable tilted her head back and pressed her lips to his. It was the first time she'd ever made an advance toward him and when he shuddered, she realized just how much she really got to him. Her stomach fluttered. "That Federation ship might come back with reinforcements," she reminded him.

He tugged her closer when she tried to step away. "Kiss me again, baby. And give it your all."

Draping her arms atop his shoulders, Sable drew his mouth down to hers. She kissed him the way she'd always wanted to, with deep licks of her tongue until she felt the full, heavy prod of his erection against her belly. She laughed. "If we keep this up we'll never get out of this Sector and I won't be able to walk. I may be a vamp, but even I need a break."

"Okay, okay," he said with obvious reluctance. "Let's get the hell out of here."

Chapter Four

Derek rose from the copilot's chair and winced as his muscles creaked in protest. They'd been held in flight for over three hours, waiting for a docking port to open on Rashier 6. Sable had the ship well in hand, but he preferred sitting with her rather than occupying himself elsewhere. That thought had him smothering a wry laugh. Everything she did fascinated him, even sitting in a chair cursing at the control tower.

"Who are we hunting now?" he asked.

Sable stood and stretched as well, her full breasts straining the front of her bio-suit as she arched her back. "Don't you have to go back to work? And what about your ship? Your belongings? You don't have any clothes beside your uniform."

"Trying to get rid of me?"

"I didn't say that, Derek."

Reaching for her hand, he laced his fingers with hers. "I took a leave of absence and my ship is docked at the field office. It'll be fine. I'll buy what I need as soon we disembark and then I'll get out of this." He tugged on the front of his uniform with his free hand.

"I think you look sexy as hell in that uniform," she said in a provocative purr that heated his blood.

He smiled. She'd softened toward him considerably since they'd gotten out of the shower.

She pressed a swift kiss to his mouth. "Thank you for taking the trouble to come after me, even if you did stow away to do it."

He liked that. She was starting to reach out to him physically. Things were progressing between them and he felt a deep masculine satisfaction that their relationship had developed so much quicker than he'd anticipated. She'd been worth the wait.

Sable tugged her hand from his. "We can't hold hands."

Derek stared at her, agape. Maybe he hadn't gotten that far after all. "Why the hell not?"

Her smile was almost...*sympathetic*. "We can't make it obvious that we're...that you and I are..." She winced.

"Dating? Fucking?" he suggested rudely. Damn it, it hurt that she wanted to hide him.

Her wince deepened. "Yeah."

"Fine." He walked away, his jaw clenched.

"Fine?"

He heard the wounded note in her question and smiled grimly. "Whatever you want, baby," he said baldly.

Derek hit the release for the cargo door and exited into the bustling terminal. He felt Sable following him and reached out with his mind, using stealth so she remained unaware of his probing. Her sadness was deep and almost tangible. Derek's chest tightened. He could deal with her anger — hell, he'd love a good screaming match right now — but her sadness ripped at his insides. That sharp flare of pain made him realize how much he cared for her.

Not that he was completely clueless. He'd known he liked her a great deal and wanted to spend some exclusive time to get to know her better, but he hadn't quite understood that she had the power to wound him, as well as arouse him. It was a risk he wasn't sure he was ready to deal with.

He stopped at the maintenance counter and made arrangements for repairs to be done to the damaged Starwing. Then he continued on to the taxi terminal.

"I'm sorry," Sable said in a whisper behind him. "I don't want it to be like this. Please believe that."

Derek gritted his teeth. Why couldn't he have felt this way

about a different woman? Someone open, with nothing to hide. Someone who wanted him as much as he wanted Sable.

He didn't speak to her again for hours.

Catching a cab, they worked their way through the multi-tiered traffic and headed toward the hotel they'd booked. The air and streets were clogged with tourists of all species. Riotous banners stretched from skyscraper to skyscraper just above the teaming transports. The overall effect of the city was one of prosperity and celebration, but the mood didn't impress upon him or Sable. After the closeness they'd just shared, this pained silence was like an ice water bath.

They reached the hotel and she blatantly ignored him as she checked in. She grabbed her keycard and left him staring after her as she ascended in the elevator without him. Just to spite her, he insisted on taking the room that adjoined hers. He'd be damned if he took a separate floor just to please her skewed sense of propriety.

Pissed off, Derek left the hotel and went shopping for clothes and toiletries. After changing in the dressing room of a clothing store, he sent his uniform and purchases back to the hotel and headed for a nearby telecomm café. Settling into a booth away from the large glass window and the prying eyes of the pedestrians on the other side, he inserted his identi-card and waited only a moment before his assistant appeared on the screen.

"Hello, sir," Charles Stein greeted with a smile. He glanced away from the monitor and then said, "On Rashier 6, I see. Great time of year to visit. They're in the middle of their Retro-bration, aren't they?"

"I have no idea," Derek said dryly. He hadn't been paying any attention to his surroundings because he was too angry at Sable. That was a sure sign that he was screwed. His entire life was centered on the need to know what the hell was going on around him. "I need all the information you can locate on a woman named Sable Taylor. Namely service work or maintenance done on her Starwing."

"Just a moment." Stein frowned, then typed furiously on his keyboard. "Well, there's not much in the Council database." Distracted, his voice lowered as he read from the screen. "In fact, there is no record at all for Ms. Taylor prior to ten years ago."

Derek scowled. "That's not possible. She's a vamp, at least a hundred and fifty years old. I've checked her file before and it was a kilometer long." He tried to remember what he could about the contents of that file and then sighed at the realization that he'd been more interested in the photos than the details about her transportation.

Stein typed some more, digging deep into the Council's records. "Sorry, sir. Her file isn't hidden, it's been erased."

Erased? Impossible. It took the authority of the Interstellar Council's majority vote to delete information from the database. "What's left in her file?"

"Her name, address and bank account info."

"Her personal history is gone?" Derek asked. "No dating history, no family records, no next of kin?"

"Nothing at all of a personal nature."

"Shit." Derek rocked back in his chair. "Who was the last person to access her file?"

Stein checked, then whistled softly. "Marius Drake, President of the Interstellar Council General Assembly."

Derek nodded grimly, not the least bit surprised, but aching with the news just the same. "And one of the few people with high enough access to tamper with the database."

"That's true. It's still illegal, but he could pull it off, if his need was strong enough." Stein looked back into the monitor at Derek. "Why would President Drake have an interest in a bounty hunter? Whatever the reason, it can't be good."

"Yeah, my luck to get involved with trouble."

"Involved?" Stein blinked. "As in a 'personal' type of involved?"

"Don't look so shocked."

"I've known you a long time, sir, and in that time you've never been 'involved' with anyone."

"There's a first time for everything."

"While I won't disagree, I suggest perhaps you should leave this particular female alone. I don't like the looks of this."

"I wish it were that easy." Derek ran a hand through his hair. Sable was into something dangerous. Had he finally fallen hard for a woman, only to have to arrest her? He drummed his fingers on the table. If Sable were involved in a criminal enterprise it would explain her desire to keep their burgeoning relationship a secret. Her dating a STF agent could get them both staked. "Keep digging, Stein. I'll check back with you in a few days to see what you've turned up."

"Of course. Perhaps you should spend the interval asking Ms. Taylor about herself. If she feels the same way about you as you feel about her, she'll tell you the truth."

Derek nodded. "She damn well better."

* * * * *

Sable eyed the slinky, silver dress on the bed warily. It was Retro-bration on Rashier 6 and she had to wear the old-fashioned thing if she wanted to fit in—whether she hated it or not. No matter what, she needed to gain admittance to the RetroBall being held in the hotel later that evening. Jeffrey Leroy had reported that he would be attending the event in the course of his duties and she planned to shadow him until she could determine what he was up to.

Sighing in resignation, she shrugged to herself. Oh well. When in Rashier, do as the Rashiens do. Or something like that.

"Put it on."

She spun to face Derek, who leaned against the frame of the open adjoining doorway.

"How do you always sneak up on me like that?" she asked breathlessly, drinking in the sight of him. He'd been gone for hours and she was so happy to see him.

But he didn't look at all happy to see her.

"Your focus is always divided."

Looking past him, she saw the bed behind him. "You took the room next to mine?"

"You're the reason I'm here," he said in a dry tone of voice that betrayed his continuing anger. "It would be stupid to stay away from you."

Wincing, Sable acknowledged that he had every right to be pissed off. She'd treated him horribly earlier and she'd had some time to think about what she'd done. One of the reasons she'd hesitated to take him seriously was because she was afraid that he would hurt her. So what did she do? Hurt him first. It wasn't right. She needed to be honest with him and tell him who she was. If he didn't want to be with her after he knew, that's just the way things were. Better to know now. Wounding him to save her feelings wasn't the way to go about it. "Derek, let me explain." She held out her hand to him.

His silver gaze narrowed dangerously. "I'm not a fuck toy, Sable."

"I never said you were."

"That's how you treat me. The only time I can get anywhere near you is when I'm fucking you."

Obviously, she couldn't talk to him when he was this riled up. His hands were balled into fists and his jaw was clenched tight.

She licked her lips and watched his eyes smolder as they followed her tongue. "We can't talk when you're this tense." She strolled toward him with an exaggerated swing of her hips. The sudden, elevated tensing of his powerful frame was tangible. "Let me help you relax and then I'll tell you everything."

"Tell me now."

"You're not in the mood to listen to me. You want to pick a fight. I'd rather use that energy doing something a little more pleasant."

"An orgasm is not going to make me feel better," he growled.

"Are you sure about that? I hope you forgive me, but I'm going to touch you anyway. You see, once you hear what I have to say, you may not ever want me to touch you again. And if that's what's going to happen, I'll take what I can get now." She pressed a kiss to his pursed lips and then sank gracefully to her knees.

"Sable." His deep voice was dark with warning. "Damn it. If you tell me the truth, you won't have to worry about me leaving you."

"I will tell you the truth. I promise. When I'm done." She worked the fastenings of his trousers slowly, drawing out his anticipation. She watched his magnificent cock swell before her eyes. "I do miss the uniform, I have to admit. But I like you best naked. You have such a gorgeous body, Derek. And it pleases me so well."

He stilled her hands with his own.

She looked up at him with pleading eyes, her breathing rapid in near panic. She'd die if she didn't get this last time with him. "Let me suck you, baby," she said hoarsely.

"What are you hiding?" Derek's large hand cupped her cheek. "Why are you doing this?"

"Wouldn't you like to come in my mouth?"

His face flushed with reluctant desire. "I want answers. I want to know what kind of trouble you're in."

"If you trust me to tell you the truth now, you should trust me to tell you the truth later." She reached into his pants and tugged out his heavy shaft. Without hesitation, she licked across the plum-sized head and down along a ridged vein.

Derek's breath hissed out between his teeth and his hips bucked forward. "Sable..."

"Shhh. I'm so sorry for how I treated you earlier. Just relax and let me apologize to you properly. You can ask me questions later." A shiny drop of fluid graced the tip of his cock and she eagerly sucked it into her mouth, shivering at the taste of him.

"Fuck." His eyes slid shut. "I'm so screwed." Despite his frustration, his hands tangled in her hair, holding her still while he slipped his cock between her parted lips.

Sable moaned at the feel of his thickly veined shaft sliding along her tongue. The skin was soft and stretched tight over the pulsing hardness beneath. She cupped his ass, kneading gently, feeling his ass cheeks clench as he thrust deeper into her mouth. She began to suck as he fucked slowly through the circle of her lips, a steady, shallow rhythm accompanied by guttural cries from his throat. She shivered at the feel of her cunt creaming with desire—a desire created by the sheer erotic delight she received in concentrating entirely on his needs. He'd spent so many hours giving pleasure to her. It was long past the time when she should return the favor.

"Harder," he gasped, his fingers drifting into her hair. "Suck harder."

Tightening her lips around him, she hollowed her cheeks, gripping his hips to hold him steady. His stamina was amazing, his desire for her heartrending. And Sable didn't take his weakness for her for granted. It was a gift and she cherished it as one. She'd find a way to prove that to him.

Derek tensed, his breath seized in his lungs and then he cried out her name as his cock jerked against her tongue, spurting his cum down her throat. Relishing his pleasure, she drank from him. Even when she felt his balls empty and his knees shake, she didn't cease the suction of her mouth.

"Enough," he groaned. "You'll kill me."

He sank to the floor in front of her, dragging her across him as he collapsed onto his back.

She folded her arms over his heaving chest and rested her chin upon them. She studied his features, darkened with passion and misted with sweat. With his eyes closed, he appeared younger, more vulnerable. Sable sighed.

"You're not just a fuck toy to me, Derek. It's never been about that."

"Liar," he retorted hoarsely.

"Well, maybe it's partly about that," she corrected with a grin. "Getting physical with you is…well, it's beyond words. But that's not all you're worth to me. Don't ever think otherwise."

His breathing began to slow. "What the hell am I supposed to think, Sable? You're embarrassed to be seen with me, you…"

"That's not true! I'm flattered you want me. I'm amazed you stowed away on my ship just to be with me. I'm *proud* of you and a bit startled that I could catch your interest, let alone keep it."

Derek opened his eyes. "Is that what this is about? You think you can't keep my interest?"

"Isn't it a possibility?" she challenged.

He held her gaze for a long time before admitting. "I don't know what to think anymore. I know you can hurt me. I'm not sure how I feel about that."

She offered a sad smile. "At least you're honest."

"Because that's what I want from you in return, Sable—your honesty."

"And I'll give it to you."

Sable pushed off him and rose to her feet, despite his protests. Walking over to the dresser, she opened a drawer and retrieved her identi-card. When she turned back to him, he was sitting up, watching her with blatant curiosity and more than a touch of wariness. She held out her hand and he rose to take it, stopping only a moment to straighten his clothing.

He looked at the card and hesitated.

"Take it," she prodded. "All the answers to your questions are right here."

He accepted her offering while tossing her a sidelong glance. With obviously reluctant steps, he walked to the comm link in the corner and slid the card inside.

"*Good evening, Special Agent Taylor,*" greeted the feminine voice of the comm link. "*You have no new messages in the IAB database.*"

Sable watched as Derek stilled, staring down at the comm link like he'd never seen one before. Then he turned to face her. His silver gaze was intent, searching. She tensed and waited for his condemnation.

"Is that what you've been hiding from me? That you're an IAB agent?"

She swallowed hard and nodded.

"Anything else you want to tell me?" he bit out. "Now would be the time."

"Well, my mission is—"

"No," he interrupted, lifting his hand. "You can tell me about your mission later. Is there any other reason why you don't want to be seen with me?"

She shook her head. "What else would there be?" She shifted nervously and confessed, "I'm crazy about you, Derek. Absolutely crazy."

"Oh, Sable." His voice turned deep and husky. "Thank God." He dissipated into mist and reappeared instantly before her, crushing her into his chest with huge hug.

She stood motionless in shock.

His large hands drifted into her hair and he pressed sweet, relieved kisses all over her face. "You have no idea what I thought… I was so worried…" He gave a crazed little laugh and picked her up, spinning her around.

"Derek?" she queried, a little worried. "You're not angry that I'm IAB? Disgusted?"

His eyes widened. "Of course not. It all makes sense now. You can't be seen with me, because it'll blow your cover."

Sable knew her smile must be radiant, because his face softened with such tenderness. "Most agents hate IAB. They don't trust us. Are you sure you really don't care?"

"Hell no, I don't care!" He laughed again. "Baby, I thought you were some kind of criminal. I was tearing myself up wondering what I'd gotten myself into." He kissed the tip of her nose. "I already knew, no matter what you were involved in, that I couldn't let you go."

Deeply touched, Sable felt her eyes tear up. Derek lived for his work and yet he'd considered setting aside his scruples just to be with her. It was a sacrifice that spoke volumes.

"Don't cry," he said hastily. "It's okay, I can help you. We'll solve your case, get you out of my field office and then we can get on with our lives. Together."

"You're so optimistic," she noted with a shake of her head. "And I'd always heard you were so cynical."

He shrugged. "We have a lot to look forward to. I can't wait until I have you all to myself for days at a time. I want the opportunity to get to know you better." His voice dripped with promise. "In every way possible."

With a gentle shove, she created distance between them and began to pace restlessly. "You may have to wait a long time, Derek." She didn't look at him. She couldn't. "And I can't ask you to do that. It wouldn't be fair."

"Wait for how long?" he asked, a frown evident in his tone.

"I've already been on this case for two years and I'm not much closer to solving it now when I started." Her hands clenched into fists at her sides. "There's a leak in your field office, Derek. One of the agents is selling sensitive information to the Federation. I'm only halfway through my investigation. I still have half the agents to investigate."

He grabbed her as she paced by him, pulling her to a halt in front of him. "Two years? That's about the time I first met you."

She nodded. "You were the first agent I investigated."

"And what did your investigation reveal?"

Sable lifted her chin to meet his amazing eyes. "That I'd met a man who made me hot. A man who made me wish for things I can't have. Things it's not possible for him to give."

"Until I met you." His gaze turned molten. "Am I cleared in your eyes?"

"Of course."

"Are you sure?" He searched her face. "You don't have any doubts?"

She met his questioning gaze head on. "I wouldn't have slept with you if I did. I wouldn't have even wanted to."

Tension visibly drained from his shoulders.

She stepped out of his embrace. "Now I have to get ready for the RetroBall. Agent Leroy will be attending tonight and he's next on my list."

"Jeff? I've known him for years. He's a good guy and he's having a rough time right now."

"I know. He's an agent in dire financial straits. His wife is dying and her medical bills are eating him alive."

"He's not the mole," he said with conviction.

Sable put her hands on her hips and arched a brow. "Listen, Derek. Don't try to tell me how to do my job. This thing between you and me won't work if you start interfering. I know what the fuck I'm doing. I happen to be a damn good agent."

Derek ran a hand through his hair and offered a sheepish smile. "I know you are."

"Leroy sent an update of his mission to headquarters this morning. He reaffirmed his pursuit of Kennedy Smith."

"Smuggler, pirate extraordinaire," he filled in. "So what? Sounds like he's on the job."

"Yeah well, Kennedy Smith has been in custody for the last two days. And this isn't the first time Leroy's lied about his missions. He's been coming to Rashier 6 at least once every six months."

Derek's eyes widened as he took in the implications of that. "Shit. So he's here for something else. I'll go with you to the ball," he offered.

She walked over to the bed and began to undress. "It would be better if you don't. Leroy will get suspicious if he sees you around."

He came up behind her and cupped her bare breasts in his hands. With a sigh of contentment, she leaned into his chest. It seemed like she'd waited forever for him to hold her like this, with lust heavily tempered by tenderness. His fingers found her nipples and squeezed, before rolling them gently. Her eyes closed on a soft moan.

"It doesn't seem fair that every other guy gets to ogle you in that dress," Derek whispered, before scraping his fangs gently across her shoulder.

Sable smiled. "I'll wear it for you later."

He stepped closer and swiveled his hips against her, revealing his renewed desire.

"Jeez, Derek." She laughed. "You don't quit, do you?"

"You wouldn't want me to." One large hand caressed the length of her torso and dipped between her legs. Two fingers parted her, while a third slipped across her clit. "Would you?"

Unable to speak, she shook her head. She widened her stance, shamelessly encouraging him to reach deeper.

"You're wet, baby."

"Yes..." Sable shivered as he thrust a long finger into her. And then another.

Derek licked the side of her neck. "Did it turn you on to suck me?" he breathed, pulling her tight against his cock and rubbing it against her. Even through his trousers, she could feel how hot he was.

"Hell, yes." Her hips moved in time with his fucking fingers. "Don't stop," she moaned, her eyes drifting shut.

"What if I'd rather fuck you with my tongue and return the favor?"

Melting at the thought of his mouth on her again, she

hummed a sound of encouragement. His hands moved to her hips and urged her toward the bed. "Get comfortable, baby. We're going to be busy awhile."

"Leroy…" she murmured in faint protest.

"Leroy can find his own pussy to eat," Derek growled.

She knew that tone of his. It was his "*You're going to come until you can't move*" tone. Her body responded instantly. Her breasts became tender and full. Her cunt creamed with excitement and a hard shudder coursed the length of her body.

"You want it bad," he teased, his irises molten with lust as he watched her arrange herself on the bed.

"Oh yeah." She spread her legs wide and arched a brow. "You're really good at this, you know."

"I'm glad you approve." Derek crawled up from the foot of the bed, his wicked mouth curved in naughty smile. "Because I'm addicted to your taste."

"Umm…" She settled into the pillows as he licked her ankle and then moved higher.

The feel of his tongue surrounded by the warm circle of his lips and the occasional tip of a sharp fang made her back arch upward, her body tensing in heated anticipation. There was a tenderness to his touch and an affection in his eyes that aroused her just as surely as his carnal attentions.

"You're killing me."

"I know." He chuckled, his broad shoulders pressing against her legs. "But I owe you a good time for telling me the truth."

"Can't you pay me back a little higher?" she complained, her pussy spasming impatiently.

His eyes flared at the sight. He turned his head and gave her a teasing swipe. She whimpered.

"Yum, baby." He spread her open with his fingers and nuzzled his lips against her, his silky hair caressing her inner thighs. "You're drenched."

"Derek..."

"Hush," he soothed, his mouth settling softly around her and suckling gently. His tongue stroked in a lazy back-and-forth motion over her clit.

She cried out, her legs trembling at the light touch. He wasn't feasting so much as worshipping and it felt so good she couldn't breathe, every cell and nerve ending waiting for the orgasm that hovered just out of reach. His lips closed, pressed a soft kiss against her, and then opened again, licking her in a patient, loving rhythm. Her hands fisted in the bedspread, her hips lifting and falling in matching tempo.

"Ready to come?" he breathed, two fingers of his free hand slipping through her cream until they were seated deep inside her. They fucked her slowly, in and out.

Sable watched and licked her fangs. The sight of him finger-fucking her was so totally erotic so thought she might come just from that. He stared back at her, his smile tender. Then he lowered his head, suckled her clit, and brought her to a powerful climax. She called out his name, her cunt clutching franticly at his pumping fingers. Derek held her there, drawing out her pleasure until she sagged into the bed with a moan. Before she could catch her breath, he made her come again.

"I need you," she begged, as his fingers worked inside her.

"These aren't enough?" he asked, his voice husky. He licked the taste of her from his lips. "I was hoping to stay down here awhile."

Shaking her head rapidly, she gave a soft cry as he screwed three fingers into her pussy. "I-I want your cock."

Derek lowered his head and sucked her off again, using a deep, drawing pull on her clit while his fingers twisted slowly inside her. Crying out in pleasure, she nevertheless beat her fists into the mattress with frustration. Her hair was drenched with sweat, her cunt swollen and desperate.

"Your cock," she gasped, her mouth and throat dry.

He pulled his fingers out and licked them clean. "Ah, what

every man loves to hear. His woman begging for his cock."

"Please." She managed a strained smile. "I'll make it good for you."

"Baby." He laughed, sliding from the bed and undressing. "There's no doubt about that."

When his trousers fell from his hips and his cock was revealed, she quivered with excitement. He was as hard and thick as if he hadn't just come moments ago. The head was engorged and weeping, the shaft thick and lined with the pulsing veins she loved so much.

"Hurry," she urged, wanting nothing more than to feel that massive cock inside her.

He crawled up the bed and knelt between her open legs. Catching the underside of her knees, Derek draped her thighs over his and took aim, rubbing the broad tip against the creamy opening of her pussy. "Watch me take you."

She whimpered as that beautiful cock sank into her with a slow, slick glide.

"Damn, Sable," he gasped. "You're soaked and burning hot." Rolling his hips, he pumped the last few inches into her. With her hips tilted up to receive him, he pressed in deep. "Fuck, I wanted this to last."

"No! Hurry."

But he didn't listen, choosing instead to pull out, and then press back slowly, massaging her deep within. Her nails dug into his thighs as he took her with an achingly patient rhythm, the tight muscles of his abdomen rippling with every thrust. Fighting against his hands, she wrapped her legs around his waist and ground onto his cock, swirling her hips.

"Oh man…" Derek breathed, his shaft jerking inside her. "Keep doing that."

"Yes!" she hissed, feeling the first flutters of her coming orgasm. Leveraging her lower body by rising on her elbows, she rode him with every bit of strength she had, her legs tightening to plunge him deep and then releasing to slip off him. Up.

Down. Up. Down.

And then she came. Hard. Clamping down on Derek's cock so hard he choked out a surprised sound before flooding her with a roar.

* * * * *

Derek wrapped a towel around his waist and said, "You sure you don't want to stay in?"

Sable laughed and left the bathroom. "Sorry, lover. I've got a mission to see to. And now I'm late."

"Alright, alright," he grumbled. "I need to feed anyway, and then I'll go back to the Starwing and look around. I have my suspicions about how those Federation ships found us." He tossed the towel in the corner and started to dress.

"You think they tracked us?" She turned to look at him.

"They must have. And for them to come after you like that…well, it was obviously a warning." He brushed the hair from his forehead. "You must be getting closer to the truth then they're comfortable with. If I can find a tracking device on the ship, maybe we can trace it."

"I don't just leave my ship open for tampering, you know."

"Never? Not once? How about when you caught Castle? You were locked up in your ship before I could catch you and I'm pretty damn fast."

"No, it was locked. I just had it programmed to open at my bio-signature, just in case my weapons drew attention from Concourse security."

"Then it must have been installed at headquarters."

Her eyes narrowed in thought. "If that's true, it would exonerate Leroy since he was already here on Rashier 6 at that time. Or," she said excitedly, "he could be working with someone else!"

She looked at Derek to see what he thought of her suspicion and found him watching her with rapt attention.

"You really like your job, don't you, baby?" he queried softly.

Sable chewed her bottom lip for a moment before answering. "I don't like finding out that someone we all trust, someone we believe is working toward the good of the Council, is actually harming us. I hate that part of my job. But when I solve a case, when I know that someone who violated the oath I believe so strongly in has been removed from the force, I love it."

Derek kissed her, long and deep, then swatted her on the butt. "Get dressed. And call for me if you need any help."

He headed toward the door. He seemed so happy and relieved that she'd told him the truth about herself, she wished she'd trusted him sooner. She shuddered to think of how different the outcome would have been had he not been persistent and stowed away on her ship. She might have lost him.

"I don't know how to use my calling yet," she called after him.

"You're stronger than you realize. Just think about me and I'll hear you. I promise." With a rakish wink, Derek left.

Chapter Five

Derek lay on his back and stared up at the tracking device in confused anger. He recognized the design and it was Council, not Federation. Sable was being tracked by their own people. But why?

With a curse, he removed the offending piece of technology, ripped off the serial number for future use and easily crushed the rest of the tracker in his hand. What the hell was going on?

He dissipated into mist and remerged in the captain's chair. There was no way in hell he was going to wait another two years to court Sable like he wanted. He'd lived several hundred years and he knew a lot of things could happen in just two. He wasn't willing to risk losing her or the wonderful feelings she inspired in him. He sure as hell wasn't going to sneak around, trying to find the time to squeeze in a little lovemaking. He'd never get enough of her that way.

Resting his head against the headrest, Derek closed his eyes and relished the fullness in his belly. It'd been as easy as usual to find a meal. In the past, he'd enjoyed the triple impalement of his cock and fangs in an eager woman who he then gifted with a mind-blowing orgasm for her donation.

Tonight though he'd only fed. He'd given his meal her orgasm with his calling and nothing more. Sable had completely drained him with her wicked mouth earlier, but even if he hadn't been sated, he still wouldn't have had the heart to fuck another woman. He'd asked Sable to remain faithful to him and for the first time in his life, he had every intention of being faithful in return.

She was his perfect counterpart, his equal. They were so

alike in so many ways—their jobs, their vampirism, their sexual appetite. Whoever said opposites attract was an idiot. He much preferred a woman who could understand him without asking and knew what he needed before he did.

Now he just had to keep her safe and get her through her assignment in one piece.

As his eyes remained closed, he felt a brush of feeling across his mind. He concentrated on it and tried to amplify it. Suddenly, he sat upright in the chair. It was Sable. Her thoughts were in a jumble, her pulse was racing and her breathing was erratic. He could sense something dark, insidious and possessive curling through her mind.

Moving too fast to be seen by human eyes, Derek flew out of the Starwing and was on his way to the RetroBall.

* * * * *

Sable stood motionless, her mind urging her to flee while her body refused to heed its dictates. She watched in stunned horror as Marius Drake approached her, his lips curved in a predatory grin of anticipation. Why the hell did he keep popping up in her life at the most inopportune times?

The expansive hotel ballroom was well lit, as befitted the RetroBall and Sable fought off the headache brought on by the unaccustomed bright lights. Multicolored streamers draped across the ceiling, and guests wore odd hats and blew on bizarre-sounding horns, all of which had her gritting her teeth.

She'd been searching the sea of guests for a glimpse of Jeffrey Leroy, when an insistent prodding in her thoughts had drawn her attention to Marius. He remained as arrogantly proud of bearing as always, his presence wordlessly conveying his power—a power it had taken her years to learn to resist. Still, Sable felt a deep fear and foreboding. She remained so untutored in the ways of vampires. She knew nothing about what rights Marius held over her.

Sable, my love, he drawled in her thoughts. *What an*

unexpected pleasure to see you again.

She eyed the handsome blond man who came to a halt in front her. Her pulse kicked into overdrive, and her skin grew cold and clammy. "Marius," she returned in an icy tone, as she ruthlessly shoved him from her mind. "What are you doing here?"

He laughed and the bitterness in the sound was harsh on her nerves. "You've gotten stronger. It took you no time at all to evict me from your thoughts. Have you missed me, my sweet novice? Are you tired yet of chasing the sewage of the universe? I am more than ready to have you come home."

"Never going to happen," she assured him. "I much prefer having my own thoughts and feelings. I enjoy living my own life."

Deep green eyes caressed her face with emotionless possession. "Your life was my gift to you. You would have been dead years ago had I not infected you with the virus."

"Your gift came with too many restrictions," she snapped, looking away as she searched the crowd for Leroy. She'd felt beholden to Marius for so long. Even now, she felt guilty for leaving him. "Go away. I'm not here for you."

"You live for me!" he hissed furiously. He gripped her elbow in what would have been a bone-snapping vise to a human. "You knew what I asked of you. I never deceived you. And you agreed to the terms."

Her head whipped toward his. "Bullshit. I was young, barely a woman, and foolishly infatuated with a handsome man who promised me the world and an eternity of his love. But you don't love anyone or anything besides yourself. You don't want *me*. You want a puppet you can control. I was *alive* before I met you. You didn't create me."

"I love you," he growled as he dragged her toward the crowded dance floor. "I've always loved you."

Sable attempted to shake off his grip, but couldn't. "See what I mean, Marius? You just do whatever the hell you please without regard to my feelings. If you truly loved me, you would see how miserable you make me and try to change it. Instead, you just want to change me."

Pulling her into his arms, Marius began to twirl her around to the ancient music he'd often enjoyed while they were together. He'd taught her how to dance, how to eat, how to have sex. He'd been grooming her to take her place at his side in the highest echelon of universe politics and prestige. But she had never wanted any of it. She'd only wanted him. But he was, and always would be, completely self-absorbed and unavailable. Nothing like Derek, who offered himself so freely and wanted her just the way she was.

Marius dipped her and kept her bent over his arm. His head lowered and he licked along her throat while taking a deep breath of her scent. Suddenly, he faltered, nearly dropping her. He yanked her upright abruptly, his emerald gaze shooting sparks in his fury. "You reek of another man. *Another vampire*," he spat. "You swore you didn't want to be with a vamp."

"No," she corrected smoothly as she stepped out of his now lax embrace. "I swore I didn't want to be with *you*." She jumped in surprise as a strong arm encircled her waist.

"Is there a problem here, baby?" Derek asked in a casual tone that didn't hide the possessiveness.

Sable glanced at him with relief. He had changed his clothes and stood at her side in an antique black-and-white ensemble that she thought was called a "tuxedo". He had never looked as seductively handsome.

She curled into his side. "Not anymore," she assured him.

"Introduce me to your plaything, Sable," Marius growled.

"Derek, darling," she cooed, deliberately goading the bristling blond man. "Meet Marius. Marius, this is Derek."

Marius extended his hand. "I am Sable's Master," he said with a satisfied smirk, watching with glee as his rival stiffened at the news.

But Derek recovered swiftly and smiled a purely male

smile. "Well then, I must thank you. Your infection of Sable allowed her to live long enough to become my mate." He bowed. "I am in your debt."

"She's not your mate, so enjoy her while you can," Marius snapped. His hands clenched into fists. "She won't be able to avoid my calling forever." He looked at Sable. "Have a care, love. For yourself and your toy."

Sable took a quick step toward him, the murderous expression on her face causing the Master vampire to take a step back. "Don't threaten me and don't threaten Derek. Trust me, you won't like the way I respond."

Derek grabbed Sable around the waist and pulled her backward. He bared his fangs in a territorial warning as Marius stepped toward them. The blond man wisely backed down—for the moment. Derek knew he would have to deal with Sable's past eventually, but tonight was not the time and the RetroBall was not the place.

Once they had retreated a safe distance away, he set Sable down and linked his fingers with hers, dragging her from the room. "Have you lost your damn mind?" he muttered.

"You heard him," she said crossly. "He was threatening us, the slimy bastard! He's lucky I didn't rip out his balls."

Derek looked at her over his shoulder and winced. "Ouch. Remind me not to get on your bad side."

She grinned. "Don't get on my bad side."

"Point taken," he said dryly, then he turned serious. "You leave Marius Drake to me. You've got guts, baby, but you're a novice and you're *his* novice. You don't have enough control yet to be tangling with a Master."

"You're a Master," she pointed out. "I think I'm pretty good at tangling with you."

He stopped and pulled her to him, lowering his lips to hers. He kissed her long and hard, with one hand at her waist and the other at her breast. His thumb stroked across her nipple until it peaked, eager for more. Instantly hot for him, she moaned into his mouth, heedless of the crush of partygoers around them.

"You don't want to tangle with him like you do with me," he murmured.

Breathless, she stared into his intent face and got lost in the swirling desire she saw reflected in his eyes. "No, I don't."

"No, you don't." He straightened and pulled her toward the exit. "I'm far older than Marius Drake. There are very few vamps who are as old as I am, so leave the heavy lifting to me."

She tugged on his hand, digging in her heels. "Okay. Slow down. I can't leave yet. I haven't found Agent Leroy."

"I saw him leaving on my way in to claim you."

"What?" Sable's shoulders slumped in disappointment. "Shit, we'll never find him now."

"Yes, we will," Derek assured her.

"Have you got a tracking device on him or something?"

He snorted. "Listen. I did find a tracking device on your ship. And it's not a Fed design. It's Council."

"What the fuck?" she stumbled to a halt, gaping at the back of his head.

"Yeah." He tugged her along again. "My thoughts exactly. When we get through with Leroy, we'll see if the serial number is registered somewhere."

"Wow," she breathed, her stomach roiling. "I don't know what to think about that."

"Don't think about it now," he soothed. "I'll take care of you."

"This has been a really trying day, Derek. Look at everything that's happened."

"You've got me, so it can't be all bad." He tossed her a careless smile over his shoulder. "And I overheard Leroy getting directions from the front desk. I know just where he is."

"Getting you is worth all this shit," she said softly, profoundly affected by that smile.

He stepped out into the lobby and headed for the elevators. "We'll go to our rooms and change out of these ridiculous clothes. Then we'll see what he's up to."

"I happen to think you look very tasty in those clothes."

His mouth curved with sardonic amusement. "I have to wonder at your taste, Sable. You liked me in my uniform too."

"I like you best naked," she purred.

The elevator doors slid shut and he engulfed her in a warm embrace. "This crap with Leroy better be over quick," he groaned, his hands caressing the length of her spine. "Yours is the only body I'm interested in chasing right now."

* * * * *

Derek kept his large form tucked closely against the wall of the small motel on the outskirts of town. Music wafted across the still night air as various room occupants held impromptu parties. Out here, away from the city, the night was darker and the sounds of transports less intrusive. Stars shimmered in the sky above, as did the moon, which hung low and full.

It was a night made for lovers.

Or hunters.

He glanced back at Sable. She moved on silent feet behind him, her hand twitching restlessly by the hilt of her lasersword, which was strapped to the side of her lithe thigh. She wore tight black trousers and a tighter black tank top, her erect nipples easily delineated through the thin fabric. As a slight breeze blew Sable's luscious scent to him, his cock swelled with an unwanted erection.

He was going to throttle Jeff.

Glancing forward again, Derek inched his way along the dimly lit outside corridor. He'd forgotten to mention to Sable what he'd discovered about Marius Drake accessing, and possibly deleting, her records. At the time, he'd been too grateful that the other man hadn't recognized him in his costume to remember to tell her.

In any case, that definitely hadn't been their last meeting.

The President was obviously not in agreement with Sable that their relationship was over. Derek intended to do something about that. Somehow, he would convince the other Master that Sable was now off-limits and by her own choice.

As they reached the motel room door that shielded Leroy from their prying eyes, he slowed and placed a finger over his lips. Sable stepped past him and took a position on the other side of the portal. She cocked her head and listened. Her nostrils flared and her eyes widened.

He's fucking someone! she mouthed.

Derek knew his face had to be as shocked as Sable's. Jeff was married for Christ's sake and had always seemed devoted to his wife who even now lay dying. Raising his brows, Derek shrugged sheepishly.

Sable snorted with disgust and walked away.

He followed. "Damn, I'm going to beat Jeff within an inch of life when he gets out of there."

"For cheating on his wife?"

"No, for doing what we would be doing, if we weren't out here chasing him down."

She laughed and Derek softened his posture. Only a few days ago she'd been openly hostile toward him. Now they shared a growing connection that he was beginning to value greatly. "Sable?"

"Yeah?" She turned those stunning blue eyes toward him.

"If I hadn't trapped you on my ship a couple of days ago, would you have come after me when your mission was over?"

She scratched the back of her head. "I doubt it."

"Why not?" He was surprised that she'd answered without hesitation. "You said you were interested in me from the beginning, that you're crazy about me."

"I was. I am." She crossed her arms under her chest. "But

you're an arrogant bastard. I had my share of inflated egos with Marius. And your reputation precedes you. You never stick with the same woman for long. My track record with men isn't very good, as you witnessed tonight. I doubt I would have thought you were worth the risk."

"I'm not arrogant," he protested.

Raising a brow, she said nothing. Which said a lot.

"And now?" he prodded. "Do you consider me a good risk now?"

She met his gaze and her ripe lips pursed in thought. Finally, she said, "The jury's still out on that one. You'll have to prove it to me, I guess."

"And how do I do that?"

"Stick around, Derek," she said quietly. "Just stick around."

He opened his mouth to speak, but she shook her head. "Do me a favor, okay? I'm beginning to suspect your friend Leroy is doing nothing more criminal than adultery. I'm not blowing my cover for that. Will you question him when he comes out? If my suspicions are correct, it will prevent the waste of two years of work."

"No problem," he agreed. "I'll come up with a good reason for being here."

"Good, I've got something to take care of." She strode down the hall.

You're just going to leave me here? he called after her in surprise.

"Sure," she tossed over her shoulder. "I trust you, Derek."

* * * * *

Sable crossed the street and entered the nearby telecomm café. She'd checked in with her superior earlier that day, but already so much had happened since then. She needed to know where IAB wanted her to go from here. Slipping into a privacy booth, she closed the door and inserted her identi-card. She was pulling on the headphones and mouthpiece to further safeguard her conversation, when Captain Donnie appeared.

"Good evening, Captain."

The jovial Donnie smiled good-naturedly. "It's barely morning here, Taylor. What have you got?"

"Another all-nighter? How does your wife put up with you?" She smiled at his grimace. "I'm not positive yet, but I'm fairly certain we can rule out Leroy."

The captain sat back in his chair and frowned. "Another agent cleared. This case has me stumped."

"Yeah, me too, but we must be getting close. Someone at the STF field office placed a tracking device on my ship yesterday."

"You told me about the tracker earlier, but you didn't tell me it was implanted at headquarters."

"I didn't know until a few minutes ago. The device found on my ship was a Council design."

"But it was the Fed that attacked you."

"Exactly. Can you imagine the ramifications if the Federation has purchased the codes to our trackers and have access to our tracking information? They could locate any of our ships, at any time. We'd be sitting ducks."

"Shit, Taylor." Donnie shook his head. "If that's true, this is a lot bigger than we thought. I'm going to assign someone to assist you in investigating the remaining agents in that field office. I don't want to step on your toes, but it would make the work go twice as fast."

Sable nodded and tried to hide her relief. If she'd been presented with that idea yesterday, she'd have been mad as hell. Today, however, she realized she was in over her head. She was proud, sure. But she wasn't stupid. "Sure, Captain. I'm all for wrapping this up as soon as possible."

"Good. Glad you're not getting territorial about this." Donnie arched a brow. "Really isn't like you to concede so easily about a case that you've worked your ass off for."

She shrugged and thought of Derek. He'd taken a leave of absence for her and she longed to do the same for him. "I'm tired, boss. I could use a little time away."

"Soon, Taylor," he agreed. "I'll give you three months leave when this is over."

"Great. Divide the remaining agents and leave a list of my assignments in the database for me to check in the morning." She stretched and yawned. "I haven't slept in days. I'm going back to my hotel to crash."

The captain nodded sympathetically. "You do that. You look tired and for a vamp, that's saying something."

* * * * *

Sable woke slowly. Opening her eyes, she could tell by the dim light creeping in around the blackout drapes that it had to be late afternoon. She stretched, grinning as her leg brushed along Derek's thigh. He slept like most vamps did, like the dead, his heavily muscled torso rising and falling with the measured breaths of deep sleep.

She brushed a hand along the rippled planes of his stomach and smiled as he groaned softly, the bed linens starting to rise with his erection. She stroked the heated length of him through the thin sheet, feeling him swell to rock hardness with a few deft squeezes of her hand.

Watching Derek as she built his desire, Sable took in the masculine beauty of his features—the full, sensual curve of his lips, the strong line of his jaw, the bold sweep of his raven brows. Just watching him so innocent and boyish in repose made her heart ache for him. He was physically beautiful, but also emotionally supportive, something she truly had never expected from him. The last two years she'd spent watching him and wishing she could have him, she'd never allowed herself to picture beyond the heartache she'd thought he would bring.

She grew wet and hot as her hands drifted with feather

lightness over his satiny skin and the light matting of hair on his chest. She wanted him. Wanted to always wake to the sight of him, gorgeous and tousled and eagerly receptive to her sexual advances. She pushed aside the sheet and licked her lips at the sight of his massive cock, fully engorged and pointing straight in the air.

As the cool air of the room drifted over his skin, Derek turned instinctively toward her warmth. Sable tossed her leg over his hip and wiggled until the hot head of his erection pressed at the creamy opening of her cunt. He'd taken her often during those two days on his Starwing. More than once, she'd woken up to the awareness of her body tensing in orgasm, discovering Derek's tongue or cock thrusting deep inside her.

It was time to pay him back.

She closed her eyes and, with a downward thrust of her hips, impaled herself on him with a tortured moan of p. Shivering as needles of sensation swept over her skin and hardened her nipples, Sable set her hands on his broad shoulders and buried her face against his chest. She breathed him in, absorbing the luscious scent that drove her to distraction and hoped with all her heart that they could make a relationship work.

Unbearably aroused, she ground downward, massaging her clit with his pelvic bone. Her face rested just inches away from Derek's and when she opened her eyes, she found herself staring into his shocked and passion-heavy gaze.

"Damn, baby," he murmured in a sleep-raspy voice, sparkling erect fangs peeping out as he spoke. "A guy could get used to waking up like this."

Sable rolled him gently onto his back, straddling his lean hips and forcing him deeper into her core. "Yeah? Well, a girl could get used to waking a guy up like this." She raised slightly, the heavy weight of his cock slipping wetly from her, then she slid down around him again, gasping at the feel of his thickness boring deep.

Derek gripped the tops of her thighs, his expression intense. "You've got a deal."

He lifted her and then thrust his hips upward to meet her downward drive. They both groaned.

She began to ride him with the same slow strokes that he liked to use on her. Torturous stokes that drove them both insane. Again and again, she rode his cock until she couldn't tell where he ended and she began. Her back arched, her head fell forward and her fangs descended. With a quick hiss of warning, she bit into his throat.

Rich and heady, Derek's blood was a nearly intoxicating delight. She reached out to his mind, feeling for the connection in the red haze of her overwhelming desire. She writhed over his body, her breasts rubbing across his chest, her stomach sticking to his with their mingled sweat, her arms wrapped around his shoulders as she held on to his bucking body with all of her strength. His tunneling cock stretched her deliciously and his warm hands firmly guided her hips while his deep voice purred encouragement in her ear. And then he was there, in her mind.

Sable, he growled. *So damn good. Nothing has ever felt this good.*

She sobbed almost desperately against his throat. It wasn't what he said, but what he felt, her mind flooding with his affection and need. Her entire body began to contract in anticipation of her orgasm and he urged her to a faster pace.

I'm here, baby. I'm right here inside you.

She'd never experienced this closeness with anyone, this need to merge completely with another individual. Derek knew what she needed and he was with her, everywhere. Over her, under her, around her, inside her.

Her body began to shake and she released his neck, pounding her hips onto his. The orgasm swept her away, hard and fierce, like Derek, who rolled her beneath him and fucked her like a beast, pumping his cock through the grasping spasms of her climax.

Sable held onto sanity by a thread as he built another sweeping tide of pleasure in her veins. Powerful and insistent, their need for each other would not be denied.

Wrapping her legs around his hips, she felt his steely buttocks clench and release against her calves as he propelled himself so deeply into her body that she felt him in her throat. She screamed as another orgasm claimed her.

Her eyes flew open in astonished pleasure and she met his gaze—dark and possessive and hot with passion. His face was flushed and sweat dripped from his forehead to splatter onto her skin. His fangs glistened in the semi-darkness and she arched her neck to him, wanting to gift him as he'd gifted her. It had ceased to be just sex and they both knew it. Better yet, they both welcomed the added intimacy.

As he pierced her skin, she felt his shaft swell and then jerk inside her, his scorching cum spurting out in powerful jets that brought her to the brink of pleasure and then shoved her over. Her back arched, her blood poured freely into his seductively sucking mouth, her pussy gripped his spending cock in a fist of silk. And in her heart, she felt Derek demanding entry.

She opened the door and let him in.

Chapter Six

Derek closed the tiny punctures he'd left in Sable's throat with reverent laps of his tongue and willed his heart to slow its fevered thumping. Making love with her just got better and better. He could feel the power her touch gave him flowering in his body. He rolled to his side, taking her with him, relishing the feel of their sweat-slicked skin stuck together.

I like the feeling too.

Derek looked down at Sable in surprised pride and awe.

She grinned at him. *I love the way you smell after sex. You smell like me – plus power and pure male vampire. It's very yummy.*

He gifted her with an exuberant kiss. "You're calling me."

She nodded shyly. "Every time you touch me, I grow stronger. I've been feeling your strength building within me since the first time we made love."

He nodded. "It's the same for me."

"What does it mean?" Her smooth brow was marred by a tiny frown. "Is this normal? I never felt like this with Marius."

Derek caressed the length of her spine. "I don't know what it is. But I like it."

"Me too." Her fingers drew invisible drawings on his chest. "So what happened after I left last night?"

He knew she was asking about Jeffrey Leroy. "You were right. Jeff is getting a little piece of action on the side."

Sable pinched his nipple, renewing the desire within him. He'd never been so physically attuned to a woman before. It was unnerving, in more ways than one.

"Where did you get that tuxedo you wore last night?"

"Someone reminded me yesterday that it was Retro-bration here on Rashier 6. I picked that costume up at a shop in town. Just in case." He smiled with lascivious intent. "You looked stunning last night in the slinky dress you wore. We'll have to keep that around for some off-duty use."

She tweaked his nipple again and blood rushed to his groin. "We may get that downtime you wanted a little earlier than I anticipated."

He shoved a pillow under his head to look into her eyes. "How so?"

"I spoke with my captain last night. He's going to assign another agent to partner with me on this case. He'll divide the remaining agents from your field office between us and hopefully, we'll get done twice as fast."

"While the news is good to my ears, I want to know how you feel about that." He brushed his fingertips along the side of her face. "I wouldn't think you'd like having to share a case you worked so hard on."

She gave a little shrug that strove to be nonchalant and almost succeeded. "I'm okay with it. Work doesn't hold the same appeal that it used to. Maybe I'm just a little burnt out."

Or maybe I'd rather be with you.

Derek kept his face impassive as her thought entered his head as clearly as if she'd spoken it. She was still so new to calling, she didn't know how to shield herself yet. And he didn't mind. His heart leapt at the simple declaration and he held her tighter. "So what's the plan for this evening, baby?"

"Tonight we leave Rashier 6." She rested her chin on his chest. "How much time did you take off from work? Do you need to go back yet?" *Please say no.*

As he felt the twinge of sadness that colored her thoughts, he kissed the tip of her nose. She still had doubts about his interest in her. He, however, no longer had any. "I have all the time in the world. It's only been a couple of days. I can stay with you."

"A couple of days. Is that all? I feel like I've known you forever."

"It's been a week since I first took you to my ship, but we had two years of foreplay before that."

Most people would consider them to be strangers, but Derek knew Sable from the inside out. They were connected so completely, he could sense her thoughts and emotions.

"Umm, foreplay," she purred.

"Not that you gave me a chance for any of that this morning." His hands drifted to the tempting curve of her ass. He pressed her into his growing erection.

"You loved it." Her mouth curved in a provoking smile. *Bet you'd love me to do it again too.*

"I'd love for you to do it again." He bit the lobe of her ear and hid his smile.

She wiggled her hips into position and pushed down onto his thick cock easily, her passage lubricated with her cream and his cum. He watched her eyes darken as he filled her. Then her voice came husky and warm.

"Derek, darling, you read my mind."

* * * * *

Sable hung the last of Derek's new clothes next to hers in the closet of her quarters on the Starwing. In a way, it was comforting to see his belongings nestled so intimately with hers. In another way, it was like an invasion. He was merging himself into her life so completely, she wondered if it would ever be the same when he left.

Maybe he won't leave, whispered a little flare of hope. But she squelched the thought. It wasn't a good idea to get her hopes up so soon. Everything was still too new.

Sighing, she exited her ship through the cargo door and searched the bustling crowds of passengers for Derek.

"Hello, Sable love."

She stiffened at the familiar voice and turned. Marius stood just inches away at the end of the ramp. Wary, she rose up on her tiptoes and glanced over his shoulder, searching for Derek.

"Your toy is still in the concourse," he assured her.

"What do you want, Marius?" she asked coldly.

He grinned and the light in his emerald eyes chilled her to the bone. "You need to ask yourself what you want—do you want to keep your boyfriend? Or do you care enough for him to let him go?"

Sable felt her stomach tighten into a knot of dread. They'd spent decades together and she knew Marius so well. He wouldn't be such a successful politician if he didn't know how to play dirty. "What are you talking about?"

"Your plaything."

"What have you done?"

Marius shrugged, his shoulder-length blond hair drifting around his handsome face. "Nothing. Yet. The choice is yours to make."

How had she ever imagined that she loved this man? "Let's not speak in riddles. Tell me what you want and how much I'll have to bleed to give it to you."

He stepped closer, curling his palm around her cheek. "If you want to stay with Atkinson, I can't stop you, but I can get you drummed off the Force. And I will."

She offered a grim smile. "Go ahead and try it. I've already proven myself to be an excellent agent. You'll have a hell of a time proving otherwise."

"I don't need to prove otherwise. You're a vamp. Since the popular opinion right now says that a predator shouldn't be guarding the prey, it won't take much to get you pensioned."

Knocking his hand away, she snapped, "Do your worst, then. But stay the hell out of my life afterwards."

"If you don't care about yourself, do you care about Atkinson?" His lips hardened into a harsh line. "I think he appreciates his job a little more than you do. Do you have any idea what he went through to get into the force? The academy was full when he applied and Captain Hoff had already begun his lobbying to keep vamps out. Atkinson slipped in when I got you in."

"You what?" Her face drained of color.

"Did you really think you got in on your own merit?" he asked softly. "Oh, you did well in the academy and Captain Donnie wanted you for IAB, but you should've gone through years on patrol with a partner and then more at a desk on the Force before moving into Internal Affairs. But I knew how badly you wanted the job and I pulled a couple of strings. You think I don't care for you, Sable, but I do. I would do anything to see you happy."

Sable recoiled, her mind in a near daze. *How long had Marius been watching her?* "If you truly wanted me to be happy, you'd let me have Derek." She lifted her gaze to meet his. "I love him."

Marius shook his head. "He's not for you. Can't you see that? He won't stay faithful to you or cherish you like I will. He's a bachelor and always will be."

"Maybe you're wrong," she whispered.

"Are you willing to take that chance?" he asked, exploiting her greatest fear—losing Derek. "You've seen how much he loves his job," he pressed. "Atkinson may not care at first if he's kicked out of the STF, but eventually he'll resent you. And you'll lose him anyway. I'm a very powerful man, Sable, and I'll do whatever is necessary to keep you from being hurt."

Marius would follow through on his threat, she had no doubt. "What do you want in return for leaving him alone?"

"Break it off with him. Now. And come back to me. I want you back in my house, back in my bed. If you do that, not only will I leave him alone, I'll help him get promoted."

She snorted. "I won't share your bed. You make me sick."

"But you'll come home?" he asked with obvious excitement.

"It's not home to me anymore, Marius. I'll have my own room and I want it in writing that you'll assist Derek with his career. You give me those assurances and I'll move back in." He'd lose interest eventually. She'd make sure of it. In the meantime, it wasn't fair to Derek to drag him into her mistakes. She had to protect him and she would. Whatever the cost.

Marius grinned with triumph. "Of course," he agreed in the soothing tone of voice one would use with a petulant child. "I don't want you unwilling. I'll change your mind, love. You'll see. You'll forget about Atkinson and remember how much you love me, how right we are together. You're mine, Sable, and soon you'll remember that. You'll ask me back into your bed. And I can wait until you're ready."

Her lips curled with distaste. "You'll be waiting forever."

He bent his head low and kissed her cheek. "It's a lucky thing we're vampires then. I have forever to wait."

* * * * *

Derek gave an appreciative whistle as he stepped aboard Sable's Starwing. She'd dimmed the lights in the main cabin and all the adjoining rooms. Scented candles were everywhere, permeating the air with a sultry scent. Through it he could smell his woman, his mate. Her seductive call lured him in and he barely remembered to close the cargo door in his haste to find her.

As he stepped into the cockpit, his heart stopped. Sable stood with her back to him, her lithe body draped with a crimson robe. She knew he was there, he could sense her instant arousal and emotional pleasure in his proximity, but she didn't turn around.

"Remove your clothes and go lay on the bed," she ordered in a husky murmur. "I'm just finishing programming the coordinates to headquarters and then I'm going to fuck you all the way home."

His cock hardened to bursting immediately. Vamps were

sensual creatures by nature, but never had he experienced this kind of instant physical response before.

"Damn, baby," he growled, stepping toward her. Breathing her lush scent deep into his lungs, he cupped the cheeks of her ass and ground his erection in the cleft between. "You can drive me crazy with just a few words."

She punched a few more buttons and then turned to face him. "That's not all I can do to drive you crazy." She dropped to her knees, hitting the catch of his bio-suit on the way down.

Eager to help, he shrugged out of the sleeves with a haste that made them both laugh. He stared down at her, admiring the way the deep crimson material looked against her pale skin and dark hair. Her luscious lips curved in a wicked smile and then her tongue darted out, just catching the tip of erection.

"Baby," he growled, shuddered from that simple, tiny contact. Then his head fell back on a groan as Sable sucked his aching cock into her hot mouth.

Damn, she was good at giving head. She sucked him off like she starving for him, her greedy mouth tugging in an erotic rhythm that made him want to come. Right. This. Minute. And she moaned as she did it, telling him that she loved the act as much as he did. The vibrations of the sound traveled through his cock, into his balls, making his knees go weak.

Soft slurping sounds filled the cockpit. It was so fucking raw and base, the sight of her on her knees, her lips stretched wide to accommodate his thickness. She couldn't take him all, not even half, but he liked that. It turned him on to see how hard he was, to see his cock shiny with her saliva and his pre-cum, which leaked profusely, because he was so aroused. He felt her tongue stroke rapidly over the veins of his shaft and then tease the tender spot just behind the head, and he tangled his fingers in her silky hair to guide her motions. He began to thrust his hips, fucking her mouth, loving how erotic it looked to take her this way.

Her hands left his ass and tugged open her robe, her long

fingers grasping her erect nipples and squeezing. Rolling. She moaned again and his cock swelled until he felt the pressure of her fangs on either side. Swiveling his hips, he deliberately scraped his skin against the tip, hissing at the slight pain, but gasping a moment later as that faint taste of his blood drove her crazy. Sable began to suck him so hard he almost thought she could suck the cum right out of him.

Too far gone with lust to control himself, Derek thrust deep, the head of his cock dipping into the tight clasp of her throat. *Oh, fuck, it was good.* He felt his balls tighten up and he spread his legs to anchor himself more firmly to the deck.

One of Sable's hands left her breast and slipped between her legs. He growled as her lithe body shivered with pleasure.

"Fuck yourself," he ordered hoarsely, knowing that if she did, he'd come harder than he ever had in his life.

Sable whimpered and widened her kneeling stance, dropping her other hand between her thighs. One finger thrust straight up into her cunt. Derek heard the wetness that greeted her and knew she was creaming for his cock. He gripped her head tightly and fucked her mouth like a man possessed. He felt the need building, his balls aching, his cock swelling. And then she took the finger out of her pussy, reached under his drawn-up balls and, using her own cum for lubrication, slipped her finger deep into his ass. He shouted as he came, his semen pumping out of him, coating the back of her throat. Over and over his cock jerked, his vision going black as she fucked his ass with her finger.

She moaned, sucking him so hard, trying to drain him. When he swayed, she pulled out of him and supported his hips with the tight clasp of her hands.

Derek pulled her head away from him roughly, still jetting his cum and he lifted her up and impaled her in one brutal thrust. As soon as her heated cunt wrapped around him, Sable stiffened in orgasm.

He watched her, startled and awed as the spasms of her

climax sucked his cock just as powerfully as her mouth had. The sex was amazing, fantastic, but it faded in significance compared to the way she looked at him. *Like she loved him.*

Driven by a frenzy of adoration and lust, he lifted her body until just the tip of his dick speared her creamy opening and then he thrust her down onto him. Over and over he lifted and impaled her, claiming her, marking her, flooding her with his cum.

She writhed on his cock and in his hands, screaming his name and he showed her no mercy, pounding her onto his erection until she came again. And still he wouldn't stop fucking her.

His mind reached out to hers and she let him in. This time, she let him in almost completely and he wrapped her in his sensual call. He felt the immediate effect it had on her, her body melting in his hands, her silken pussy gripping him like a vise. And he felt something else, something dark and very desperate, as if she were pulling away or hiding something. It wasn't something he could take, not when he was lost in her, totally crazed for her.

Keep coming, he urged, determined to get past those last shields. *That's it, baby. Damn, that's so good… Squeeze my cock with that tight cunt.*

And she did, endlessly, her juices dripping down his straining thighs, her throat closed on a scream.

Derek kept her under his spell, refusing to spend himself again even though her pussy worked greedily to milk him. He kept his dick hard and kept pleasuring her with it, because her satisfaction was paramount, more important than his own.

In the part of his mind that still worked, he thought if he could sate her enough, she'd have to admit how she felt. He'd make her admit it.

She was so beautiful in his arms, her black hair damp with sweat, her pale skin flushed with passion, her lips swollen and shiny with his cum, her lithe body impaled on his own. He'd never felt like this in his life—filled with his lover in his mind, his body, his soul, his heart.

Derek's eyes widened.

His heart.

He *loved* Sable.

Joy, fierce and wild and sweet, welled within him and he longed to share it with her. *I love you*, he declared with every fiber of his being. *Baby, I love you so much.*

And deep inside her, he felt something die.

Chapter Seven

Sable heard Derek's passionate declaration and felt his love shining brightly in her mind and in her soul. Her love for him rose in a fierce tide, threatening to overflow and wash them both away. But she bottled it up, hiding it, knowing that if Derek were to sense the depth of her affection, he would never let her go.

And he had to let her go.

Despite how much she wished they could be together now, she wouldn't ruin his life for her own selfish desires. It would be wrong to take his love and hurt him with it, and that's just what would happen if she didn't take care of Marius now.

Having seen Derek in action over the last two years, she knew he was good at his job and that he loved it. Maybe more than he loved her. She was new in his life and he was used to living without her. She'd rather leave with him loving her, than lose him to a festering resentment in his heart because she'd cost him a livelihood that meant so much to him.

But for tonight he was hers and she would love his body until morning and his soul until forever, even though he would never know it.

She wrapped her arms around him and suckled the side of his throat, not biting or feeding, just loving. He released her slowly, allowing her legs to touch the cold metal floor. She could feel the full, heavy prod of his arousal brush against her hip and realized that he hadn't come again. Her eyes lifted to his and her breath caught in her throat at the love she saw shining there. "Derek?" she queried, confused.

He kissed her forehead with such tenderness she wanted to cry. "I'm saving it for you, baby," he told her as he led her, fingers linked, into the bedroom. "I intend to pleasure you all night."

"You always do."

Lifting her feet from the floor, Derek set her on the bed. Sable scrambled to her knees. As much as she wanted to love him, to hold him with tenderness and speak her heart, she couldn't. In fact, it was best if she started to push him away now, so when she left tomorrow, it would not seem such a big surprise.

"I love you." He cupped her face and kissed her long and slow. "I love everything about you."

Her heart tightened painfully and she covered his mouth with her fingertips. "Please."

"Please, what?"

"Don't say that."

Derek frowned as he looked at her. He searched her face, his silver gaze too perceptive. "Why not?"

She felt him in her mind, probing, seeking. "It's too soon," she blurted out, pushing him from her thoughts. "You don't know how you feel. And it makes me…uncomfortable."

His features gave away none of his thoughts, but she felt what he did and knew she'd hurt him. She wanted to cry, to scream, to confess. Instead, she shifted nervously. "After Marius, I just don't—"

"Hush," he soothed, the tense line of his jaw softening. "It's okay. I can wait however long it takes for you to believe in me."

Eyes burning with unshed tears, she gripped his swollen cock and stroked, relief flooding her when she felt his focus alter. A girl could always distract her man with sex. "I want you again," she murmured, moving into position on her hands and knees. She looked over her shoulder at him. "Now."

Derek stood behind her, the touch of his hands on her hips sending his thoughts and feelings pouring into her. He kissed upward along the length of her spine, the depth of his feeling covering her in a safe, warm blanket. "You have me," he said softly and then he slipped his cock into her in one slow glide.

She gasped and arched her back, heat immediately flaring across her skin, flushing her. His large body came over hers, his hands over hers, his body caging her to the bed. His hips moved his cock in shallow massaging strokes. The connection between them deepened, until she felt echoes of what he felt—the tight clasp of her swollen tissues, the liquid heat of her cream.

"Wow," he breathed, his cheek resting against her shoulder. "Feel that?"

"Yes…"

"I want to feel everything with you."

Sable closed her eyes, knowing there wasn't time to share everything. They only had a few hours left.

Derek rose up, his hands caressing her quivering thighs, and then he rubbed a thumb along the tight rosette. "Would you let me take you here?" he rasped. "I'd love to feel that."

Swallowing hard and unable to speak, she nodded, clenching tight around him as he swelled inside her. He continued that gentle, teasing rubbing and she shivered at the sensation.

"Have you taken a man here before?"

"No."

"It hurts the first few times," he warned, but the tiny tremors in his hands betrayed how much he wanted this.

"You're big."

"Yes." He slipped out of her and she protested with a plaintive whimper. Sitting on the bed next to her, Derek drew her into his lap. Lifting her chin with a gentle finger, he brought her gaze up to his. "Whether you're ready for it or not, I love you. You don't have to say it back and you sure as hell don't have to prove it. I'm happy being with you just the way you are. The happiest I've ever been. I'm completely satisfied, Sable."

Unable to help herself, she allowed a little of the love she felt for him to shine in her eyes. "Do you have to be so damn wonderful?"

He laughed.

"I want to give you this, Derek. Something I've never given anyone. Wouldn't you like that?"

"I'd like it so much it would probably kill me." He kissed the tip of her nose and hugged her close. "But I don't want to hurt you. It takes time and preparation. Lust is riding me pretty hard right now and I don't think I'm capable of the control initiating you requires."

"I'm a vamp. I heal quickly."

He pulled back and searched her face again. "Is this what *you* want? Or are you only offering to please me?"

She wiggled her ass against the burning length of his cock. "I suspect I'll like it. With you." Her voice lowered. "There's oil in the drawer."

He gave a wicked chuckle, returned her to the bed and held her down when she tried to roll onto her stomach.

"Don't move," he ordered as he stood between her thighs and lowered his head for a kiss. His sweetly seductive mouth pressed gently over hers, coaxing her to relax with teasing strokes of his velvety tongue. His thoughts caressed her mind. *Easy, baby. Concentrate on the feel of my hands, the touch of my lips, the warmth of my body pressed against yours.*

"Mmm," she moaned into his mouth as his skilled hands caressed the underside of her breasts, the callused pads of his thumbs brushing against her nipples. They peaked hard and tight, addicted to his touch. Even when Derek was apart from her they craved the pinch of his fingers.

Her hands drifted to his back, massaging the muscles she felt flexing as he gentled her. His skin was so warm, so sleek and fluid over the tight ropes of sinew underneath. His body was as gorgeous as his face, a work of art in its sheer perfection. She gave herself up to that body, to the seduction that it wielded with such consummate skill.

Seduce me, she pleaded. *Make me forget everything but you.*

Sable felt his answering love in the very marrow of her bones. Then his sensual call wrapped around her like a thick fog, obscuring her restlessness, erasing Marius and his threats just as she'd hoped. Deeper and deeper he drew her under his spell, warm and welcoming and wondrously arousing on the deepest level. He didn't probe or pry, merely surrounded her in his affection.

Suddenly, his hands felt as if they were everywhere at once, his mouth sucking and moving across her skin in a thousand different places at the same time. His scent was so wonderful, like sex and vampire. He tasted so good, like chocolate-covered sin. His lips, those beautifully sculpted lips, were opened wide against hers, so soft and sensual.

Sometimes, he thought, *I want you so badly I can't think.*

Sable closed her eyes and engulfed him in her very essence, wanting to touch him all over as he was touching her. Derek groaned, the sound so erotic that goose bumps spread over her skin.

It's never enough, baby. I can never get deep enough.

His hot mouth left hers, traveling across her jaw and then lower, licking along the vein in her neck, making her body weep with a rush of moisture. Reaching her breasts, he surrounded her nipples, holding one gently between his teeth while his tongue flicked across the tip until she mewled like a kitten and twisted restlessly in his arms. Then he paid the same loving attention to the other one. His warm hands caressed the length of her torso, kneading and petting in maddening rhythm until they slid between her thighs, spread them wide and found her dripping with need.

His long fingers spread the folds of her cunt and slipped inside, one swirling around her clit, two more penetrating her deeply. She moaned uncontrollably, calling his name. Derek was mouthwatering, the beautifully delineated muscles in his arm flexing with every deep plunge, his touch so reverent and possessive.

I love this, your cunt filled with my cum. I need to fill you everywhere.

Covered in her cream and his seed, his lubricated fingers slid lower. He caressed the tight rosette with soothing circles. The soft swirling of his fingers was endlessly arousing and yet completely wicked. But she wasn't afraid. How could she be? This was Derek and he loved her, adored her. He would never hurt her and she could sense his expectation, his careful control. He wanted her this way, wanted it so badly he was almost shaking with the anticipation. He was a Master after all, a vampire used to having his own way. And she controlled him completely, ruled him in the most base of ways. This was her gift—her complete submission—and he knew her well enough to recognize the level of trust she gave him.

One finger pressed firmly against the tight rosette and with a gasp of pleasure, Sable relaxed and it slid deep inside.

Hot. So tight. Fuck, Sable, you're going to burn me alive.

She lifted her heels to the edge of the mattress and moaned, her hands going to her breasts to massage their swollen ache. *Take me.*

Soon. His finger withdrew and then returned.

He growled when her cunt spasmed.

She groaned.

It was strange, odd. A burning pressure, but not too painful. He worked his finger faster, fucking her until her hips rolled desperately. Then he retreated. Derek reached for the single drawer that protruded from the wall and found the oil. He rolled the bottle between his hands, warming the golden fluid. Then he opened the top and drizzled the liquid between her spread legs. She whimpered, one hand going between her legs and massaging her throbbing clit.

Don't come, he warned. *Not until I'm inside you.*

"Derek!" she protested, near mad with lust. Two of his fingers were fucking her tight hole, stretching and yet pleasing. It was almost painful, but she was shielded by his calling, wrapped in his love. Three fingers. Burning, more stretching. But she was wet, so wet that her fingers pumping into her pussy were drenched and her hips started a gentle tempo in time with his thrusts. He bent over her, his mouth capturing a stiff nipple and suckling. His erection was rock-hard and stabbing into the back of her thigh, weeping rivulets of pre-cum.

Now? he asked, concerned and yet so eager she could feel it.

Yes, now. She wanted him so badly, wanted to feel him inside her.

He stepped back, just enough distance to position the thick length of his cock at her tight, well-oiled rosette. His slick hand worked his cock, lubricating it. The sight of his masturbating almost made her come and she bit hard into her lower lip to prevent it. She was desperate for him, so aroused she could barely breathe.

Hurry.

Soon, baby.

Now!

And then he was there, huge and so hard, pressing for entry. Pressing until the tight hole flowered for him and the thick head of his cock popped through the tight ring. Sable gasped and writhed as he entered. So slowly. Pain grew and spread. She turned her head into the pillow and whimpered,

I can feel it, he thought. *Relax, baby.*

Clenching her sheets, she forced herself to relax.

Derek paused, his breathing harsh, his palms damp where he held her thighs open. *Do you want me to stop?*

No, she moaned, feeling his cock against her fingers through the thin membrane that separated them.

Let me in, Sable. I can take the pain away if you let me in.

The warm blanket of his call wrapped even tighter around her and she felt nothing but the heated length of him, tunneling deep with infinite care.

Mine.

Yes.

Forever.

And Sable said nothing, could say nothing. She wanted to shield her thoughts, but Derek had taken over, controlling her mind as he controlled her body, sliding home balls-deep in the depths of her ass. Pleasure poured from his consciousness into hers. The muscles of his stomach were clenched tightly as he began to thrust, gently at first to allow her to accommodate him, and then faster.

Hot, so tight and sweet, he groaned, sweat dripping from his forehead onto her belly. *I love you. I love you so much.*

Spread wide, she was pinned beneath him, his cock stroking through the oil into the dark depths of her. She moaned, lost in the pleasure, feeling him glide past her fingers on every deep plunge.

Sable shattered in orgasm, bursting into a million pieces. Lost in his love, her love, she felt his cock jerk and his cum spurt in hot bursts, filling her ass with his seed. And through the blinding power of their mutual orgasm she was flooded with his thoughts.

So good. Yours, I'm yours. Never get enough. Want you more. Need you. Love you. Love you. Mine. All mine, my love.

Her heart broke.

* * * * *

Derek woke up with widest grin. He knew he must look starstruck, but he couldn't help it. He felt boneless and sated to his very soul. His chosen mate knew how to please him very well. Sable had slept for an hour at most and then she'd woken him to a hot cleansing cloth wrapped around his cock, which was later followed by her hot mouth.

Insatiable, she'd fucked him repeatedly throughout the night and he'd given himself completely into her hands. She had drawn him into her calling, drenched him with her luxurious sensuality and loved him to his core. His grin began to hurt, it was so big.

She loved him. Sable Taylor loved him.

She hadn't actually said the words, she hadn't even thought the words, but he'd felt it just the same. Her love for him was a precious thing. His most cherished possession.

He reached for her, but didn't sense her. Derek frowned and sat up, searching for her with his eyes and his senses. "Sable?"

Silence. In the room and in his mind.

He tossed the covers back and swung his legs over the edge of the bed. A rustling noise stilled him. He dug through the covers until he found the note.

Derek,

We're docked at your field office headquarters. I've gone. Don't come for me. It's over between us. I could never feel for you what you claim to feel for me and it wouldn't be right to lead you on or give you hope for things that can never be.

I don't want to make this harder for you. I'm sorry if you became more emotionally involved than you should have. It was never my intention to hurt you, but after Marius, your love is not something I want.

Thank you for your assistance in my investigation. Thank you for everything.

— Sable

Derek shook his head and blinked rapidly. Was he having a nightmare? He looked at the open clothes locker and saw that all of Sable's belongings were gone.

Had she gone insane? Had he fucked the sense right out of her brain?

He must have, if she thought he was going to buy this shit. She loved him. He had no doubt about that. None.

He'd sensed her turmoil all night, had wondered about it

and in the end had dismissed it as nerves. She was falling deeper and deeper in love with him, and he knew that scared her.

He crumpled the note in his hand.

He sighed in resignation as he got out of the warm bed that smelled so strongly of sex and Sable. They were going to have to work on this fucking him and leaving bullshit.

Damned impossible woman.

Chapter Eight

Derek walked into the quiet squad room. A quick glance at the monitor told him all of the other agents were out in the field. His name on the roster was dimmed, showing his leave of absence status.

"Atkinson."

He turned to face Captain Hoff. "Yes, sir?"

"Is that Sable Taylor's Starwing in docking bay 7?"

"It sure is."

"Where is she?"

Shrugging, Derek said, "Hell if I know."

"Is she in the med-lab?"

Derek turned and leaned back against the counter, his arms crossing his chest. He eyed the captain carefully. "Not that I'm aware of. Why would she be?"

Hoff smiled easily. "Glad to hear that. I'd heard there was a spot of trouble with her ship. I'm relieved to hear she wasn't injured."

"Umm," Derek hummed. This was getting interesting. "I thought you didn't like vamps?"

"I don't. On the Force. She's a bounty hunter and a good one. She's helped us quite a bit, don't you think?"

"Sure. I'm just surprised to hear that you do." He pushed away from the counter. "Well, it's been fun chatting with you, Captain, but I'm still on leave, so I'll be heading out now."

"Are you leaving with Taylor?"

Derek studied the captain again. "Why would I do that?"

A red brow arched sardonically. "You came here in her

ship."

"You sure know a lot about what happens with her," Derek pointed out.

"That's my job, Atkinson. I have to know what's going on with everyone who enters this building." Hoff walked toward his office. "Enjoy your vacation."

Derek watched the captain walk away, frowning at the thought that entered his mind. Hoff was far too interested in Sable, always had been. She was constantly being detained, sometimes for hours. In the past, he'd always assumed that her unconventional methods of capture had attracted the unwanted attention. Now, he wondered if there was more to Sable's case than she'd let on.

How many secrets did she have?

* * * * *

Derek settled into the captain's chair of the *Viper* and established a secure comm link with his assistant. He was not in a good mood. In fact, he felt murderous. He'd figured out where Sable had run off to. She was with Marius Drake. And he'd been chasing the two of them for almost three weeks. To his fury, he always seemed to be a step behind them.

Marius was a wealthy man with a dozen different residences scattered all over the galaxy. Unfortunately for Derek, he seemed determined to take Sable to each and every one of them, causing Derek to slowly lose his mind. So far he'd been able to detect by scent that Sable was using her own room and Marius was staying the hell away from her, but how long would that last? Loving Sable like he did, Derek knew it must be torture for Marius to have her so close and not take her. But if the other man touched her… And if she let him…

Derek growled.

The screen before him lit up with the image of his assistant and he offered a curt greeting.

"Good afternoon to you, too, sir," Stein returned. "On the

Viper again, I see, and from your tone, I take it you were unsuccessful at catching up with them."

"Not for much longer," Derek muttered. "Did you discover anything interesting since the last time I spoke with you?"

"Quite a bit, actually." Stein fumbled around on his cluttered desk. "I managed to hack into President Drake's file."

Derek grunted. "About damn time."

"My job is not as easy as it looks, sir," Stein retorted. "However, despite the delay, I think you'll be pleased. Once I gained access to the file, I located Ms. Taylor's. He hadn't erased it as I'd originally thought, merely swallowed it into his."

"Son of bitch," Derek growled.

"There were some very interesting things in there. First of all, it appears that Ms. Taylor has been a project of the President's almost since birth."

"I knew that already. He's been grooming her to be his mate. He just wasn't counting on her having any backbone."

"Well, were you aware that he's been tracking her?" Stein asked. "He's had a tracking device on every one of her ships since she broke off their personal relationship."

Derek's eyes widened. Marius had put the tracking device on her ship? "I think that tracking device almost got her killed."

"So you said. I researched the schematics of the particular devices used on Ms. Taylor's ships. The President had them specially designed so that the authorities wouldn't be able to pick up the signal. It could only be read by a special receiver, one that he alone possesses."

"Damn, so the Federation didn't find her that way."

"It doesn't appear likely," Stein agreed. "As I searched deeper into the President's account, I noticed we aren't the only ones who've been delving into his information."

"Hoff."

Stein's mouth fell open. "How the hell do you do that?" he asked, startling Derek with the rare curse.

"Hoff asked me some odd questions the last time I saw him and he knew about the attack against Sable's ship."

"So you've discovered the culprit. Ms. Taylor was the key after all."

"I suppose that's true, but not in the way I had originally assumed. Can you prove Hoff had access to the tracking device information?"

"Without a doubt. I'll send a security team to apprehend him immediately." Stein smiled. "Now that the traitor's been discovered, sir, will you be dropping your cover and returning to the Security Council?"

"Soon," Derek said evasively. He damn well wasn't returning anywhere without Sable. "Did you get a copy of the video from the concourse on Rashier 6?"

"Yes, sir. I downloaded it to your ship just a few moments ago."

"Excellent. I'm on my way to Sarjon to check on another Drake residence. Comm me if you have any trouble with Hoff."

"Of course. Good luck, sir. I'm looking forward to meeting Ms. Taylor. She sounds like a remarkable woman."

"She is," Derek murmured. "Atkinson out."

He took a deep breath before playing the video taken by docking security on Rashier 6. Even though he knew deep in his soul that Sable loved him, part of him still feared what he would witness on the video.

He froze as the screen flickered and Sable appeared, standing on the cargo ramp of her Starwing speaking with Marius Drake. Stein had done an excellent job of filtering out the background noise and Derek listened in rapt attention as Marius blackmailed Sable into breaking off their relationship.

"*I love him*," Sable told Marius on the tape.

And Derek's heart swelled. He hadn't misread her. He rewound the video and played her words again. And again.

The tiny seed of doubt that had tried to take root, insidious and punishing, urging him to think that maybe Sable's note had been the truth, withered and died and would never return.

"I'm coming for you, baby," he whispered to her beloved face, frozen on the screen. "I'm coming."

* * * * *

It was approaching midnight when the transport cab pulled away from the large house. Sable waited a few moments more before leaving her hiding place in the bushes, just to be certain they wouldn't return for something they'd forgotten. She'd finally solved her investigation. Now she had only to capture the culprit. She'd wondered how this hunt would go down when Captain Hoff had come out of his house with his family in tow. But then he'd kissed them goodbye and sent them on ahead.

Now it was just the two of them.

She crossed the moonlit circular driveway and rounded the side of the house. Knowing how trigger-happy some agents were, Sable had waited until just a few moments ago to comm in her call for backup. She couldn't risk them arriving too soon and scaring her prey away. Not after the last two years of hard work.

Marius had done his worst to screw up her life, so it was ironic that he'd really helped her instead. Living with him had given her access to his computers and his passwords. With those advantages, she'd planted information under his access code. She'd created two secret Council files—one with a reference to a fabricated new weapon and one with a nonexistent "cure" for vampirism. Knowing that both of those items would be invaluable to the Federation, she'd deliberately left a back door to those files open and waited for the traitor to make their move.

It had been a risky gamble, but one that paid off. The traitor hadn't bothered to hide his personal information when he'd downloaded the files. It would have taken weeks to circumvent the Council anti-hacker programs with an anonymous identity, and since Sable had set the files for automatic deletion in a couple days, she'd forced his hand. He'd used his own unique access code and revealed his identity in his greed.

And now his gig was up, as the archaic saying went.

Sneaking into the house through the kitchen door, Sable moved into the living room and crawled up the wall to the ceiling. She could hear Hoff packing quickly, shoving documents into a bag along with a few articles of clothing. Her fingers twitched restlessly around the hilt of her laserword, preventing it from slipping out and crashing to the floor below. She walked toward the hallway with noiseless steps.

Waiting.

Hunting.

Hoff fell silent and her senses heightened. She crouched low, hugging the ceiling, as the hairs on her nape stood on end. And then she heard it, the sounds of transports moving into the drive.

Damn it, how did the Task Force get here so fast? With a smothered curse, she crawled from the ceiling to the floor without a sound. Preparing to pounce, she was startled by a steely arm wrapping around her throat.

"Vamp bitch," Hoff hissed in her ear. "I'd hoped those Federation ships would kill you! They would have too, if you hadn't had Atkinson on board to assist you."

Sable stilled, but she wasn't afraid. She could easily break the human male in half with her bare hands. "Not a wise move," she said casually. She felt a sharp prodding against her back.

"Feel that?"

"Yeah, don't rip my tank. It's my favorite."

"I'm going to rip your heart out," he growled. "And then I'm going to stake it through. The Federation is working on a program to eradicate your kind. I can only hope the information I sold them will speed up its inception."

Sable rolled her eyes, grabbed the arm that crushed her windpipe and broke it.

The wooden stake in Hoff's other hand pressed against her

skin and then sank in an inch. It burned like forged metal and she hissed, her fangs descending, her animal nature springing to the fore. She spun on him, furious and prepared to kill. Vamps didn't get defensive. They killed. Fully a predator, she lunged for his throat and was tackled from the side, the force of the blow carrying her across the room. In pain from the stake wound, Sable fought viciously against the men who held her down.

"Taylor!"

As she registered the sound of her captain's voice, she felt the red haze of fury drain from her. She stared up at the STF agents who struggled to restrain her.

"I'm fine," she growled. "I said I'm fine!" she repeated when they refused to release her.

"See?" screamed Hoff. "You can't trust them! You can't control them! They're infected, diseased, rabid animals that need to be put down. They'll kill us all. We're nothing but food to them."

Sable leapt to her feet and glared at the wild-eyed, red-haired man who struggled between the grips of two agents. "Get him out of here."

Captain Donnie stepped into the doorway after the agents dragged Hoff away. His countenance was grim as he came toward her. "What the hell is the matter with you, Taylor? You've never lost control like that before."

She winced. The captain was right. She'd let her personal turmoil affect her actions at a time when she should have been in control. And she knew why. Living with Marius was driving her insane.

"I'm sorry, Captain. You're right." Her shoulders drooped. "I've been having some…issues. They got the better of me."

Donnie shook his head and sighed. "I promised you three months leave of absence when this case was over. Why don't you start them now? Just send your report to me by the end of the week."

Sable nodded. "Thanks, Captain."

Then she headed home to Marius.

* * * * *

Sable entered one of the dozen ostentatious, opulent mansions that belonged to Marius Drake and was grateful that she'd never have to enter it again. While she'd been in the database under Marius's access code, she'd stumbled onto something that had shattered her heart. Derek wasn't at all the man he'd said he was. She'd been staying with Marius trying to protect Derek and it turned out he didn't need her protection at all. That meant neither of the master vamps had a hold on her anymore. She was free and once she packed up her stuff, she planned to hole up for a while and wait for her broken heart to heal.

She was two steps up the staircase on her way to pack her bags when the growling and crashing in the expansive ballroom halted her ascent. Weary, but curious, Sable lifted her nose and sniffed the air. She smelled the two Master vampires immediately. Their territorial hormones filled the air, their heady and intoxicating blood pervading her senses, making her heart race and her palms damp.

She moved to the open doorway of the ballroom and surveyed the damage. The place was a mess. The heavy, three-story tall velvet drapes hung in tatters and every piece of furniture in the room lay smashed to pieces.

Her gaze searched for and found the combatants over twenty feet above the floor. They were clinging to opposite walls of the room, panting and snarling, their handsome features distorted with rage and bloodlust. Both of their nostrils flared as she entered, smelling the blood from her wound. They became even more enraged, more animals than men, their hormones and instincts running the show. By her assessment, the battle for a mate had begun hours ago.

The battle for her.

She drank in the sight of Derek, noting the minor injuries he bore. He was obviously winning, because Marius was in far worse shape. A relieved breath escaped her in a sigh. She was furious, yes, and terribly hurt, but she would never wish him harm. In fact, she couldn't bear it if something happened to him.

If Marius weren't so stubborn, he'd admit that she wasn't the mate for him. He needed a wife who relished power and politics as much as he did. Sable liked action and a hands-on approach. Political sidestepping just wasn't something she could spend an eternity doing. They also didn't love each other anymore, if they ever truly had. It was time for him to move on, too.

And Derek... What the hell was he doing here? Hadn't he gotten everything he needed out of her? The hollow ache in her chest became nigh unbearable and she lifted a hand to shelter her heart. Her stomach did a little flip at the thought of him coming after her and fighting for her, but she squelched the tiny hope ruthlessly. He'd lied about who he was, he'd used her body to get what he wanted, he'd demanded the truth from her and then hadn't given her the same courtesy. Everything they'd shared had been a lie. It didn't matter if he still wanted to fuck her. He didn't love her. Not like she loved him.

Despite all this, her body softened, responding instinctively to the scent of her mate and the pheromones he exuded in his battle to win her. Looking at him and needing him with every breath she took broke her heart a little more. She loved him desperately, but she couldn't trust him and there was no future to be had with someone you couldn't trust.

She remembered their conversation in the hotel on Rashier 6...

"At least you're honest."

"Because that's what I want from you in return, Sable — your honesty."

"And I'll give it to you."

What a fool she'd been. And these two were even dumber

for fighting over her when she didn't want anything to do with either of them.

"You're both idiots," she said scornfully.

Then she turned on the heel of her boot and left.

Chapter Nine

๛

Derek's senses were inundated by his mate's proximity, his body recognizing her scent and adjusting to it. He stared at Sable's beautiful face with a soul-deep longing. Three weeks. Three damn weeks since he'd last seen her. He waited for her to smile, to show some pleasure at seeing him again. Instead she looked at him impassively for only an instant before leaving the room.

Filled with the animalistic need to claim his woman, he was no longer even remotely human. Moving with extraordinary speed, he crawled along the wall and out of the room, following her up the staircase. Marius did the same, wisely keeping to the opposite wall.

The blond Master was badly cut and bleeding profusely, but remained determined to fight. Derek felt a reluctant admiration and a tiny grain of pity for the other man. To have once had Sable and then to have lost her—he could only imagine the pain of that. But his imagination was enough.

Sable climbed the stairs with a casual, unhurried stride. She had to sense the two territorial Masters crawling along the walls above her, but she ignored both of them. That worried Derek a lot, but not nearly as much as he worried about the scent of her blood.

Sure, she was tough and could take care of herself, he wouldn't try to shield her because she'd hate that and resent him. Still, he knew he was going to be terrified every time she was endangered. But he accepted that, because he loved her the way she was.

As she entered her bedroom, she left the door open and Derek preceded Marius into the room behind her. As she pulled a bag out from under her bed and began to pack, Derek felt the rage boiling in his blood reduce to a steady simmer. He shot a glance at Marius. "She's coming with me," he growled triumphantly.

Marius hissed at him and crouched for another lunge when Sable's calm voice stilled them both.

"No, I'm not, *President Atkinson*." She snorted in disgust. "You're so damn arrogant you didn't even attempt to disguise your name."

Derek winced. Shit, shit, shit. She'd found out before he could tell her.

He felt his spine straighten, his muscles lengthening, his fangs and claws withdrawing, as the animal retreated and allowed the man to emerge. He reached out to her with his calling, tossing it over her like a warm blanket. *Sable, love…*

She tossed it right back. *Nice try, lover, but the mission is wrapped. Haven't you heard? You don't need to seduce me anymore.*

Marius growled, remaining in his combat form out of sheer self-preservation. "Sable, we have a deal," he reminded her in a guttural voice no human could comprehend.

"Deal's off," she said coldly. She continued to pack without looking at either one of them. "Didn't you hear me? Derek isn't a STF agent. Fuck, he *controls* the STF. He's President of the Interstellar Security Council. He's just as powerful and connected as you are. In fact, I can't believe you didn't place his name and face. You can't do anything to him and you can't do anything to me. Not anymore. Not ever again."

"I'll protect you," Derek assured her smoothly, still trying to connect with her, but ramming into the impenetrable wall she'd erected against him. Her ability to block his calling was amazing and impressive. As she aged and matured, she would become a formidable vamp the likes of which Derek had never seen. And he wanted to be there with her on every step of the journey.

"Of course you'll protect me," she agreed, pressing a button on the side of her bag, which compacted it to a quarter of its former size. She brushed past him. "You wouldn't want word to get out about how you seduced your way into an IAB agent's bed just to solve a case."

His hand snaked out and clutched her elbow, halting her retreat. He searched her sapphire gaze, and found it icy and remote. "Damn it, Sable. That's not true!"

Fury blazed in her eyes. "Are you denying that you went undercover and followed me for two years?"

His jaw tightened. "No, but—"

"Are you saying that when you detained me aboard your ship after the Windemere incident your intention wasn't at least partly to fuck information out of me?"

His nostrils flared. "Partly, but then—"

"And are you trying to tell me that when you stowed away on my ship, your intention wasn't to decide once and for all if I was the agent selling information to the Federation?"

He swallowed hard. This was bad. She knew everything. "Fuck, it isn't what you think."

"It's exactly what I think," she retorted, before yanking her arm from his grip and storming out.

Marius moved first to follow her. "Sable. I tried to warn you about him."

She continued downstairs, leaving the two men to trail behind her. "Go to hell, Marius. How do you think I discovered who he was? You kept popping up in my life in all the wrong places. The first thing I did after I moved in was use your computer to access your records. I know all about the tracking devices you've been planting on my ships."

"I can explain—" he began.

"Don't bother," she said curtly. "In a way, I'm grateful, even though that damned tracking device almost got me killed by the Federation. Once I got into your records, I saw a Charles Stein poking around in there. I looked him up and found out he's the assistant to Security Council President D. Atkinson, presently on a mission of Interstellar Security. It didn't take me a second to put it together. Maybe if you'd been doing your job instead of stalking me, you would have remembered voting him into office." She threw her free hand up in the air. "I'm done with pushy, overbearing, domineering, lying, bullshitting vampire Masters. I think I'll find me a nice docile human male for once. Someone *I* can push around for a change."

"Sable!" the two Masters cried in stunned horror.

She waved at them over her shoulder and slammed the front door shut behind her.

* * * * *

Derek stood on the edge of the expansive ballroom in the Interstellar Council Headquarters and watched the hundreds of dignitaries and their escorts swirl by on the dance floor. From the corner of his eye, a glimmer of golden hair caught his attention.

Marius Drake danced by with his fiancé, a beautiful woman who looked very much like him—cold and blonde. It had taken the other Master less than a month to find a newer, more docile mate after realizing that Sable was far more vamp than he could handle. Marius had tolerated her walking out on him once, but the second time was too much for his monumental ego.

Derek groaned inwardly. He, on the other hand, was still pining away for his one true love. He'd waited seven hundred years to find her and he would love her forever. He'd tried to track her down, but she'd simply disappeared and he had no idea where to look. When Sable Taylor wanted to hide, she knew just how to do it.

He turned away from the festivities and headed down the hallway toward his offices. Work was his entire existence lately. All work and no play made Derek a very grumpy vampire. He hadn't gone this long without sex in over six hundred years and it showed. He was curt and short-tempered, and since he'd ordered half his staff to scour the universe for Sable everyone knew why.

He strode through the open door leading to his outer offices and then further into his own expansive suite. He went straight to his desk and checked his messages. Sixteen agents had reported in, but the results were all the same—no sign of Sable.

He slammed his fist onto the desk. "Damn it, baby, where are you?"

I hear you've been looking for me.

He looked up in shock, then shot to his feet. Sable lounged in the doorway, her long legs crossed at the ankles, her torso encased in the old-fashioned silver dress from Rashier 6. Her hair was piled high on her head, and she was gorgeous. Breathtaking.

"You came back," he whispered, insanely worried that he'd frighten her away.

Pushing away from the doorjamb, she sauntered in with an exaggerated sway of her hips that made his cock harden instantly. "Why did you suspect me of treason?" she asked in a conversational tone of voice that couldn't hide the hurt in her eyes.

"Your file was incomplete, with large gaps and inconsistencies. In fact, Captain Donnie hid you so well, I recently promoted him. He had you listed in the IAB database as a droid, an area I'm ashamed to say I never thought to look in, so I never caught it. As far as I knew, you were a bounty hunter, but unlike most, you didn't take breaks after every capture. You never stopped hunting. It was a red flag to me that you needed so much money and despite how many captures you made, you never seemed to get ahead financially. The leak was coming out of the Gamma Sector field office and that's the one you worked out of the most. It was reasonable to investigate you."

"I see." She licked her bottom lip. "When did you realize you were wrong?"

"After those two days on my ship." He rounded his desk.

"When I established our first mental connection you were distant and secretive, but I sensed nothing but good in you and a strong desire for justice."

"You still thought I was a criminal."

"There were too many questions, baby, and you block me very well. Too well. But even if you had been involved in something illegal, I would have found a way to keep you."

The left strap of her dress slipped down her shoulder, displaying the creamy swell of her breast. "Why didn't you tell me who you were when I told you I was IAB?"

Derek swallowed hard and leaned back against the front of his desk. "I was already falling in love with you. I knew what you would think if I told you. I was afraid you wouldn't believe my interest in you was genuine. And you see I was right. You broke it off with me as soon as you knew."

Her steps slowed. "Were you ever going to tell me?"

"Sure. Right after the wedding."

The other strap slipped and the dress hung onto her torso against the laws of gravity, barely clinging to the mounds of her breasts. His fangs descended as his cock swelled.

Her sapphire gaze narrowed. "Don't you think that's a little arrogant?"

He shrugged, pressing a palm against his straining, painful erection. "What better way to prove my love?"

As soon as he said the words, he felt her sensual call swirling around him— hot, misty and alluring. Sweat broke out on his forehead.

"I do love you," he whispered fervently. "If you can believe anything I say, believe that."

The dress fell to floor and Sable was gloriously naked beneath it, baring her firm, high breasts with their berry-colored nipples, her sleek abdomen and her impossibly long legs. All taut and toned, covered by creamy pale skin.

Damn, he loved her body.

"I realized you must care, at least a little," she murmured.

"More than a little, baby. More than anything."

"Otherwise, I wouldn't have come back for you."

Derek tore his silver jacket, the symbol of his station, away from his body. His pants also fell in tatters to the floor. And still she stood, unmoving, waiting.

Waiting for what?

"Let it out," she urged in a throaty murmur. "Like the first time you took me and made me yours. You claimed me then, like a beast. And I loved it."

He watched her hungrily, memorizing her just as she was now, then his eyes slid closed. He felt his power and need rising inside him, heard her blood pumping through her veins and smelled her arousal. The animal tore at him, fighting to be freed, and he struggled to restrain it, to control it. It began to radiate through his cells, growing in strength.

Then she said what he'd longed to hear.

"I love you, Derek."

And he couldn't hold it back any longer.

* * * * *

Sable felt the energy building within her mate. It poured from him in hot, steadily radiating waves. She smelled him—pure, potent vampire male. Her vampire. Her Master. Her slave. Her love.

Everything. All things. I'll be all you need. All you want, he promised. Then he leapt at her.

She watched him in a daze, as if time had frozen, contained in a bubble. Strong, powerful, beautifully masculine, his body stretched through the air. And then suddenly the bubble burst and she leapt to the top of his desk, neatly avoiding his grasp.

He growled, a deep rumble that vibrated through the air into her body. Cream flooded between her legs as her nipples hardened and her mouth watered at the sight of him. His magnificent cock was so hard, it curved upward to nearly touch his navel.

She crouched and her lips curved in a come-hither smile. Moving slowly, carefully, she twisted to sit on the edge of the desk and spread her legs wide, letting him see her welcome. She leaned her weight on one hand, while the other reached between her legs and stroked her swollen clit.

She watched his nostrils flare, watched him lick his fangs with a loving caress of his tongue. His eyes were molten silver, his muscles bunched and thickened, his cock swelled and wept. And through his heat and mindless lust she felt his love, powerful and true. She lifted her heels to the edge of the desk, opening herself completely to receive his mounting. *Fuck me.*

Derek's haunches bunched tighter with his crouch and then he sprang. She closed her eyes and forced herself to relax. She'd asked for the beast and that was exactly what she was going to get—a raw, primal claiming.

The only warning she got that she'd miscalculated was the hot steam of his breath across her inner thighs an instant before his tongue slipped inside her. Gasping in surprise, Sable lifted onto her elbows, affording her a breathtaking view of his gorgeous face buried with enthusiasm between her thighs.

His tongue, elongated by the vampirism within him, laved the creamy walls her pussy with surprising tenderness in his animalistic state. Lapping, licking and fucking, he goaded her desire, built her passion. He latched onto her clit as two fingers slipped in through her cream and began to plunge slowly. Sable cried out as she spasmed in climax, her cunt rhythmically sucking at his thrusting fingers. His mouth moved to the pulsing vein on her inner thigh and he struck deep with his fangs.

Instantly his sensual call enveloped her and she was lost in the mindless pleasure of his fucking fingers and the deep, erotic pulling of his warm mouth on her skin. She came hard, her orgasm blinding her with pleasure.

When he finally released her, Sable collapsed backward

upon the desk. Her heart pounded hard against her rib cage, her thighs trembled and her entire body quaked in the aftermath of her powerful release. Derek crawled over her, his eyes lit with masculine satisfaction, and his seductive grin was feral and predatory. He gripped his thick cock in one hand and started to enter her when she pushed him away with such force he sprawled on his back on the floor. She pounced on him and laughed.

"Not so fast, lover. This time, you're mine."

* * * * *

Derek looked up at the beautiful woman who caged him to the floor with her body and fell even deeper in love. Sable had let her own animal loose, releasing her power and desire to soak the air around them.

Everything primitive and fierce within her answered the call of everything base and carnal within him. She was his mate, his better half, his truest love. She complemented and completed him. And she had come back to him.

She loved him.

In one fell swoop, she thrust her hips downward and engulfed his cock in the heated, creamy embrace of her cunt. His back arched as sharp pains of pleasure flared out from his groin and fired every nerve ending in his body. But Sable didn't give him time to recover, her cunt slipped up and down his erection at a rapidly increasing, superhuman pace. He'd never been fucked by a vampire in her full animal state before. It was glorious, primordial. He could feel every inch of her and experienced, through her thoughts, how he felt inside her. How he stretched her and filled her perfectly.

Pumping and gasping, Sable rode him hard and then harder, claiming him. His balls tightened, his cock swelled, his eyes clenched shut along with his jaw. Derek felt her mouth suckling his neck the second before her fangs sunk deep. Her head remained motionless as she drank from him while her hips continued the wild fucking of his shaft. She called to him, sweetly brushing across his mind and his soul.

I love you love you love you love you love you.

Growling and snarling and cursing, he exploded in orgasm with hard, pulsing jets of cum, spewing his essence directly into her core, branding her from the inside. His claws ripped into the rug beneath him. Pleasure inundated him, pouring out of him and into her mind. Sable screamed, her cunt clamping onto his jerking cock as she joined him, still chanting her love, while soaking up all of his.

* * * * *

Sable stirred slowly, nuzzling her mouth against Derek's damp chest. Deep within her body she could still feel him pulsing and deep in her soul she felt the warmth of his love.

"Will you marry me?" he asked as his hands stroked the length of her spine.

"Of course."

He kissed the top of her head. "I have another proposition for you as well."

"Really?" she drawled, rising onto her elbows to look at him. For the first time the affection in his eyes brought her joy and not pain.

His sexy mouth curved in a smile. "I want you to work for me."

"Hmmm."

"I want to keep you close by. I have an idea that'll keep you busy and out of trouble."

"Trouble?" She arched a brow. "I'm never in trouble."

Derek rolled his eyes and laughed. "Hear me out. We have to make preemptive strikes against the Federation. They know half the Council consists of vamps. If they find a way to kill us it will disrupt the entire universe. I've decided to establish an elite corps of vamp agents to handle missions that require superhuman skills and the utmost secrecy. And I want you to help me train the agents I select."

Sable shook her head sadly. "The Council will never go for it. Vamps are facing too much bigotry and opposition as it is. To create a group that excludes humans because they don't possess our skills will be political suicide for you."

He grinned. "That's why no one is going to know the corps exists except for you and me."

"And if we get caught, Derek? What then?"

"I can afford to support us indefinitely, but it won't happen." He licked her lips. "What do you think? Ready to take on the universe with me?"

She brushed back a damp lock of hair that had tumbled onto his forehead. "I think I love you. And if I can take you on, I can take on anything."

He growled. "Is that a yes?" He grew hard again inside her.

She rolled her eyes. "Are you always going to use sex to get what you want from me?"

Rolling her beneath him, he gifted her with a devilish smile. "That's my intention."

She purred. "How can I refuse an offer like that?"

KISS OF THE NIGHT

Dedication

୫ଠ

This story is dedicated to my fabulous editor, Briana St. James, after whom my heroine is named. She pushes me to reach a little deeper, and in doing so, she makes the stories I share with you better.

Thanks, Bree.

Chapter One

༃

Alex Night's entire body hummed with anticipation as the lovely blonde cut through the crowded lounge and headed directly toward him. The dancing throng parted for the tiny woman without protest, her presence so compelling it demanded respect and received it without question.

A moment ago, the popular band had held his complete attention. Now his keen hearing tuned out the music and focused instead on the steady, rhythmic tapping of her high-heeled boots upon the vented steel floor. Dressed in a black bio-suit that hid her rank, Representative Briana Michaels had forgone her customary tight chignon in favor of soft, shoulder-length curls. She'd made no overt attempt to mask her famous features, but the difference wrought by her clothing and hair was remarkable enough that she went unrecognized by everyone but him.

She looked harmless enough, cute actually, if one failed to note the blaster strapped to her thigh. A newer model gun, by the look of it. Briana was a deadly beauty with a razor-sharp mind—a potent combination for a man like Alex.

Proceeding with the mission when the brain in charge was between his legs broke every protocol in the database. But then Alex wasn't known for following protocol, which was why he'd been chosen to handle such a delicate undercover assignment to begin with. Failure was not an option and the Special Task Force wanted an agent who would go the distance, using whatever means necessary. Alex had been their first choice and when he learned Briana Michaels was the target, he'd leapt at the opportunity.

Rolling a small, cylindrical data chip between his palm and the cool metal table, Alex kept his eye on his mission as she swayed toward him with slender hips and narrowed green eyes. The press loved to portray Briana as a woman whose passions were incited only by political debate, but Alex saw untapped sexual passion in her full red lips and arrogantly arched brow. Just looking at her heated his blood and made his jaw ache.

He closed his eyes and savored her smell—spicy but a bit tart. *Oh yes.* He'd been spot on, as usual. Chief Donny swore a man couldn't tell a damn thing about anyone from watching them on a vid unit, but Alex knew better. A vamp didn't reach 223 years of age and not learn how to read women.

"Taking a nap, Captain Night?"

Ummm... Her voice was divine too. Just the right side of prim with a raspy inflection.

He'd been in lust with the powerful politician from the moment he first saw her on the vid comm. Her endorsement of vampiric rights and controversial medical research that could lead to reproductive capability in vampires intrigued him. But the reality of her physical presence was far more alluring than any monitor could portray. He was attracted to her convictions and political fearlessness, but when such admirable traits were packaged in a body like that...

Ah, hell. He wanted her bad.

"If you prefer," she continued. "I can hire another smuggler to perform the tasks I require."

Alex raised his lids slowly and lounged deeper into the bar booth. His fingers curled around the data chip and then slipped it into the chained holder he wore around his neck. "Ah, sweetness. I'm more than willing to perform in any way you desire."

"I bet." Briana slipped into the booth across from him, her long legs brushing against his, causing a deeper sensual awareness. She flipped open a comm link and spun it around so he could see the split screen.

"Duncan Chiles and Mitchell Sandoval," he said, eyeing the relay. From the looks of it, the other men were seated in the same bar. They were waiting for Briana to make her appearance, just like he had been. He schooled his face to remain impassive while inside he admired her initiative. However, he couldn't allow her to hire them. Unlike Alex, they were criminals. "Very good smugglers. But not the best, which is why you need me."

"Yes, I'd heard your skill was matched only by your ego. Having witnessed one, I'm suitably impressed by the other."

He laughed. She would be fun, in more ways than one.

"One hundred thousand credits," Alex said, getting straight to the point so they could go straight to his ship. The bar was packed and the band played too loudly for a proper seduction. It wouldn't be easy to woo her into his bed. He'd have to finesse her properly and that took time. An impatient man by nature, he was eager to get started.

She arched a dark blonde eyebrow and his heart rate picked up. "Fifty."

"You're out of your mind," he scoffed. "To get you to Simgan 2 without hitting any checkpoints will force us to go through the Ligerian Ice Field, Federation space and the Council's largest waste dump. One hundred thousand is a steal."

"Seventy-five."

He straightened, relishing the barter. She was gutsy for a human. "One hundred."

"Eighty or I'm hiring Sandoval."

"Ninety and you have a deal."

She laced her fingers on the tabletop. "Eighty-five."

Alex laughed again. "Eighty-five and a half."

"Done." Briana smiled and for the first time in many decades he momentarily lost the ability to think.

Her seat as Interstellar Rep of the entire Delta Quadrant, the largest quadrant in Council territory, made any hint of softness a weakness she could ill afford and Alex understood that. She rarely smiled and never laughed, but he liked the challenge she presented. He would elicit the gamut of emotions from her during the flight to her homeworld and enjoy every moment of it.

She slid the comm link over. "Enter your info and I'll pay you now."

Once he'd done as she asked, he held out his hand to seal the agreement, an ancient practice he employed simply to touch her. She hesitated and then slipped her hand into his. Alex savored the moment. With a simple touch, he could sense the rapid beating of her heart and her quickened breathing. He felt the steadiness of her grip and the dryness of her palms.

The highly esteemed politician was aroused, but not surprised to be. In fact, he suspected she liked the feeling. Maybe she even liked him.

Without releasing her, he asked, "Can I ask why you prefer to sneak into your own quadrant rather than take the more efficient and comfortable diplomatic route?"

"You can ask. Doesn't mean I'll answer."

"I'd like to know what I'm risking my neck for."

She pulled her hand away, her fingertips drifting across his palm. Her eyelids lowered, shuttering her thoughts. "Maybe I'm just avoiding the press. Taking a break."

"While the House is in session?" he asked dubiously.

Briana turned her head and said nothing.

Alex drummed his fingers atop the table to ease the tingling her touch had left behind. "I don't like the media either, but it would take a hell of a lot more than a need for privacy to make me risk death."

"Ah yes," she purred dryly, shooting him an amused glance. "About eighty-five thousand credits."

"And a beautiful woman," he added.

"My PA warned me about you." She breathed an exasperated sigh that did nothing to distract him from her blush. "He should be here in a moment, once he sends Sandoval and Chiles on their way. Then we can get out of here."

"Wait a minute. No one mentioned two passengers."

She arched that brow again and his cock twitched with interest. "I never travel anywhere without my assistant."

He scowled. "I have a perfectly acceptable unit on the ship."

"James has all of my preferences and contacts programmed," she argued, as she snapped the comm link closed and bent over to tuck it in the thigh pocket of her bio-suit.

"I don't care if—"

The sudden flare of blaster fire lit up their booth and left a gaping hole in the back of Briana's seat. Exactly where she'd been sitting just a split-second before.

"*What the hell?*" Alex leapt from his seat and placed himself between Briana and the rest of the room. The music continued without pause, the majority of the lounge occupants paying no attention to the danger in their midst. He scanned the room quickly, using both his eyes and his instincts. He detected nothing at all, no touch of malice or wicked intent, which couldn't be correct. If it was, they were in a hell of a lot more trouble than he'd like to admit.

Reaching a hand behind him, he was relieved to feel her returning grip. "Jump on," he ordered. His free hand held the hilt of his laser sword, ready to deflect another shot. She crawled onto his back, her lithe thighs gripping his waist with easy strength, her full breasts pressed tightly against him. If he weren't so concerned, he'd have a hard-on. "Hang tight."

He leapt over the dancers, landing first on the bar before lunging out the swinging door to the darkened night outside.

Thieves' Cove was a frightening city for most respectable citizens, but Alex had been working undercover here for most of the last decade. He knew the maze of back alleys as well as he knew the curves of a woman's body, and that was saying something.

The cool night air flowed over them, ruffling his hair and hers. In the distance, various sounds fought for dominance — the sounds of music, laughter, shouting. Sounds of the city. But Alex was aware only of Briana and the lush weight of her body on his back. She remained silent throughout the journey even though he knew the speed with which he moved would disorient any human.

It was dark with only the stars to light their way. He could see perfectly, jumping over discarded crates and waste with ease, but a human wouldn't be able to see his hand in front of his face. Despite this and the fact that he was a stranger to her, when he searched her mind, Alex found that Briana was unafraid. She was as tough as the media claimed and Alex didn't find that intimidating in the slightest. In fact, the longer he knew her, the more he liked her.

It took only moments to reach the private docking bay where his early-model Starwing waited. He set her on her feet and rounded on her. "Are you alright?" His gaze raked her from head to toe.

She nodded.

"You mind explaining what just happened?"

Swallowing hard, Briana met his gaze without flinching. "What's to explain?"

Probing her mind, Alex sensed minor evasiveness but no intent to deceive. "Someone just came damn close to killing you." He grabbed her elbow and led her up the cargo ramp into the belly of his ship, wanting her inside where it was safe.

"I noticed that," she said with only a tiny waver in her voice. "And I'm used to it. I'm not a very popular person, if you hadn't noticed."

"*Mistress!*"

They both turned, Alex with his sword at the ready. He gaped at the sight that greeted him. Striding toward them was a man about his height, though not nearly as large, with gleaming blond hair and bright blue eyes.

"*That's* your PA?" Alex snapped. "It looks like a sex droid."

"Well…" she hedged.

He turned his head to stare at her. "You've got to be kidding me."

"What?" she grumbled defensively, a soft pink flush sweeping over her cheekbones. "Have you seen the latest personal assistants? They look like accountants. I have to work with him all day. Why make him hard on the eyes?"

"Is that all he's hard on?"

Alex sank his fangs into his lower lip as self-punishment for letting that comment slip out, but he couldn't have helped it if he tried. Sharing the lovely Representative with a sex droid/PA was not his idea of a good time. She deserved better.

"That's none of your business!" she retorted, hands her hips.

He leaned over her, his nostrils flaring. "It is when it's on my ship."

"Then I'll commission another ship."

"Go ahead!"

Her mouth fell open and then she snapped it shut. "I will!" She stormed back down the ramp.

"Your stubbornness is going to get you shot," he called after her. *Like he'd ever let that happen.*

She ignored him, but drew her blaster from its holster, her grip steady and light. Briana Michaels knew how to defend herself, a fact Alex carefully filed away for future examination.

He waited until the heel of her boot hit the bay, and then he closed his eyes and released his calling. He sent it out slowly, seductively, like the ripples on a lake. Soothing her first, he then turned up the heat, revealing a bit of his desire and attraction to lure her back to him.

He could hide what he was doing, make her think the urge to return to him originated with her, but instead, Alex caressed her with his essence, steeped her with it so there was no doubt in her mind that he wanted her back. He sensed the moment she became aware of him, felt the answering spark of lust and he smiled.

"That's unfair," she muttered as she spun about. She glared at him a moment and then stomped past him into the ship. By *her* will, not his. "There should be a law against vampires who look like you."

Staring after her, Alex licked his fangs and admired the curve of her ass until she disappeared from sight.

"Thank you," said James as it came to a halt next to him.

"For what?"

"For saving her life. She was frightened."

One of the things he disliked about droids was the implant that allowed them to monitor the thoughts of their owners in real time. Sure, it increased their efficiency, but at what cost to privacy? Droids could be stolen and the information they carried could be accessed.

"I'll take care of her," Alex said sharply. "But I need to know what's going on." He stepped into the ship and hit the lock pad, waiting until the cargo door was secured before moving into the cockpit.

"Which room is mine?" Briana yelled from down the corridor.

"Whichever one you like best," he yelled back, secretly hoping she picked his.

"It is my job to care for her," James said. "Your job is simply to transport her to where she wishes to go."

Snorting, Alex dropped into the captain's chair. He ran a scan to check for any foreign devices and then started his preflight routine. "You sound mighty possessive for a droid."

"She had me programmed that way."

"What the hell did she do that for?"

But when Alex turned his head, the unit was gone.

* * * * *

Lust and decadence.

Those were the two descriptors that came to mind as Briana stared into the captain's quarters and drooled. Decorated in rich jewel tones and voluptuous hanging materials, the room looked nothing like the rest of the ship. She felt as if she were standing on the threshold of an ancient harem—a purely masculine retreat with all the comforts a woman could desire. Add Alexei Night to the picture and a woman would have everything she needed to be sated.

Releasing a deep breath, Bree leaned against the doorjamb and pictured the infamous pirate reclining on the bed, spread out for her pleasure. Alex's dark, dangerous presence would be showcased beautifully in such a bedroom. She closed her eyes and breathed in his scent, remembering the feel of him between her thighs, his powerful body flexing and bunching beneath her as they flew through the night. Never in her life had she experienced anything so thrilling, the world racing past her in blur, leaving only Alex as the one solid thing she could hold on to. Even now, the memory of him in her arms made her wet, made her breasts swell and grow heavy, the tips aching.

When she'd set out on this course of action, she'd told herself he was the obvious choice because he was considered the best and she tried to believe that was the only reason she'd hired him. But that wasn't entirely true. From the moment James had opened the data file she'd been captivated by the rakishly handsome captain.

The seductive promise in his gaze and wicked grin had riveted her, causing her pulse to leap to attention just from the sight of his pilot's photo. She should have known the reality would be so much better—after all, who looked good in their license picture? Alexei Night, that's who. And the damned thing was, it had been a bad photo.

Briana had wanted him on sight and when his expertise had been proven, it had given her the excuse to have him. She'd dressed especially for their first meeting, choosing her attire and hairstyle to be more appealing. Her mission was vital and her primary focus would remain on its successful completion, but in the downtime she wanted to be seduced. Truly, completely awash-in-lust seduced by a master lover. She wanted, just once, to experience the sort of mind melting pleasure she'd read about in erotic romance e-books and Alex Night was more than enough vamp to give her what she wanted. The question was, would she be able to give him what *he* wanted?

She was damn well prepared to try. As many times as necessary.

He'd had centuries of experience while she, a mere human, had only a dozen or so liaisons in her lamentable sexual past. None of them had been extraordinary. Thankfully, the vampire was interested, but she wanted him more than interested. She wanted him panting and hungry for her. Desperate to fuck her. She wanted to unleash his animal side and leave a memory behind that he wouldn't soon forget.

That would take more than a quick capitulation. Alex would have to earn the right to take her. He was going to have to work for it. Then he would appreciate it, which in turn would make her more appreciative.

The powerful engines rumbled to life and snapped Bree out of her reverie. She turned to find another room and ran headfirst into soft pseudo-skin covering solid titanium alloy.

"Damn it, James!" she complained. "You scared me half to death. How can you walk so silently when you weigh so much?"

He smiled with endless charm. The only way one could tell he wasn't human was by the lack of matching warmth in his blue eyes. "Your thoughts are naughty, Mistress."

Bree wrinkled her nose and muttered, "You don't know the half of it."

"Not true. I detect your rapid pulse and quickened breathing. Those physical reactions are not due simply to the recent danger." He shook his head. "When will you learn that you cannot hide things from me?"

"It's an archaic expression, James darling," she explained with a sigh.

"Your father will be fine."

Her throat tightened. It still disconcerted her to realize how deeply James could read into her thoughts.

"It's all my fault he's in danger," she said bitterly. "I knew my position on vampirism would make me plenty of enemies."

"But you never knew it would come to this."

Bree arched a brow. "But you did. Anyone using logical reasoning would have known that if they couldn't get to me personally, they'd go after my family. Being shot at, being hunted… Hell, I'm used to that. I even expect it. I accepted the inevitability of my early demise long ago. But my family…?" She shuddered.

"Your family is the reason you are doing this, Mistress. They knew the risks and they support you completely."

"Because I swore they'd be safe. I told them I would protect them."

Three years ago, when her younger sister Stella married a vamp, Bree had known something had to be done to further the rights of vampires. They were banned from certain sectors, denied jobs and provided the bare minimum of health care. Sure they had healing skills that were far beyond human capability, but the virus that infected them also prevented them from bearing children and some humans wanted to keep it that way, afraid vampires would take over and the human race would become extinct.

James circled her and placed his hands on her shoulders. "You did the only thing you could think of to help your sister have the children she wanted. As the Delta Quadrant Representative your power is almost limitless."

Like any politician worth their carbon, she'd lied, cheated and deceived her way into the position. Basically, she'd played the dumb blonde role to perfection. She'd allowed the powerful lobbyists who could have kept her from winning to think she'd be easy to control and too stupid to make her own decisions. Then, once she'd won the election by a landslide, she did whatever she wanted. She did what was right.

So many of her peers started their careers with such high hopes, but eventually the need for reelection campaign funds drove them to sell their votes to the highest bidder. Briana was lucky that vampires, her largest contributors, had a tendency to be very wealthy. Based on firsthand historical knowledge, vamps were highly cognizant of monetary forecasts. They could almost predict changes in the market and adjusted their finances accordingly.

Kneading her tense shoulders, James murmured, "With the massive financial support behind you, Mistress, you are not susceptible to bribes. You are untouchable, unbeatable and determined to get your way."

"I'm determined all right, determined not to let my family suffer because of vamp haters. They want to hit me where it hurts? I'll hit them right back. Twice as hard."

"And you will succeed. I have no doubt."

She sighed. "I wish I could be as sure."

"You are tense," he purred in her ear, "which makes it hard to think clearly. Would you like me to relieve you?"

Closing her eyes, she let her head fall forward to better enjoy the magic of his massaging fingers. "Ummm... That sounds divine." She knew how good his hands felt all over her body.

Alex may not like the idea of turning a sex droid into a personal assistant, but there was no way a PA droid could offer such comforts. It just wasn't in their rigid programming to learn ephemeral pleasures. Sex droids, however, were built to please and if that meant handling communications and data in addition to their other duties they did so with only a minor adjustment to their processors.

Bree stepped away from James and moved down the corridor to find another room.

"How about these quarters, Mistress?" he asked behind her. "They look comfortable and spacious."

She paused, thinking she didn't much care where she slept. If she had her way, she'd be sharing the captain's quarters before too long and Alex Night could make her forget, if only for an hour or two, that the choices she'd made to help her family had now put them in danger.

As the ship lifted from the private landing bay and began its two-week journey to her homeworld of Tolan, Briana undressed and began to plan her lines of attack—one against the yummy Alex and the other against the forces that wanted his kind eliminated.

Chapter Two

Alex glanced around the dining area one last time, making sure that everything was as perfect as possible. He'd dimmed the cabin lights, turned on soft music and prepared Briana's favorite meal. The last had been the hardest. Since he couldn't sample the food, he had no idea if he'd cooked it right or not. It smelled…edible. However, if it was really bad, he'd purchased enough space rations to keep her alive.

He shrugged. He could always seduce her into forgetting about his questionable cooking skills. Hell, he planned to seduce her anyway. A long, slow seduction. Keeping Briana on edge was the best way to stay in control, which was a necessity. Regardless of the lust he felt for her, he had a job to do.

Her work in the Council was of unparalleled importance to the entire vamp race and he was charged with the task of keeping her safe until the threat against her family could be resolved. It was an assignment he took seriously. The mistakes of his past hadn't faded and they never would, but he could lift himself above them if he worked hard enough. He'd been given a second chance and no matter what, he would prove himself worthy of it.

Still, he didn't see the harm in enjoying her. If *he* called the shots.

With a multitude of tantalizing thoughts in mind, Alex moved down the corridor to Briana's quarters, his senses coming to a heightened awareness as he drew closer. It had been a long time since he'd felt this kind of attraction. He'd forgotten what a rush it was. It flooded his mind with decadent pleasure, like warm hands coursing across his skin, kneading his flesh, making his spine arch…

Oooohhhh… Harder, James…deeper…

Alex stumbled to a halt.

What the hell?

The sensations he was experiencing were not lustful imaginings but feelings radiating from Briana.

He swore as his fangs descended. There wasn't another woman in the universe like Briana Michaels. Physically she was no more or less than any other female he could have, but who she was inside was completely and beautifully unique. She laid her life on the line for a cause that wouldn't benefit her at all simply because it was the right thing to do. Correcting an injustice and fighting prejudice were all she cared about and because of that, Alex cared about her. It was a potent combination, her unwavering convictions, the power she wielded so easily and her passionate nature. Quite simply, Briana was one of a kind.

These next few weeks were all the time he would ever be allowed to have with her. His work and hers were literally worlds apart. After this mission he'd never see her again, so having his fill had to happen now. No way was he getting usurped by a droid. Not after all these months of waiting and planning and dreaming.

Within seconds Alex was standing inside the door to her quarters watching with possessive eyes as the blond droid straddled his naked woman.

A snarl was the only warning he gave before leaping into action.

* * * * *

Bree drifted into a state of half-awareness, imagining hypnotically dark eyes and erect fangs attached to the hands that were presently moving all over her back. The chip in her mind signaled her preferences to James, whose motions went along with her thoughts, facilitating the massage until she was completely relaxed.

Then suddenly he tensed, his body becoming a crushing pressure against her thighs. She felt him pitch forward and she screamed, knowing the droid's heavy weight could kill her.

But before that could happen, the burden was snatched away with a snarl. She rolled over, confused, and barely caught sight of James' bent legs moving horizontally out the door.

"Hey!" she yelled, leaping from the bed and dragging the sheet with her. She covered herself as she ran out to the corridor. Alexei was already halfway down the hall, her droid tucked securely beneath his arm. Bree gaped. James weighed a ton, but the vamp carried him as if he weighed nothing.

Her bare feet slapped against the cool metal floor as she gave chase. "What the fuck are you doing?"

"This thing's got to go," he muttered.

She studied the odd stillness of her droid. "What did you do to him?"

"Shut it off."

"You can't do that!" she protested.

"I just did."

Alex rounded the corridor and entered the cargo hold. Finding a neglected corner, she heard him drop James unceremoniously to the ground.

"You're going to break him," she complained, stumbling blindly into the darkness behind him.

He rounded on her, dark eyes flashing red in the unlit interior. "If only I could be so lucky."

Bree scowled. "What's your deal anyway?"

The laser brightness of his gaze grew more intense, signaling that he was moving closer. She stood her ground and lifted her chin even as her heart raced with excitement.

"I'm not sharing you with a droid. Got it?"

She blinked in surprise and then bit back a smile, grateful he couldn't see it.

"I love your smile," he purred, moving closer. "Even when it comes at my expense."

Choking, she took rapid backward steps. *Damn!* She'd forgotten he could see in the dark.

"No need to make me jealous," he said softly, the foreign inflection in his words making her nipples hard. "I'm easy."

At the reminder, she snorted and spun on her heel.

"Hey!" Now he was chasing her.

"Go away, Alex."

She shrieked as her feet left the deck and she was swung up into his arms.

"Don't be mad at me, sweetness," he said, nuzzling her throat. "I can service you much better than a droid could."

"No doubt," she said petulantly. "With your experience."

He moved down the corridor, walking straight past her room. "Isn't my experience something you want?"

Bree glared at him. "Stay out of my head, captain."

"Call me Alexei, like you do in your thoughts."

"Listen…" she began, but then fell silent as they entered the dining area. Turning her head, she gazed around the room and her mood switched from irritation to blossoming pleasure. The mess hall, normally a stark utilitarian space with metal bulkheads, chairs and tables, was transformed. "Wow," she breathed.

A small table set for one was draped in a multitude of colorful scarves and softly lit by dimmed overhead lights. She inhaled the luscious scent of curried Tolan fowl and her mouth watered.

"Do you like it?"

Looking up at him, she was arrested by his boyish, hopeful smile. Black, silky hair fell across his forehead framing his exotically handsome face with its sensual lips and thickly lashed eyes. She was suddenly aware of the way her right breast was pressed against his chest and how her hip rested against the rippling expanse of his abdomen.

"Oh yeah, I like it." She wasn't talking about the food. And he knew it.

"Good." Alex carried her to her seat and set her down.

"Shouldn't I change?"

"Unless you're offering to lose the sheet, the answer is no."

Holding back a grin at his arrogance, Bree admired the seductive grace with which the vamp took the seat next to her. Dressed in a deep red torso-hugging vest and loose flowing pants, Alexei Night was the epitome of flamboyant male sex appeal.

"Drakish," he said in answer to her unspoken question about his heritage. "On my mother's side." Lifting the lid on the warming pot, he ladled her food into the shallow bowl in front of her before relaxing.

"That explains your coloring. I've never seen such beautiful skin on a vampire before. It's very appealing."

"Would you like to see more of it?" he asked solicitously, his long fingers reaching for the single button that held the flaps of his vest together.

She gave a breathless laugh. "Behave."

"Why?" Sprawling loose-limbed in the chair, he reached for the glass in front of him and then draped the arm that held it over the backrest, canting his body toward her. The pose caused one side of his vest to gape open, affording her an unhindered view of his powerful pecs. The air around them was thick and humid with his blatant sexuality. Her mouth watered.

Swallowing hard, Bree forced her gaze away. She had a goal and she was sticking to it, even if her pussy disagreed by throbbing and growing damp. "Curried fowl is my favorite."

"I know." The deep tone of his voice swept across her skin and left goose bumps in its wake.

"Did you read that in my mind too?" she asked, reaching for the spoon.

"No, I read it in your bio in the Council database."

"Really?" She stared at him. "It has such personal stuff in there?"

"Really." He took a sip and wrinkled his nose. As he righted his goblet, she watched the way the viscous liquid clung to the side of the glass.

She had yet to meet a vamp who didn't dislike the taste of stored blood. "No groupies?"

Alex chuckled at her irreverent reference to the vamp followers that offered their blood in return for sexual pleasure. Most vamps had one or two with them at all times. Highly sexual beings by nature, vampires relished the opportunity to have fresh blood and easily accessible orgasms. "Not on this trip, no."

"You're either a masochist or awfully sure of yourself where I'm concerned."

"*'If one believes strongly in a cause, one should dedicate themselves to it fully. By leaving room for failure, you invite it to occur.'*"

Briana stared. She'd given that speech last year at the dedication of the new vampire embassy built adjacent to Council headquarters. "I've never had someone quote me to my face before."

"Does that bother you?" he asked, twirling his goblet by the stem.

She shook her head. "No. Actually, I'm really flattered." Scooping up some curry, she brought it to her lips. The richly spiced broth exploded with flavor in her mouth and she moaned her appreciation. "You've got a great cooking unit. Most can't get the curry ratio right."

"I don't have a cooking unit."

She frowned. "You don't?"

"What would I do with one?"

"Oh yeah…"

He must have cooked the meal himself then. After researching her favorite foods. Her stomach fluttered and she set her spoon down. "What do you want from me, captain? Blood? Sex? Both? And why go to all of this trouble?"

Alex studied the contents of his glass with undue attention. "Does my occupation bother you?"

Bree tucked the sheet tighter between her breasts and avoided his question as he'd avoided hers. "Does *my* occupation bother *you*? Considering what I do for a living, does it make you uncomfortable to have me on board?"

"No." He took another drink. "I admire you, Briana. I respect you and the strength of your convictions. Even if you championed a different cause I would still feel the same." The quiet dignity of his tone told her he was serious.

She bit her lower lip before asking, "What do you transport? Usually."

"Illegal aliens, contraband goods, Council Reps."

"Ha ha. Funny. What about drugs? Weapons?"

He was silent for a long time, so long she wondered if he was going to answer. Standing, Alexei drained his glass, set it down and moved to the window. "Would smuggling those items affect your decision to take me to your bed?"

"Yes."

"Because of your career?"

"I doubt *what* you smuggle would be of any importance to my political enemies, only the fact that I'm consorting with a known criminal would matter." She released her breath in a rush. "Illegal drugs and weapons serve one purpose—to hurt people for profit. I couldn't sleep with a man knowing he took part in that, regardless of how much I was tempted to."

Alex locked his hands behind his back, bringing the muscular beauty of his biceps and shoulders into stark relief.

Heavens, he was gorgeous. A living work of art.

Her fingers toyed with her spoon before she began to eat again. She was so nervous she couldn't even enjoy the food, but going through the motions gave her something to do.

"I could lie to you, Briana, just to fuck you." His blunt statement was punctuated by a rapid succession of images in her mind—images of his mouth on her, his hands on her, his tongue licking her nipples and lapping up the cream between her legs. She saw him as he was dressed now and herself as she was dressed now. He clutched her to him and pinned her to the bulkhead. She could feel him, all of him, his cock driving into her aching pussy with such force her feet left the floor.

Sweat broke out on her skin as her spoon clattered into the bowl. "Oh God…" she moaned, her entire body shaking with lust as the pictures came in a torrent so forceful she could scarcely register them all.

"Or I could make you want me so badly that what I do for a living wouldn't matter to you." His low voice was accompanied by the feel of talented fingers plucking at her nipples, then moving between her legs.

It was all in her mind, she knew. The scent of his skin…the warmth of his breath…the expertness of his touch…

Briana pushed back from the table so fast she knocked the chair over. Alexei turned to face her in a graceful movement, completely in control.

"Stop it," she said, in a shaky voice.

With an arch of his brow, the images and sensations disappeared.

Leaning against the table with one hand, she took shuddering breaths, willing her pulse to slow.

"I wanted you to know, Bree, that I have no reason to lie. You'd spread your legs eagerly if I wanted you to. You might hate us both in the morning, but if all I wanted was to fuck or feed, that wouldn't matter. Vamps have their calling for a reason—to survive. Subduing prey is nothing to us."

He moved toward her with predatory grace, the wide legs of his pants swirling around his bare feet. "But your feelings do matter to me, so I'll tell you the truth. I don't smuggle drugs or weapons any longer, but I did at one time."

"Damn you." She shivered with desire. "You could have just said what you meant and not tortured me first."

He reached the table and began clearing it, moving the dishes to the sideboard. "But then you couldn't be certain."

"How can I be certain now?" Frustrated by his calm in the face of her falling apart, she cast off any illusions of hiding her thoughts. "I want you. I wanted you before, but now it's unbearable. I'd fuck you on a crate of blasters at this moment and you know it." Briana straightened and moved away with rapid strides, determined to get to her room and take care of herself.

But Alex moved too quickly. Before she knew what hit her, she was flat on her back on the table. "Damn it!" she snapped, hitting his rock-hard chest ineffectually with her hands. "I wanted you to wait for it. Beg for it!"

As if he would. He could get it from anyone.

"I only want it from you," he murmured, catching her flailing fists and kissing the knuckles.

"Why?" She stared up in him, startled by the sweet gesture.

"Does there have to be a reason?" Nimble fingers dipped into the valley between her breasts and lifted the two halves of the sheet away. His breath sucked in sharply at the sight of her nakedness. For a moment she was cold and then the heat of his gaze chased the chill away. She watched in stunned, aroused amazement as his fangs descended and then very slowly ascended again.

"What the…?"

Shaking his head, Alex spread his fingers and ran them over the swell of her breasts until he reached the tips. "Not tonight." He met her gaze. "Not ever, if you don't want." He licked his lips and then bent his head, his tongue swirling around one hard, aching nipple with breathtaking skill before moving to the other.

Bree arched upward helplessly. She wanted him to wrap his mouth around her and suck. She wanted his fingers on her skin and inside her body. She wanted him to fulfill those images he'd shown her earlier. Damn it, she *wanted*. Badly.

"Uh-uh," he said softly. "Not tonight. You're too worked up, too hot for it. You're not thinking clearly and you'll need to be in order to make up your mind. I don't want any regrets between us."

She pressed her breasts into his hands. "You want me to beg."

"No, sweetness. I've got no problem doing the begging. In fact, I'm looking forward to it." Alexei leaned over, resting his cheek on her bare stomach, his talented hands kneading her flesh. His tongue snaked out and dipped in her navel. "When you're ready and not a minute sooner."

"I'm ready." And she was. She believed him completely and she trusted him. How could she not? He'd stood between her and a blaster shot after she'd already paid him. He'd had nothing to gain. His concern today had been genuine.

"No, you're horny," he argued with a low chuckle. "That's not the same thing."

She shifted her fingers through his dark silky hair and sensed the lust he held tightly restrained. There were depths to this man she hadn't considered, because she hadn't known about them. She'd been captivated by his physical beauty, but there was so much more to learn, like the glimpse of tarnished honor that surprised and pleased her. He could fuck her now, but he held himself in check. For her.

Alex straightened and removed his vest, arresting her attention with the rippling muscles of his torso. As he lowered himself over her, Briana spread her legs to make room for his body, absolutely and completely unconcerned that she was laid out for him like a feast. The hard, clenched planes of his stomach made contact with the damp flesh between her thighs and she groaned, the fever in her blood rising until her skin was covered with sweat.

Alex's hips undulated, sliding his ridged abdomen along the folds of her pussy and she gasped as another wave of heat swept through her.

"Could I make you come like this?" he wondered aloud. Resting his elbows on the table, he reached for her nipples and shimmied again. "Just our bodies touching, nothing more?"

"I don't know," she said breathlessly. "Could you?"

When he arched a brow, she explained. "Unlike you, I'm not easy. It takes a lot of work to make me orgasm. Most men get frustrated and give up."

The smile that curved his lips took her breath away. "I won't give up." He rolled her nipples between his fingertips, his grin widening as her eyes half closed on a pleasured moan. "I have forever, sweetness, but it won't take nearly that long."

"It's not my fault." Bree sighed. "I love sex and I love to orgasm. I just can't seem to do both at the same time."

He chuckled. "That's the problem with you humans. You're always in a hurry. Some things take time and an attention to detail."

Time. She always wished she had more of it. Especially now. Alexei Night was a luxury to be savored.

Her hands moved from his nape to stroke his spine, loving the way he arched into her touch. She'd heard vamps were very responsive and sensual creatures. She'd like to test that theory by tying Alex to his decadent bed and having her way with him for hours.

"I'd like that too," he whispered.

"No fair." Her lower lip stuck out in a pout. "I don't have the ability to know what you're thinking."

He licked her lip and then began to move, stroking his torso along her clit, inciting a riot of sensations that tightened her womb and made her breasts swell in his hands. His taste—dark, exotic and richly intoxicating—flavored her mouth. Bree wanted him to kiss her and let her taste him more deeply, but he wouldn't give her what she wanted. And he was doing it on purpose, she knew.

"I'm thinking patience isn't one of your virtues," he teased. "I'm thinking you like hard, quick fucks, but you don't get enough foreplay beforehand to orgasm from them. I think your skin feels like satin and smells delicious."

Bree groaned. She was dying here and he was far too collected for her tastes. Hoping to goad him out of his rigid control, she moved sinuously beneath him, her nails raking his back, her legs wrapping around his lean waist. She lifted her head and bit his earlobe. "You feel so good," she breathed.

The tightening of his muscles was the only indication that she'd moved him at all.

She rubbed her aching nipples against his chest, torturing herself in her attempt to torment him. "I've dreamed of you, Alexei."

"Lay back, Bree," he said, his voice maddeningly calm with a hint of indulgent amusement. "Just enjoy it."

She fell back onto the table. "You suck."

He laughed. "I will later, if that's what you'd like."

Closing her eyes, she concentrated on the feel of his body stroking her pussy and the tight clench of his fingertips on her nipples. Drenched in sweat and aching all over, she arched her neck and whimpered in pleasure.

Yes. Alex's low purring voice floated through her mind. *Don't think about me, sweetness. My pleasure will be found in yours.*

"I wanted to please you."

You do.

"I-I want to be special."

You are. His tongue licked the column of her throat, tracing the line of a rapidly pulsing vein.

Locking her ankles together, Briana rocked in counter-rhythm to his movements, allowing the stark eroticism of the moment to sweep through her. Alexei was in her arms, just as she'd longed for him to be, and the pleasuer of his embrace went far beyond what she'd imagined.

His hot, wet mouth closed around her breast and sucked leisurely, a slow insistent tugging she felt all the way to her core. The need to come became a driving force and she writhed beneath him, scratching his back, struggling for it, hating the desperation she felt at the thought that she might not make it there. Again.

I'll take you there, he soothed, his mouth working her nipple expertly. *Just relax.*

"Now, Alexei!"

Patience.

Frustrated tears squeezed past her lashes and fell into her hair. Her skin was too tight, too hot. Her cunt spasmed desperately. Aching...needing...wanting... She bucked beneath him. "Fuck me!"

Alex's arms shot underneath her hips and lifted her higher. He altered position, aligning his rigid cock to her slit and thrust through the lips—once, twice, thrice—the material of his pants creating a luscious friction on her clit.

That was all she needed to come.

"Oh God!" Briana bowed upward with her orgasm, her cunt grasping greedily for his cock and finding nothing to hold. Sensing her need, he slid one hand underneath her thigh and thrust two fingers into her drenched pussy. He continued to rock his cock against her clit, taking her from one tantalizing release to another. And then another. Starved for him, she took everything he offered and demanded more.

He rode her until she begged him to cease, her skin so sensitive she couldn't bear to be touched. Lowering her to the table with infinite care, he brushed the curls from her face before kissing her softly. His fingers left her cunt and she whimpered at the loss. Then she shivered as he put them in his mouth and sucked them clean, his tongue swirling around each one with a soft, pained groan.

The solicitousness of his movements angered her. She was naked, sweating, *vulnerable*, while the devastating vamp looked no different than he had at dinner—cool, calm and completely in control of his desire. Before he could step away, Bree cupped his cock with her hands, not at all surprised to find his pants soaked with her cream.

No! He caught her wrists.

"Yes," she insisted, fighting his grip. She lifted her gaze to his, her determination obvious.

She held on. He held on. Between them raged a silent battle for control.

"I just had a brutal lesson in patience, Alexei. I may not have forever to show you what I learned, but I do have two weeks."

As he breathed deep, his nostrils flared. His eyes narrowed and burned with something not quite human, but she wasn't afraid. She knew without a doubt he would never hurt her. It was strange to be so certain about an almost complete stranger, but she was.

Smiling, she teased, "Don't be so stubborn."

His hands tightened a moment and she thought he would refuse, and then they fell away.

Hurrying before he changed his mind, Bree tugged at his waistband. The comfortable material stretched and lowered, catching on the tip of his upthrust shaft which tented the front. Pulling harder on the elastic, she freed him and gasped.

"Wow." She blinked, awed at the sight of him. Alexei Night was thick, *very* thick and long. She licked her lips and he groaned. "No wonder you're so cocky." She giggled. "No pun intended."

Fascinated by the size and perfectly formed beauty of his cock, she stroked it, admired it and coveted it. He clasped his hands behind him, granting her permission to do whatever she wished. Pleased, she looked up at him. And stilled.

Alex stood unmoving, his jaw clenched so tight the muscle ticced in protest. As she watched him, he shuddered, the momentary break in his reserve betraying a wealth of desire ruthlessly leashed. He wasn't in as much control as he tried to appear. In fact, her best guess would be that he was teetering on the verge of losing it.

And she wanted to push him over.

Tracing the thick veins that lined the proud shaft, Bree marveled at the silken texture and unbelievable hardness. She reached lower and cupped the heavy sac below, testing its weight. "You have no hair here," she noted, her palms tingling wherever she touched him.

Do you like that? Even in her thoughts, his voice was strained.

"Oh yes. What's not to like?"

He shuddered again and his balls drew up tight in her hands. Gripping his cock with two fists, she began to pump. He hissed and threw his hips forward.

Harder.

She gentled her touch.

Faster.

She slowed down.

Damn it, Bree!

She grinned. "Not so much fun when you're the one waiting, eh?"

Then a picture of Alex formed in her mind. She saw his powerful frame tensing in orgasm and felt the hot release of his cum splashing across her breasts. The sounds of his pleasure echoed in her mind and her heart welled with tenderness.

"Would you like that?" she asked breathlessly, her blood heating with renewed desire.

Very much.

"Would you beg me for it?"

His wicked mouth curved, revealing sparkling fangs. "Please."

Briana's heart leapt. It was simply unfair for one man to be so achingly perfect. "How could any woman refuse a plea like that?"

Tightening her fists, she began to work his cock with hard tugs, using the sounds of his guttural cries to guide her speed and rhythm.

"Does that feel good, baby?" she asked hoarsely when his last grunt was loud and tormented.

You know it does. Too good.

He felt so hot in her hands, so solid and thick. She shivered. "Damn. I can't wait to fuck this cock."

Bree… He swelled in response to her words, his voice gritty with need. Knowing he was close, she urged him on.

"Do you know how tight I'll grip you, Alex? It's been a long time since I was with someone, and he wasn't anywhere near your size. You'll have to stretch me, make my cunt fit you, but I'm so wet. Dripping. That will help. Can you imagine how it'll feel?"

"Ah, fuck!" He gripped her shoulders and began to fuck through her fists while she pumped his shaft in counter-tempo. His pace was frenetic, his lust palpable. He growled just before his cock jerked violently. Briana watched in an agony of lust as he came, his cum shooting across her breasts in hot, steady bursts. His thighs quaked, his fingers dug into her skin with bruising force and he chanted her name in her mind—*Bree, Bree, Bree*—so she knew, even though his eyes were shut tight, that he was with her in his pleasure.

Awash in his delight with her nipples peaked tight and his cum dripping from them to splash on her lap, her breathing was as labored as his. He finished finally, his heavy balls hanging empty beneath his semi-hard cock. He was glorious, naked from the waist up, his body lean and tight and glistening with sweat.

"Bree," he gasped, his eyes opening and then glowing possessively as he stared at his primitive claim all over her chest. His large hands reached out, cupping her breasts, kneading his cum into her skin.

"That was awesome," she said, with a wondering laugh. "Wow."

"You're telling me?" He arched a brow as he pulled up his pants, scooped her into his arms and carried her down the hall to his room. "I can barely walk and I'm a vamp. That should tell you what kind of shape I'm in."

"Where are we going?" His bed, she hoped.

"The shower."

"Oh." She couldn't hide the disappointment in her voice.

Alexei laughed, a deep husky sound that fueled her growing affection for him. "Did I not give you enough orgasms, sweetheart?" He kissed her forehead. "I'll have to work on that."

Flushing in embarrassment, she buried her face in his shoulder. "I can't help it," she mumbled against his damp skin. "That was the hottest thing I've ever seen."

I'm glad you aren't offended.

"Huh?" Bree lifted her head and met his smiling gaze. "Who would be offended by having a gorgeous guy so hot for her that he gets off without sex?"

I think, he drawled, *that some women would have found that very un-PC.*

"Sucks to be them," she dismissed with a shrug. "Count me in the camp of women who find blatant displays of testosterone sexually exciting."

As he stepped into his decadent quarters and then into bathroom, he hugged her tight. "You're different than I thought you'd be."

"Oh yeah?" She swayed a little as he set her down and he steadied her before dropping his pants. Moving into the shower,

Alex turned on the water and she tried not to drool. "Is that good or bad?"

"It's great."

Turning around, Bree took in her surroundings. She'd traveled in a great many transports and one thing they all had in common was "the head". Usually the room was a metal box with a sink, a toilet and a rectangular metal-lined shower. Alexei's private bathroom was as far removed from those spaces as it was possible to get. Taupe-colored stone with golden veins covered the floors and walls, and when she finished her circle, she noted the shower was lined too. It also had no door.

Alex, completely naked and dripping with water, held out his hand in invitation. Achingly aroused all over again, she gladly accepted.

"You're just so serious on the vid unit," he said. "So formal and—"

"Uptight?" Sighing at the feel of warm water coursing down her back, Briana closed her eyes and tilted her head back under the spray. Then she moaned as Alex caressed her breasts with soapy hands. "I have to be on my toes all the time. My opponents are always looking for any weakness to exploit."

"It's got to be hard for you." He tugged at her nipples with his fingertips and the sensation coursed down her body, making her cunt clench in response.

"I hope so," she breathed, opening her eyes to stare up at him as she took his cock in hand. He swelled instantly at her touch. "Great recovery time."

His mouth curved and he reached between her legs, his soap-slick fingers parting her and then rubbing her swollen clit. "I've waited a long time for this. It's inspiring to finally have you here and naked."

Widening her stance shamelessly, she clutched the top of his shoulders for support as her knees went weak. "W-what?" She shivered at a particularly skillful stroke. "We just met."

Alex reached around her, cupping a butt cheek to support her as he rinsed off the soap. Then he thrust two fingers into her, studying her response intently. "Ready for those orgasms you wanted?"

"Oh hell..." She sagged into his embrace as he began to fuck her with his fingers, stroking as deep as he could.

"You're right about being tight," he growled into her ear before biting the lobe. "And you feel like silk inside. Drenched silk." His tone was harsh, almost brutal, and she remembered suddenly that he wasn't human, not anymore.

As his thumb found her clit and rubbed in time with his pumping fingers, she tried to hold off the orgasm, wanting this moment to last. The feel of his skin, slick with water, and the fog around them, created a scene better than any she'd ever read about. "What do you mean you waited for this?" she gasped.

"I've watched you on the vid for a long time."

Lifting her head from his shoulder, she gazed up at him. His eyes were dark, the irises thin rings around enlarged pupils. "And you wanted to fuck me?" Bree couldn't believe it.

"Oh yeah." His wicked smile revealed his fangs. "Hard. Bent over your desk, your tight ass in the air, your cunt creamy..." Alexei twisted his fingers inside her as her mind flooded with images of his fantasies. "And hot around my cock. Your voice hoarse from screaming my name."

She whimpered and moved her hips in rhythm with his thrusting.

"Jack me off again," he ordered, his voice so guttural she could barely understand him.

The crude command coming from any other man would have ended the encounter immediately. But coming from Alex, it was so arousing she almost had an orgasm. She not only had the right to touch him, but he *wanted* her to. Desperately. None of her fantasies could come close to this.

The dreams she'd had were of hot, sweaty, messy sex. She hadn't imagined the darkly seductively scent of him or the rough satin feel of his golden skin. She certainly hadn't imagined his touch, so gentle and reverent, like she was valuable to him for more than her money.

Her touch, when she reached for him, was just as affectionate as his. She grasped the heated length of his cock and stroked him lovingly. Longingly.

"You're so beautiful," she breathed, watching the way his abdomen muscles laced tight with tension.

"I'm glad you think so."

Lifting her chin, she met his gaze again. She let him see the entirety of what she was feeling—the wonder of discovery, the pleasure in his touch, the lust inspired by the feel of his thick cock pulsing in her hands.

Alex shuddered. "When you look at me like that…" His cock jerked.

"What? What happens?"

He shook his head, but she knew. There was too much…*emotion*…between them. Her throat ached, her eyes burned. Bree was grateful for the shower mist that hid her sudden tears. She wanted to keep him, damn it. Not just to have a gorgeous man in her bed, but because he'd cooked for her. Because he'd been protective in the bar and jealous over James. Because he cared enough about her to want her memories of him to be good ones.

And that was all she could have of him. Memories. Would he remember her a century from now? Two? Several?

They were strangers. Why did she care?

Spread your legs.

As he finger-fucked her with greater urgency, Bree hooked one leg over his lean hip and rode his hand. "Oh God…" She was so close to coming, but she didn't want to go alone. They were in this together, whatever *this* was.

Yes.

That dark whisper was raspy, and grew even hoarser as she pleasured him ruthlessly, both of her hands pumping his cock in just the way she'd learned earlier.

"Fuck yeah…" he groaned, stroking her cunt in the same rhythm she used on him. Their hips rocked softly, their bodies straining. She offered him her mouth, desperate for a kiss. Instead he pressed his cheek to hers so that his labored breaths gusted across her ear.

"I want you," she gasped, wanting his kiss and his cock and a bed to roll around in. She wanted comfort and an end to this feeling of being rushed. She wanted to silence the driving voice in her mind that said this bliss was only temporary, but it increased in volume, crashing against her in hot waves of need.

It took her a moment to realize it was Alexei she was hearing.

From then on soft and sweet wasn't possible. Their mutual drive to come was raw and hungry, both of them running away into the forgetful arms of climax. But as they reached orgasm together, their bodies shuddering against each other, her cunt drenching his hand, his cock spewing its seed, the tenderness with which they held each other was undeniable.

It wasn't making love.

But it was awfully close.

Chapter Three

෨

What the fuck just happened?

Alex ran a hand through his wet hair and felt like he'd just been run over by a transport. He'd really like to sit down for a moment and consider the mess he was in, but the insistent beeping from the comm link wouldn't allow him to do so.

Falling wearily into his chair on the bridge, he activated the comm and watched as the President of the Interstellar Security Council came into view.

"What the hell took you so long, Night?" Derek Atkinson barked. "You were supposed to check in hours ago. Did you make contact with Representative Michaels?"

"Yeah, she's on board. We're on our way."

Derek's steely gaze narrowed. "Your hair is wet." His lips twisted with wry amusement. "Damn, you move fast. I thought she'd resist you for a day or two at least."

Scowling, Alex said, "I took a shower."

"Sure. Whatever you say. What you do with Michaels on your own time is your own business. Just don't let it interfere with the mission."

"You're not worried I'll lose my edge?" Alex asked with raised brows.

The president laughed. "You, Night? Hell no. And certainly not with a human."

Leaning back in his chair, Alex wished he could say the same with as much conviction. Unfortunately for everyone involved, his objectivity was shot to hell. What was supposed to have been two weeks of pleasure with a woman he admired had turned into something he didn't quite understand.

"Besides," Derek continued. "Intimacy with her will make it more likely she'll trust you. We need to know what she's expected to give in return for the safety of her family."

Alex's jaw tensed. He'd been distracted by lust earlier, but Briana's love for her family had shone through. She was terrified for them. "Are they safe?"

"To the best of my knowledge, yes. Her father hasn't been seen at his residence lately, but I'm still not certain if that's a bad thing or not. He may have just gone away, I'm looking into it. Representative Michaels sent her sister and brother-in-law on a trip. She may have done the same for her father. Apparently she hasn't disclosed anything to them, so they don't know they're in danger. If things heat up though, I'll have to place them all in protective custody."

"That's where they should be now."

Derek arched a brow. "If we move them, we'll risk discovery, you know that. If I simply wanted to keep them safe, I wouldn't have you sent you in undercover."

"Then Briana's safety isn't your primary objective?" he asked grimly.

"*Briana*, is it? Yes, Rep. Michaels' safety is of paramount importance."

"But her family's isn't."

"No," Derek agreed. "Her family's isn't."

Alex didn't know why he was surprised. He knew the ins and outs of his job. That didn't mean he had to like them. In this case, he definitely didn't, but he owed Derek Atkinson his life, so he kept his thoughts to himself. He'd puzzle out a way to keep Bree's family safe when he had some time to think.

"Find out what she knows, Night. And check in with me daily. Things may be happening here that you don't know about."

"Yes, sir."

"I'm relieved she's safe with you."

"She almost wasn't." Alex drummed his fingers on the console. "Someone attempted to assassinate her at the meeting point. A blaster shot missed her by a hair." His stomach clenched at the memory. He'd nearly lost her.

The momentary silence that greeted his disclosure was deafening. "That location was a carefully guarded secret," Derek said tightly.

"She brought in Chiles and Sandoval as bargaining chips to negotiate my fee. I'm sure they bragged. Just being asked by her was a huge coup."

"Damn. She's got balls."

"Yeah and a new PA droid, which explains why we weren't aware of the appointments with the other two smugglers."

"I'll look into it. We'll need to tap into the new droid and see what events we might have missed since she replaced the old one. I'll send you the schematics once I have them." Derek glanced away from the screen. "It must have been a very recent purchase. I have no mention of it here, which worries me. If my sources are faulty, there might be a lot more we don't know, which leaves us vulnerable. Any idea who the assassin was? Did you see them?"

Alex shook his head. "Not a clue. But I've got a feeling it was either a droid or a Shinite-trained professional."

Derek whistled.

The Shinites were an ancient race known for their deadly fighting abilities. They became so focused on their missions they mentally disconnected, making it impossible for a vamp to detect them.

"You didn't sense anything at all?"

"Nothing."

"Damn. Shinites cost a fortune, so do droid assassins. If you're right, this isn't one person we're talking about, but a group. I'll assign more agents to back you up in Tolan. In the meantime, watch your back, Night. And keep me posted."

"Yes, sir. Will do. Night out."

The screen went black as Alex signed off. For a moment, he looked over his semicircular console at the view of space outside the bridge window.

What the hell was he going to do? He had no fucking clue.

Standing with a weary sigh, he moved back down the hall and entered Bree's room. He stood over her sleeping form, taking in her damp curls and barely parted lips. Deep inside him a wealth of compassion swelled, threatening to overflow. She looked so soft and innocent in slumber, nothing like the vixen who'd very nearly brought him to his knees in the shower, although he liked that side of her too. A lot.

He'd been forced to put her to sleep, something all vamps had the mental ability to do, when she'd tried to coax him into bed with her. He'd been so close to losing what little control he had and fucking them both out of their misery. A tantalizing prospect, but he had to earn her trust first. Once he got her into his bed, he intended her to stay there for the duration of their journey and he didn't want her feeling remorse about anything that happened between them.

Derek wanted him to earn her trust for the mission's sake. Alex wanted to earn her trust for himself. He hoped like hell she realized what it had cost him to deny them both tonight. His hunger for her was a driving force, making his jaw ache and his entire body tense. Lust, he knew well. This kind of need was completely unfamiliar, goaded as it was by respect for her strength and tenderness for her vulnerabilities.

Blood and sex. That was all he could have of her.

He prayed that would be enough to sate him.

* * * * *

Wielding her flashlight carefully, Briana made her way through the pitch-black cargo bay until she found James. She wrinkled her nose at the sight of him frozen in his kneeling position between two crates, his eyes open and sightless. The poor thing looked so sad and kind of creepy. She searched along his nape until she found the tiny reset button. James blinked and then scowled before rising.

"I do not like Captain Night, Mistress," he grumbled.

"I'm sorry, James. The captain turned out to have a bit of a possessive streak."

"He has no reason to feel any ownership of you." He paused a moment with his head cocked to the side. "All systems are working correctly and the link between us was not broken, but if something had happened to you, I would have been unable to respond."

"Nothing happened," she soothed, running a hand along his arm. "Let's get out of here. This place gives me the willies." With its three-story-tall ceiling and massive cranes, the vast space made her shiver.

James followed. "Quite a bit happened. You and the captain are now involved."

Blushing, Bree shut the cargo door behind them. "I wouldn't say that. We—"

"Became intimate," he said flatly. "I knew you had considered that scenario a possibility, but I had hoped your better sense would assert itself."

"Excuse me?"

Droids were programmed to never aggressively contradict their owners. Because of her passionate nature, she'd had James' programming altered a little to facilitate discussion, knowing that listening to a purely logical viewpoint would help her considerably. However, discussing her sex life was not one of the things she'd wanted to debate. And discussing the intimacy she'd shared with Alex seemed…*wrong*. It was too private to share.

"I apologize," he said quickly, reading her irritation. "How you handle your personal affairs is for you to decide. It is simply beyond my reasoning to understand why you would invest so much of your life and risk your very existence for a cause, then jeopardize it so easily by aligning yourself with a known criminal."

"I'm not aligning myself with him!" she argued and then her face heated again. They'd aligned all right. Perfectly. She shivered in remembrance. She'd known Alex would be an expert lover, but to make her come repeatedly without using his cock? Hell, she'd had the best orgasms of her life last night. What would it be like when he actually did fuck her?

"I am equipped with all the tools needed to please you just as well as Night can," James said, his hand coming to rest on the small of her back. But unlike when Alexei touched her, Briana felt no thrill of awareness or spark of heat. Some owners had been known to fall in love with their droid companions, but Bree had never been able to look past the fact that James' emotions were not real and with a simple code change or two, he could care for another owner just as well as he cared for her.

"I know your thoughts, Mistress, and because of that I can touch you in just the way you desire at just the moment you desire it. No one else can do that for you."

"Thank you for the offer, James, but you know how I feel about that."

"Sex with a living being who does not love you is better than sex with a droid whose sole purpose for existence is to serve you?"

Disgruntled by his strange mood, she asked, "What is up with you today?"

James shrugged. "You seem determined to ignore your own doubts. I am simply repeating your thoughts aloud."

"I'm not thinking that at all," she denied. She remembered clearly the sight of Alex's fangs descending when he'd seen her naked and the way he'd fought back the primal instinct by retracting them again. Bree knew enough about vamps to know that must have been painful and yet he'd done it. For her.

He'd also performed some mind trick to put her to sleep. They'd be exchanging some words about trying *that* again, but she knew it was another sacrifice he'd made for her, a way to give her the self-control she hadn't been capable of last night. Alex didn't love her, but he did respect her, which was more than a droid was capable of.

"Alexei Night is a criminal, Mistress. I hope you keep that in mind. He is very wealthy and a very talented pilot. There is no reason for him to live his existence outside the law, but that is what he chooses to do."

Bree bit her lower lip. She'd already planned to ask Alex about his choice in occupation. There were alternatives she could offer him, if he was interested. She hoped he was. The Council could use his skill and he would be a valuable asset to them.

Pausing in the corridor by her room, Briana heard Alexei singing from his seat on the bridge. They'd entered the Ligerian Ice Field early that morning. Traversing through the monstrous, free-floating glaciers was beyond treacherous. A great many pilots had met their end here and yet Alex's skill was such that she'd scarcely felt a bump since they entered. The fact that he was singing told her how relaxed he was under pressure. She paused a moment on the threshold of her cabin, listening to the beautiful sound of a foreign tune sung in his baritone. He was a man of many layers and she knew she'd barely scratched the surface. She was eager to scratch some more.

"James," she murmured, her thoughts half distracted with her desire to watch Alex in his element. "Were you able to receive deep space relays while in stasis? We haven't missed any more demands, have we?"

"I have been monitoring the news, but no further demands have been made through your private channels. Your sister sent her grateful regards and said she is enjoying her vacation with her husband. The networks have been reporting illness as the reason for your absence from the House floor, just as you'd stated in your press release. That excuse should continue to work for another few days at least, perhaps even longer."

"Excellent. Keep an eye on that for me. Adjust the reports from my office as necessary to keep the impression going. Also at the end of every session, I want the minutes downloaded and ready for my review. My absence will create an opportunity for one of my opponents to present their agenda. I want to know the minute they make an attempt."

"Of course." He caught her arm as she stepped away. "Do you think it is wise to distract the captain at this moment?"

She looked over her shoulder at him with a frown, still trying to get used to having her thoughts spoken out loud. "I won't distract him, I just want to observe."

With that absolutely delicious thought in mind, she left James in her room and went to ogle a very sexy vampire.

* * * * *

Alex was grinning like an idiot. He knew it and couldn't stop it.

Briana's lust and admiration saturated the air around him, coursing over his skin like warm water and causing his breathing to quicken. Anticipation thrummed through his veins, just as it did in hers. She'd been watching him for the last hour, completely silent except for the strength of her thoughts, which were powerful. Watching him at the controls had turned her on and her desire had ignited his.

Over the last two centuries, he'd been desired for a great many things—his vampirism, his wicked reputation, his looks. Never could he recall being wanted because he was talented at something. Never had a woman grow soft and wet simply because he knew how to fly and knew how to do it very well.

"We're in the clear," he called softly, leaning back in his chair. "You can come closer, if you like."

As she approached, the tart scent of her skin grew stronger and Alex took a deep breath, absorbing her arousal into his blood.

The hunger inside him stirred in response. Flying through the Ligerian Ice Fields was always a rush, but it had never been as exciting as when Bree watched him do it.

"That was awesome," she breathed, her voice low and throaty. "I'm so damn impressed I don't know what to say." Coming around his chair, she came to a halt directly in front on him.

Alex gripped the armrests to prevent himself from snatching her close. This time, the first move had to be hers. "Thank you."

Her eyes sparkled with appreciation and then warmed as she raked him from head to toe. He almost purred with delight. Dressed in short shorts and a tight combat tee, Briana looked ready to take on the world. He'd settle for her just taking on him. And when her lips curved in a slow inviting smile, he knew she was prepared to do just that.

She leaned her hip against the console, showing off her long, lithe legs. "Can I ask you something?"

"Sure. Ask me anything." *Ask me to take you to bed, to make love to you for days, to…*

"You are the most amazingly gifted pilot I've ever seen. Why are you smuggling?"

He sighed. "Why don't I have a respectable job, you mean? Why am I a criminal?" Alex ran a hand through his hair. "It's a long story."

"I've got nowhere to go." She arched her brow and when she did that, he couldn't deny her anything. Damn, he loved it when she looked like that. That light touch of haughty arrogance made him want to fuck her so hard she wouldn't be able walk. It was such a sham, that cool disdain. She was all fire and passion under that façade, as he knew firsthand.

"I grew up poor," he began. "Very poor. My father ran off when I was a kid and my mother could barely scrape a couple of credits together. We were hungry most of the time, and my brother and I couldn't do the things other kids got to do. It was miserable and I spent a lot of time dreaming about escaping that life. All I wanted to do was be a pilot. Getting out of there, seeing the universe… I would have done anything for that.

"At the time, two hundred years ago, the cost of flight academy was so high it made it an unattainable goal for me and the military wanted advanced schooling that we couldn't afford. When my older brother said he knew of a way I could make enough credits to support our mother and learn how to fly at the same time, I leapt at the chance." His lips twisted ruefully. "Of course, there was a price."

"Uh-oh." Bree's lips made a moue in sympathy. "That doesn't sound good."

"Depends on how you look at, sweetheart. My brother introduced me to the leader of a local gang called The Crew. They were very successful smugglers. The money was good and steady, and all new recruits were sent to flight academy. The Crew only wanted the very best pilots. In return for the job, the money and the schooling, I had to accept the virus and give up my mortality. I had to dedicate myself to The Crew for eternity."

"Wow." She stared at him with wide eyes. "That's steep for hazing."

"At the time, it seemed like a dream come true—become a pilot, build up my credits and take care of my mom. Not to be crude, but the women were plentiful and the thought of living forever in the prime of my life sounded pretty good." He shrugged. "As you said last night, what's not to like?"

She blushed and Alex laughed. Briana was lovelier today than she'd been yesterday. There was glow to her and a sweet familiarity brought on by their intimacy of the night before.

"And so you're in this trade forever then?" she asked, trying to hide her disappointment and failing.

"No." He smiled at her sudden hopeful interest. "I got caught."

"How?" Her obvious surprise was very flattering.

"My brother sold me out. Evan brought me into The Crew to get out of one scrape and then sacrificed me to worm his way out of another."

Briana gaped. "How could anyone do that to a family member?"

"Not everyone has the sense of familial loyalty you do. It's one of the many things I admire about you."

Pushing away from the console, Bree came over and put a gentle hand on his shoulder. The small gesture of comfort hit him with such force, he was glad to be seated.

He swallowed hard and looked away, staring out the bridge window at the endless space beyond. "Evan tapped into my cargo droid and downloaded all of my routes. Then he asked me to switch runs with him. He said he had a girlfriend on Rashier 6 who was getting upset that he was visiting so infrequently. His route paid more than mine so I traded without question and considered myself lucky. But he was under investigation and I was taken into custody in his place. I spent three years on Hazin Prime."

Standing, Alex moved to the window and put distance between them. There was too much he couldn't say and his attachment to her was strong enough that she would sense his turmoil if he stayed too close.

He couldn't tell her how Derek Atkinson had come to the vamp penal colony and offered him a second chance to live a worthy life. He couldn't tell her that he worked on the same side of the law as she did. He couldn't tell her that his interest in her went far beyond money, blood or carnal pleasure. The most he could do was take a deep breath and pray that she would want him anyway.

"Why didn't you start over when you got out?" she asked behind him and he could feel her despondency. She didn't know that he'd begun his life anew. And he couldn't tell her.

"It's hard to find gainful employment when you have a record. No one trusts you."

"By all accounts, you have enough credits to quit."

"I couldn't quit flying. It's in my blood. It's as much a part of me as my vampirism."

"What about the tourist trade?"

"I don't qualify for a permit." Alex turned around and his heart clenched at the sight of her distress. It took everything he had to hold his tongue when all he wanted in the universe was to tell her that he *was* the type of man she wished he was. "Is it that important to you to that I fall into the status quo?"

Briana held out her hands to him. "I want you to work for me. I could use a private transport and—"

"Are you insane?" he asked with wide eyes.

"It was just a bit of smuggling, not—"

"It wasn't 'just a bit of smuggling', Bree. Those blasters you mentioned? I had those on board plus half a hold full of photon torpedoes." Of course, The Crew had led him to believe he was helping the Gorans fight ethnic cleansing, but then he hadn't done the research to verify that. In truth, he hadn't wanted to know. He'd just wanted to believe.

"Oh." She sank into his captain's chair.

Mentally kicking himself for saying the words that would push her away, Alex turned his back to her, his fists clenching with frustration.

"I don't understand," she said softly behind him. "I just can't picture you doing those things without a qualm."

"Why not?" he bit out.

"Because I just can't."

"You don't know what I'm capable of. You don't know me."

"I know you had enough honor not to have sex with me last night, even though I begged you to, just because you didn't want me to regret it." Her voice drew closer. "I know you put yourself in harm's way for me yesterday, for no good reason at all."

"Don't you think you might be rationalizing goodness in me when there isn't any, just so you feel comfortable wanting to fuck me?"

"Hmmm…" Her fingers brushed along his wrist, instantly turning his ire into heated lust. "So we're at an impasse. You can't sleep with me because you want to earn my trust and I can't sleep with you because if I do, my trust becomes questionable. Either way we're screwed, but only in the figurative sense."

Bree started to move away and the loss of her presence caused a physical ache. Alex spun quickly, clutching her slight form to his chest. "You have to want me for who I am, Briana. Record, career and all."

"I do." She stared up at him with an earnest gaze. "But that doesn't mean I can't wish for our situations to be different."

He searched her face with its determined chin and carnal mouth, features that no vid unit could do justice to. In person, she was stunningly perfect. "Why? How will that affect what happens over the next two weeks? You wanted a fantasy. Let me give it to you."

Her hands stroked the length of his spine. "Maybe I want the fantasy to be real."

Stiffening in her embrace, he began to pull away. That was his fantasy, too. Damn, how he wished he could keep her! But that would never become a reality.

"I'm sorry." She released him without protest. "I shouldn't have said that. No pressure or anything. I just—"

Alex dropped to his knees before her, unable to fight his attraction when she looked so forlorn. "I want you." He raised his gaze to lock with hers.

"Wow." Stunned green eyes stared down into his. "This is…totally unexpected. And really hot."

"*You're* really hot. For the first time in my life, I'm pretty sure having sex with a beautiful woman is a bad idea." He kissed the inside of her thigh. "But I can't resist doing it anyway."

Her fingers drifted into his hair and kneaded his scalp. He purred in pleasure. "That was actually a pretty romantic thing to say, Alexei. In a fucked-up kind of way."

"Who knew it was in me," he teased.

"You're not normally so charming?" she asked with a dubious arch of her brow.

"I don't usually have to use charm at all."

She sighed and shook her head. "Yeah, just whip out that cock and they probably stampede. It must be pretty wonderful for a guy to be so gorgeous that women just fall into bed with him."

"It's pretty wonderful if the woman he wants does that. Otherwise, it can be annoying."

Briana laughed. "Now you see why I wanted you to beg for it."

"You've got me on my knees, sweetness." Cupping her ankles, he slid his hands up, following the graceful curves of her legs. "You're in great shape."

"Yeah. With all the sitting around I do, you would think I'd be fat."

"You keep fit on purpose and you carry a blaster with obvious skill. When we ran through Thieves' Cove you moved with me—"

"That was amazing," she interrupted with a smile that would have brought him to his knees, if he hadn't already been there.

Standing slowly, Alex tugged her body against his. Whatever he'd felt for her last night was nothing compared to what he felt for her today. And they were about to have sex— full on sex with his cock buried deep inside her. He knew when they were done he'd be in a lot worse shape. "How much trouble are you in, Bree?"

She swallowed hard and pulled back a little. "Who says I'm in trouble?"

"You trust me with your body." His hands cupped her breasts, squeezing the firm flesh gently. "But not your secrets?"

"Don't worry about me. I can handle it," she breathed, her eyes drifting closed as his thumbs brushed across her nipples.

His palms tingled, then burned as her skin warmed to his touch even through her tee. "Perhaps I want to help you handle it."

"Perhaps I want you to stop talking and just handle me."

Alex fought the urge to bare his fangs, to exert his dominance and stake his claim. There wasn't any need to do that. There were other, less frightening ways to make her his. He could inundate her with pleasure. He could join their bodies so completely she wouldn't be able to tell where she ended and he began. "Undress."

Bree's eyes flew open. "What?"

"Take. Off. Your. Clothes."

She snorted. "Shouldn't you do that?"

"Certainly." He shrugged out of his flight vest.

"I meant, shouldn't you do that to *me*?"

"If you want to wear that sexy outfit again," he said gruffly, dropping his trousers, "I suggest you do it. If I touch you, I'll shred it."

"Oh." Her gaze dropped to his cock like a magnet to metal. She licked her lips. "You think I look sexy?"

Damn. It drove him crazy when her tongue darted out like that. Pretty soon he was going to feel that lush mouth slick and hot around him. "Hurry," he ordered. "And I'll show you what I think."

He'd never seen a woman strip so fast in his life.

"You know," Bree grumbled, hopping on one leg to get out of her shorts. "In romance novels, the hero slowly undresses the heroine and it's totally erotic."

"Then they fuck and the heavens open up and stars explode and galaxies collide." He snorted and stepped closer. "The real thing is better."

Her voice was muffled by her tank as she pulled it over her head. "For men, maybe." She tossed the shirt aside and shook out her curls. "You guys always get off."

Alex gripped her by the waist and stepped forward until he'd pinned her to window. He paused a moment, taking in the view of her naked upon the backdrop of black space and sparkling stars. Then he spun her around so she could see too.

Briana squirmed between his body and the glass until he bent his knees and slipped his cock between her legs. "Oh hell…" Her voice was a breathless gasp. "I think a star just exploded."

Inclined to agree, he nuzzled her ear and breathed in her scent. "Let's see how much damage we can do."

Chapter Four

઼

Bree shivered as Alex's voice, low and seductive as sin, brushed across her ear and echoed in her mind. Behind her, the heat and hardness of his cock burned between her thighs. The feel of his muscled chest pressed to her back made her wet. The chill of the glass, in stark contrast to his warmth, made her nipples hard. "You feel awesome," she told him, thinking he should know that.

His hands slipped upward and cradled the curve of her breasts. "You know," he said, his voice husky, "I don't have any jobs lined up after this run." He pulled her away from the glass and fondled her nipples. Rolling them with his fingers, he pinched and tugged until she whimpered with pleasure. "I could stick around and help you out."

"Oh my God. How can you think at a time like this?" She was having trouble even breathing.

"I'm thinking about you. Everything I do is about you. Trust me."

Leaning her flushed cheek against the glass, Bree closed her eyes and willed away the emotion she had no business feeling. "You're being romantic again, damn it."

Alex's chuckle made her ache all over.

"Let me turn around." She wanted desperately to get her hands on him.

"Lesson Number Two in patience—when a vamp has a hard-on like I do, you don't want to incite him further."

The softly menacing tone to his voice made her so hot, she writhed against him. "Why not? I'd love to see you lose control, get a little wild, turn things—"

Bree gasped as two sharp points scraped along the top of her shoulder. She stared at his reflection in the glass and saw the deadly glint of his fangs and the laser brightness of his gaze.

"*That's* why," he said softly, staring back at her. "One hunger feeds the other. Left unchecked, the man you know will give way to the animal you don't. I won't risk hurting you."

"Wow, I can see you."

"No, I'm making you see me. I don't want you to freak out."

"Oh, Alex…" Something inside her turned all soft. He was hiding the very essence of who he was, because he didn't want to scare her. "You make me want everything you can dish out. Try me. I can handle it."

With infinite care and a reverent touch, his palms slid down her rib cage and between her legs. He parted the lips of her sex and slipped through the moisture there. "No. You can't. You're human—soft and sweet and fragile. You've never seen a vamp male in full territorial rut or you wouldn't be asking for it."

"T-territorial?" God, that sounded sexy as hell. She spread her legs and moaned as he slipped a long finger inside her and then another, stroking deeply, just where she ached for him. She'd loved this last night, the feel of him inside her. Even this small little bit of him made her feel less empty, less alone.

"Yes. I'd want to mark you, claim you, make you mine. I'd frighten you, because I wouldn't look the same. I'd be larger and far more powerful. One wrong move and I could kill you. I could drink too much from you, fuck you too hard, cut your satin skin. It wouldn't be me in control anymore, Bree. I wouldn't know what I'd done until it was over."

"So you only fuck vamps then?" The sudden image of him with another woman made her grit her teeth.

"I didn't say that." Alex rubbed the heel of his palm against her clit making her pussy clench hungrily around his pumping fingers. "Damn, you're tight."

"Then what's different about me?" she argued even as her legs wobbled precariously. "I'm not weak."

He tightened his grip to support her. "I didn't say that either. I'm the one who's weak, sweetness. I haven't wanted a woman this badly in…well, in forever." He licked across the fluttering pulse in her neck and he shuddered, his thrusting fingers working faster, making her cream. "You have no idea how badly I want to pin you to the floor, and sink my cock and fangs into you. I've never been territorial with anyone, but I would be with you. I can feel it."

"You've never…? *Ever*?"

"Never ever."

His softly spoken words were devastating. Suddenly this wasn't about sex anymore and everything between them changed in the space of one breath. Things she'd never thought to offer any man became necessary gifts.

"Do it," she dared, the image of him straining over and inside her body making her impossibly wetter. "Take what you need. I bet I could handle it." Her voice wavered. "I-I want to handle it."

Alex growled as she soaked his hand. "You don't know what you're asking for."

"I'm asking for *you*, all of you. Don't hide a part of yourself away from me."

He nuzzled against her with a low moan. "Arch your back and brace yourself."

"Here?" she croaked, his rough command taking her to the brink of orgasm.

His fingers withdrew and she moaned in protest. Gripping her hips, he lifted her feet from the floor, stealing her balance. She squealed as her palms hit the window and the broad head of his cock breached her. She barely caught her breath before he lowered her onto him, the awesome width and hardness of him pressing relentlessly into her.

"Ah fuck." His arms shook as he took a step forward, using the weight of her body to drive himself deep. Her feet couldn't touch the deck, he was so much taller than she was, but he held her aloft with the effortless strength of a vampire.

Bree hissed and clawed at the glass as she seated fully onto him, his heavy balls resting against her clit. "My God! Did your cock grow overnight?" Writhing in an effort to accommodate his size, she was so painfully acutely aroused she thought she was losing her mind.

"Does it hurt?" he gasped, his lips brushing over her shoulder in a tender caress.

"God, no. It feels wonderful."

"Yes... No, don't move. Hold still. Give me a minute."

"Please," she begged as he remained completely still, his damp cheek resting against her shoulder, his chest heaving against her back. She reached behind them and tugged at his ass. His tight, taut, gorgeous ass.

"Bree... Damn it!" Alex caught her wrists and pinned them above their heads, holding her body above the floor impaled on his cock.

"Are you trying to kill me?" she complained, her pussy quivering around him, desperate for some friction. She curled her feet around the back of his knees, trying to find the leverage she needed to ride him.

Finally, he began to move in short, hard digs, rubbing more than thrusting. She came immediately, the pleasure moving outward from the place where he filled her, curling her toes and tensing her frame. Her cunt tightened around him in rippling spasms as she cried out his name and struggled against the slick glass.

"That feels fantastic," he groaned, switching to a faster pace. "Keep going."

As if she had any choice. The blissful waves of orgasm rolled and crested, easing slightly only to return in greater force as he swirled his hips and plunged deeper. So deep. Without her arms or her legs, she could only take what he gave her, her body helpless and spread for his slick rhythmic drives.

Lacing her fingers with his, Bree held on, clenching her inner muscles as he shafted her in long lunges.

"Oh yeah," he breathed in her ear, sweat from his skin binding them together. "You're making me come." He shuddered, his cock swelling before he spurted in hard, powerful bursts, flooding her so full she cried out in orgasm with him. Harsh sounds of pleasure tore from his throat, guttural and unbelievably exciting.

"Alex…" She closed her eyes as her body went languid, boneless in the wake of his infusion of heat. And still he kept going, pumping his cock through their mingled cream. "Don't stop. It feels so good, I'll die if you stop."

"I won't," he promised hoarsely, maintaining the slow, deep fucking, his shaft still hard as steel. "Now that the edge is off, I can do this for years."

He released her hands and thrust hard. "Hands and knees."

She gave an incredulous laugh. "How the hell am I supposed to do that?" She couldn't move. Besides, they were vertical.

"Trust me, sweetness. You have to learn to trust me."

His hands moved quickly, so quickly it seemed one moment she was standing and the next she was positioned just as he'd wanted. Dropping her head, she looked between her spread legs startled to see the floor a few feet below them. "Wow."

"Ummm," he agreed. "Now I can really take you deep."

Briana stared for a moment in shock, her body rocking as he began thrusting steadily. Her eyelids grew heavy as he stroked deep inside her, rubbing against places no man had ever touched before. She barely moved, arrested by the sight of his straining thighs and heavy sac as he pumped into her with a languorous, seductive tempo. It was so damn erotic watching him fuck her, her cunt fluttered around his cock as he swiveled his hips and screwed deep into her.

"Like the view?" he purred, his fingertips drifting along her spine.

"I like *you*," she admitted. Too much. Far, far too much. Alexei was such a blatantly sexual creature, she couldn't help but adore him.

Maybe even more than adore him.

It's okay, sweetheart.

"It's so *not* okay."

I adore you too.

"Damn it," she complained, her eyes misting with tears. "You're getting romantic again."

* * * * *

Romantic.

That wasn't the way Alex was feeling at all. Possessive and needy, maybe. Hungry and horny, definitely. But romantic?

Briana moaned his name and his gut tightened. *Ah hell, who was he kidding?* Romantic was frighteningly accurate. It was only the depth of his affection that allowed him to keep the hunger repressed and under control. His fangs ached and power rippled beneath his skin, but he restrained them all with a tight rein, because his feelings for her were stronger than the animal within him. In over two hundred years, he'd never been able to say that about any other woman.

She thrust downward against him, taking all of him, and he shuddered at the feel of the slick lips of her cunt kissing the base of his cock. Her creamy heat closed around him like a velvet-gloved fist. He'd just had the orgasm of his life, but you couldn't tell now. His cock was swollen to painful proportions and his balls were threatening to crawl inside his body.

"Easy," he growled when she began to rock hard, directing all of his energy into keeping them suspended above the deck of the bridge. It was the only way to keep the hunger occupied so he could make love to Bree like she deserved, slow and tenderly, instead of fucking the hell out of her.

She made another soft whimper and he cursed, the need to orgasm rising every time he sank into her. Her thoughts, hot and sexy and filled with fondness for him, drove him mad. Her fingers clawed at the glass, leaving damp trails of sweat behind. "Make me come again," she pleaded. "I'm going crazy."

Curling his body around hers, Alex shortened his strokes and reached between her legs. He circled her clit with the pads of his fingertips and groaned at the feel of her slick with his seed.

"Yes…" Bree swiveled her hips in time with his tempo, her cunt rippling along his shaft before clenching tight around him. Pure pleasure centered at the base of his spine. His cock filled with lust and desire before exploding in release, draining him of all the emotional barriers he'd set in place between them.

* * * * *

Taking care not to wake her, Alex slid his arm from beneath Briana's head and slipped quietly out of bed. He stared down at her for a long moment, taking in the gorgeous way she was displayed on his sheets. Lost in a sea of blood-red satin and jewel-toned pillows, her pale skin and golden curls made his mouth water.

He was tempted to lean over her and steal a kiss, an act he'd successfully managed to avoid so far, because he knew already that a taste of her would lead to a hunger for more. His animal would awaken and want her blood, want her cunt, want her body writhing beneath his, completely at his mercy. He couldn't take the chance that he'd hurt her. Not for anything in the universe.

With a sigh, he forced himself to step away. He tugged on a pair of trousers and left the room. Padding softly down the corridor, he made his way to the bridge and sat down at his console with its multicolored lights. Alex took a moment to think, his brain gradually clearing of Bree's addicting scent. Then he hit the comm and waited for Derek to answer.

The screen lit up almost immediately, revealing the stern countenance of the Security President. "How's everything progressing, Night?"

"As well as can be expected."

That answer sounded better than, *I'm falling in love with my mission, how about you?*

"Has she told you anything?"

Not a damn thing and that was really starting to bug him. It meant there was a trust issue between them. Not that he blamed her with the information she had about him, but he was arrogant enough to wish that whatever she felt for him would be enough to get past it. He'd got what he needed by probing her mind, but he wished she'd had the faith in him to talk about her troubles out loud. "They want her to withdraw her support of the Eastern Bill."

Derek frowned. "Why? It's a minor piece of legislation that doesn't hurt anyone's interests. If I remember correctly, it just calls for opening a remote sector of the Gamma Quadrant for travel."

"Apparently there is a small colony of nomads in that sector who display remarkable regenerative qualities. They can cut off a limb, let it die, then reattach it and it will regain its function."

"Shit." Derek fell back in his chair. "I take it Representative Michaels hopes to open the route to researchers?"

"That's the plan. Briana thinks if they can determine how the regeneration works, they can regenerate the reproductive systems of vamps. She knew opposition would be high if her true intent was revealed so she's kept it under wraps."

"Well, someone figured it out," Derek growled. "I'm really starting to feel out of the fucking loop here. I went through every report on Rep. Michaels and the only droid purchase I could find was a sex bot a few weeks ago."

"That's the one I was talking about."

"You said a PA droid."

"That's what she's using it for," he grumbled. "She's had its programming altered."

Derek threw his head back and laughed. "What I wouldn't give to be on that ship! I've never mixed it up with a sex bot and I sure as hell wouldn't let one anywhere near Sable, but the idea is intriguing. You can tell me all about it and I'll live vicariously through you."

Alex snorted. If anyone even looked at Sable wrong, Derek got pissed. Alex had always thought that kind of protectiveness was funny. Now that he was on the possessive side himself, it wasn't such a laughing matter. "That damn droid is in the cargo hold where it belongs. It's lucky I didn't eject it, like I have half a mind to."

"Uh-oh. Sounds like somebody's getting attached," Derek chimed in softly. "Don't forget she's human, Night. The fact that she's not a vamp helps our cause immeasurably. There's no future with her. You're immortal, she's not."

"I know that." But it was too late to stop the way he felt about her. He suspected he'd been half in love with her before they'd even met. The heat, the need between them...hell, *the mind-blowing sex* had finished him. "How's her family?"

"Fine. For now. Listen, Night, are you planning on telling her who you are? She hasn't notified anyone about the threats to her family, including her own personal guards. She obviously didn't trust anyone to assist her. Are you certain she trusts you?"

No, he wasn't certain and he hated that. "I won't jeopardize the mission, sir. I know what the risks to her are if she handles this alone."

"Don't discount the risks to our kind. We need her."

Alex took a deep breath and willed away the frustration that ate at him. "I know."

"Good. I trusted you with this assignment. Don't fuck it up by getting emotionally involved. Understand?"

"Yeah," he bit out. "I understand."

"I don't have the schematics on the sex droid readily available, but I'll get them to you in an hour. And your hunch was right about the would-be assassin. A traveler bearing a Shinite passport went through Thieves' Cove port the same time you were there."

Alex kept his face impassive, but inside him everything changed. Shinite assassins didn't fail. The blaster shot in the bar had either been intended as a warning or it was only by a whim of fate that Briana was alive today. Either way, she was in deadly serious danger and that knowledge solidified his next course of action.

"I've got all my security safeguards on their highest levels," Alex said grimly. "But I'll run through them again every day. I won't take any chances with her life. And you were right about her dad. He's hidden himself away at her request. Even she doesn't know where he is."

"Good. That takes care of that concern. Tap into the droid at your first opportunity. We need to know everything it knows. Atkinson out."

Derek signed off and the comm screen went black.

Alex double-checked the navigational settings and did a quick sub-space scan, before rising from his seat and heading back to Bree. In a little over a week they'd be in Tolan. Somehow he had to make her fall in love with him before then. She had to trust him implicitly or the mission could fail, and he couldn't let that happen. This wasn't about doing his job anymore or impressing Derek. This was about Briana and protecting the woman he cared about more anything.

His heart ached as he entered his room where the scent of sex and her skin inundated his senses. If she grew to love him, it would rip him apart to say goodbye to her. But he'd suffer the pain gladly if it kept her and her family alive.

* * * * *

"Ugh! Get off," Bree complained. "You're crushing me."

James rolled to his back beside her on the padded mat. "We should continue this another time, Mistress. You are too distracted to fight properly."

"I am not distracted."

"You have yet to knock me down and we have been sparring for hours." He stood and held out his hand to her.

She blew the hair out of her eyes and then brushed the strands away that clung to her sweaty skin. *Alex. Alex. Alex.* He was all she could think about and it was affecting everything, including her ability to concentrate.

"I'm just not used to fighting in artificial gravity," she muttered, using his proffered help to pull up to her feet. "That's all."

"Your excuse is dreadful," he scoffed.

"Bite me."

"That's a pleasure I reserve for myself," Alex said behind her. Startled, Bree spun swiftly to face him.

He lounged in the doorway with his arms crossed, the picture of seductive leisure in his sapphire-colored vest, loose trousers and bare feet. He looked like he'd just rolled out of bed, which he had. Since she started sharing his quarters a week ago, she'd learned another thing about vamps—they slept like the dead. He hadn't moved a muscle when she'd slipped out of his cabin earlier.

His dark eyes never left hers. "Send that thing away. I'll spar with you if you like."

She snorted. Alex was never going to accept James. He'd been furious to discover she'd reactivated her droid and it had taken a hefty dose of carnal persuasion to cheer up her vamp again. "Sparring with you won't help me. You have abilities I can't compete with."

"Then send it away and we'll get our exercise in more pleasurable ways." He pushed off the doorjamb and came toward her with a sultry stride she knew. *Let's fuck*, it said, and she always responded immediately.

"You're a menace," she grumbled as her body shivered in anticipation, her breasts growing heavy, the nipples beading up tight. She'd wanted hot sex and orgasms with a gorgeous guy and that's exactly what he gave her. But she hadn't expected Alexei Night to be so tender. She hadn't known he would want to be with her as often as possible, that he would want to feed her by hand, wash and brush her hair, hold her close while sleeping...

What did you expect? His voice, low and throbbing with something that made her sweat, curled in her mind and the way he looked at her made her breath catch. *Did you think I'd only pay attention to you in bed?*

"You said you didn't have to be charming."

He arched a brow and came to a stop before her. Lifting his hand, he brushed the backs of his fingers across her damp cheek. "I don't *have* to be anything, sweetness. But I choose to be everything for you."

"Why?"

"Because it gives me pleasure to do so." His firm lips brushed along her eyebrow. The sex appeal so innate to his kind was magnified in Alexei. She could almost breathe it in, almost taste it.

Bree lifted her face for his kiss, but he licked the corner of her mouth and then moved away.

She groaned in frustration. "Why won't you ever kiss me?"

His hands circled her waist and he stared down at her with a smile. "I thought you wanted to fight?"

"No," she said slowly. "I want you to kiss me."

"Can I choose where?"

"On the lips."

"My thoughts exactly." The wicked glint in his eyes told her they weren't thinking about the same lips.

Shoving out of his embrace, she turned away. "Go walk on the ceiling or something, Alex, and leave me in peace." She was so sick of the tight control he kept himself under. It wasn't natural, and they both knew it. Every time they made love—and it was definitely making love—he restrained his baser instincts. Every time they ate, he suffered through stored blood when she would have given hers gladly. His reticence was a barrier between them, a huge one, and she couldn't live with it anymore.

He sighed. "Bree—"

"Don't '*Bree*' me! What is it with you and your fucking control? You want a certain level of intimacy and that's it. You decide the level for you, but you want everything from me."

"It's not like that and you know it."

She rounded on him. "I know you won't kiss me! Sorry, but to me, kissing is far more intimate than fucking."

"Mistress," James interrupted. "I need to speak with you."

Alex turned. "Get the hell out of here!"

"Don't talk to him like that," she snapped, silently ordering James to her room.

"Why?" Alex asked. "I can't hurt its feelings."

She shoved past him, intent on following her droid. "Don't be an ass."

"Where are you going?" He caught her by the elbow.

"To my room."

"You mean *our* room?" he bit out.

"No, I mean *my* room." Bree tried to shake him off. "The one I slept in the first night."

He drew himself up and loomed over her. "Why can't you discuss whatever needs to be discussed in front of me?"

Titling her head back, she stared up into his gorgeous face with its tightly drawn lips and intense gaze. His grip was unrelenting. He wasn't hurting her, but neither could she escape.

"Because it's none of your concern, Alexei. You draw the intimacy line at kissing. I draw it at discussing Council business with a criminal."

Bree felt the frustration and hurt ripple through him. Every day she spent with him made his emotions clearer to her. She knew he could read her just as well, even better, since he could read minds and she couldn't.

"What does it matter?" she asked, lifting her chin even higher. "Whatever you want to know, you can find out by eavesdropping on my thoughts."

His jaw clenched. "I want you to talk to me. I want you to share things with me. I want you to trust me."

"Like you trust me?" she challenged, arching her brow.

"Damn it, that's different. I could kill you, Briana, if I'm not careful."

"Perhaps what I have to say would kill you too."

"That would be stretch," he said dryly, "since I'm very nearly immortal."

"In space maybe, where you're surrounded by metal and no suns. Tolan is a whole different world. We have two suns there and one of our largest exports is trees." She watched him run an agitated hand through his hair and released her breath in a rush. Her heart ached. "Any way you look at it, we're from two different worlds."

He shot her a narrowed glance. "What the hell is that supposed to mean?"

Bree waved a hand between them. She had to swallow hard before she could speak. "Whatever's happening between us is hopeless. I want more than you can give. I shouldn't want more, it's ridiculous to want more, but I do. We should just end this now."

Suddenly his grip hurt. "What do you suggest we do?" he growled. "Reach port and say, '*Goodbye, thanks for the fuck of my life*'?"

"I think that's best, don't—*Mmff…*"

Alex's mouth swooped down to hers—hard, expert, demanding. His hands moved to her wrists and held her absolutely still, his head tilting to deepen the angle of the kiss.

Dark, rich and exotic, his flavor flooded her mouth and made her dizzy. His tongue swept past her lips and into the deepest recesses, licking and tasting as if he were starving for her. He wasn't the gentle, considerate lover she'd known the last week. This Alex was harsh, almost brutal, his tongue fucking her mouth in a desperate, frantic rhythm.

Bree sensed the control he wielded and felt the battle that raged inside him. Encouraged, she brushed her tongue past the sharp tips of his fangs and leaned into him, pressing her breasts to his chest, telling him silently to give it to her. *I dare you*, she taunted in her thoughts, her hands cupping his ass and squeezing the firm flesh.

He growled into her mouth, flooding her mind with images of him as a ravening beast and her as a helpless, frightened victim of his lust.

She fought back with her own visions, pictures of her giving as good as she got, taking everything he had and asking for more. Straddling him, taking him, fucking *him*.

His grip on her wrists tightened until it was bruising. *You want a taste of what it would be like?*

Before she could think her reply, he was moving. He ripped at her clothing, razor-sharp claws shredding her shorts and scraping briefly across her skin. She shivered and moaned, his need for her sparking her own for him. With impatient hands, she yanked down his trousers, freeing the cock she couldn't get enough of. Crowding her, he stepped out of his pants, forcing her to take rapid backward steps. Unwilling to give him any advantage, she reached between them and cupped his balls. His snarled response wasn't even remotely human, but she wasn't scared. She could never be scared of him.

Alex pulled her to the floor, his mouth locked with hers. The kiss she'd longed for cut her lips with her own teeth. The palm that cupped her breast squeezed with painful pressure and the hair-dusted thigh that thrust between hers was rough in its intrusion. Locked together, they rolled and strained to get closer, every touch and movement filled with an underlying desperation.

And then with startling suddenness he thrust away from her.

"Go." His breathing was harsh and loud in the padded room. "Run."

"No, damn you." Scrambling to her knees, she crawled toward him. "Don't push me away again."

"Get out of here!" He curled away from her, the skin of his back rippling as he struggled to contain his hunger.

"You stop now, Alexei Night, and I'm going to kick your ass. And don't think I can't do it either. You won't fight back and I'll just keep on punching."

He shot a glare at her over his shoulder, revealing glowing red eyes and bared fangs. Against her will, she shivered.

Last chance... he warned.

Bree steeled her nerves. This was Alex. She knew him. She trusted him. "Bring it on."

Before she could blink he was on top of her. *Open your legs. Now!*

She'd barely spread her legs before he plunged desperately into her cunt, digging deep with that endless length of thick cock. Moaning into his mouth, she couldn't catch her breath, he gave her no chance to adjust. He fucked her like a madman and she could only hang on, her hands clutching his flexing ass as he reamed her with unbelievable speed, spearing her high and hard. Bree writhed beneath him, begging for air, but he dug his claws in the padded mat to anchor them in place and only shafted her harder.

"Oh God…oh God…oh God…" He was killing her with pleasure, forcing her to take it, punishing her for wanting too much from him.

More, he growled.

"W-what?" She couldn't take any more.

His forearms pinned her shoulders down, holding her immobile, and then he rammed into her, forcing her thighs brutally wide so he could thrust deeper. *More!*

She screamed and came hard, her cunt clutching his pumping cock in hard convulsive shudders. Suddenly her mind filled with him, she *became* him. She felt the drowning pleasure he took in holding her, in fucking her, in tasting her kisses. She saw how deeply he craved her and wanted her on every level possible. She saw the respect he held for her and the need he had to protect her. And when he groaned into her mouth and flooded her with his cum, she saw something else too, something that filled her with equal parts joy and despair.

Alexei loved her.

Oh God…

But there were dark parts to him as well, hidden parts that he refused to show her. Despite the depth of his affection, it wasn't enough. Tears slipped past her lashes and salted their kiss.

He ground into her, stroking his cock with her spasming depths until he'd emptied himself. Then he pulled his mouth from hers and stared at her with torment in his eyes, his chest heaving with labored breaths.

"I can't give you any more than I have." His voice was hoarse and raw as he pulled out of her deliciously bruised pussy. Leaping to his feet, he tugged up his pants and kept his gaze averted. "I've already given you everything." He turned on his heel and left her there on the floor.

Devastated.

Chapter Five

Briana stumbled down the corridor, her hand running along the cool metal wall to support her weak legs. It wasn't love. It couldn't be. Not so soon. They hardly knew each other.

But the reckless beat of her heart called her a liar and the dizziness that accompanied her gasping breaths said the same. Alexei couldn't deceive her about something so important. Could he? Before she'd begun this journey she'd been certain she knew everything about vampires, but she'd been wrong. She didn't know if they could lie through a mental link. It wasn't something she'd needed to know. Until now.

The door to her old room slid open silently and she stepped inside.

"I have news to share," James said quietly.

Wrapping a towel around her waist, Bree walked over to the bed and sank onto the edge of the mattress. Her hand fluttered to her heart as awe penetrated her consciousness. Alexei Night loved her. And that scared the shit out of her.

"You have received another demand." James took a seat next to her.

"What?" She turned to face him, thoughts of Alex driven from her mind. "What did it say? What do they want? Oh God, my family… Are they okay?"

"Mistress, calm down." He placed his hand over hers. "They have done nothing to your family, but they know your sister and brother-in-law are staying on Rashier 6."

"No…" She'd arranged a trip off-world for them, taking great care to hide their departure. Using a generic name, she'd purchased a private service to transport them. She'd told them she wanted to hide them from the media attention brought on by her position, but all her efforts had been for nothing. They'd been discovered anyway.

"What do they want?" she asked starkly, her pulse racing in near panic. If anything were ever to happen to Stella she didn't know how she could bear it.

"They know you are en route to Tolan and they are not pleased that you have disobeyed their request for you to wait for instructions."

Bree stood and began to pace. "How they hell do they know that?"

James rose to his feet. "There is an information leak somewhere, Mistress. It is the only logical explanation."

Throwing her hands in the air, she shot him an arch glance. "No one knows, James. You and me, that's it!"

"Night knows," he said softly.

She stilled, astonished. "Oh hell, give me a break! Alex wouldn't sell me out."

"Why not? Because he says he loves you? A known criminal who has spent years doing unsavory acts for money?"

"You don't know him," she argued, even as her stomach turned.

"Neither do you. A week's acquaintance is all you have to base your conviction upon."

"In most cases I would agree that isn't long enough." Bree resumed her fevered pacing. "But he's shown me things, shared things…"

"Has he shared with you the reason for the ten-minute gap in my memory banks?" James asked.

Scowling, she stopped pacing again. "What the hell are you talking about now?"

The droid stood stoically, his classically handsome features impassive. "I hesitated to tell you, because I did not want you to doubt my ability to perform. But in light of the recent demand, I have to disclose the anomaly. There is a ten-minute period of time three nights ago that I cannot account for."

"What does that mean?"

"It means I have run multiple queries and while my database appears undisturbed—"

"Then don't worry about it," she dismissed. "What was the demand?"

"I am unable to account for ten minutes, forty-three seconds," he continued obstinately. "Exactly the amount of time it would take to download all of the information I have acquired since you purchased me."

Her hand moved to her stomach, which suddenly felt queasy. "Is that what happened? Have you been tampered with?"

"There is no record of a download in my database, but I was curious." James moved to the door and locked it. "So last night while you and Captain Night were sleeping, I searched the bridge. I found a synapse interrupter, Mistress. It was set at just the right frequency to disengage me. None of the other droids or programs on this ship would require that particular frequency."

"Oh God." Swallowing hard, Bree shook her head, refusing to believe it. James was designed to see only the facts. He wasn't capable of factoring in the effect of emotions. Alex would never set her up. He would never hurt her so badly.

"What other explanation is there?" James asked.

"I don't know. But there has to be one."

"The message was very clear. Your exact location is known to them. They are aware that we will enter Tolan orbit in a few hours. They insisted you leave Captain Night behind and land on the planet alone. From there you have been instructed to travel to a local public transport hub near your father's home where you will receive instructions by public comm link. You are to leave this ship without delay and await their approval before taking any further action. You are to dress in the clothing that displays your rank and present yourself as you would on the House floor. You are to go into the hub without my escort and—"

"This is too much," she snapped, her hands going to her hips. "These nitpicky demands are simply designed to oppress and frustrate me into doing something stupid. They asked me to back off the Eastern Bill and I agreed. I'm not giving them any more than that."

"You never intended to give them even that much," James pointed out. "You merely made the appearance of capitulation until you could ensure your family's safety."

"Damn straight! I won't be dictated to. If I give in once, what's to stop them from demanding more? I'll be trapped in a vicious cycle, nothing more than a pawn used to achieve their ends."

Bree clenched her fists. Despite her frustration, she was going to do as they asked. She'd never spoken to them directly before and she couldn't pass up the opportunity. This situation couldn't be allowed to go on indefinitely. Talking to them would bring her closer to discovering who was behind these threats.

Moving to the round window, she stared out at the starry space beyond. Only days ago she'd enjoyed a similar view, drenched in pleasure as Alex made love to her that first time, moving inside her with breathtaking skill. She'd wanted the moment to go on forever, the joining to last beyond the temporary physical rapture. Known for her pragmatism, that was the one time in her life when she'd lived for the moment.

Now that moment was over. It was hard to believe when Alex's cum was slowly leaking down her thighs, but there was no denying it. He was a vamp with an endless life. She had another fifty years left, give or take a decade if she wasn't assassinated first. And he couldn't be himself with her anyway. What kind of life could they have if he was always living with only half of himself?

She took a deep, shuddering breath and rested her palms on the ledge. The metal was cool to the touch and soothing, reminding her that some things were solid and unmovable in a world that was suddenly careening around her.

Snorting, Bree rested her hot forehead against the cool glass. She'd lost her focus for a while and allowed a seductive vamp to distract her from a matter of grave importance. She'd thought this task would be so easy—hide her family, thereby taking away the leverage of the people who threatened her. Then she could approach them on equal footing. Once her family was safe, she'd have nothing to lose.

But they'd outsmarted her somehow. Now it was time for her to outsmart them.

"How far away are we from Tolan orbit?" she asked, coming to a decision.

"A few hours." He nodded as he read her thoughts. "An excellent plan. I will go and disable the alert systems for the shuttle pod. Captain Night will be unaware when we leave."

"You'll have to keep him occupied for a bit. If he comes near me, he'll know. I don't want to drag him into this."

"Of course. I will take care of him." James unlocked the door and left silently, leaving Briana with her tumultuous thoughts.

It was wrong to sneak away from Alex, she felt it in her bones. But she needed a clear head now, and her sparring session with James had proven what a distraction the vamp was. Alex was never meant to be more than a temporary pleasure—they'd been doomed from the start—and now the present circumstances were too dangerous. She knew he wasn't the one directly responsible for the leak of information, but someone he told was. And after their encounter in the workout room, he'd become a liability she couldn't afford. She cared about him too much to get him involved with this. Who knew what would happen?

Lifting her chin, she moved into the head to take a shower and wash his scent from her skin. As she stepped under the spray, she hardened her aching heart and steeled her resolve.

She hadn't reached her level of power by wavering or allowing her emotions to rule. She'd always relied on her wits to survive.

And if she could stop thinking about Alex, maybe she could actually use them.

* * * * *

Alex awoke to the headache from hell. His hand reached up and touched the rapidly healing bump on the back of his head while his senses searched for Bree's presence. He paused, frozen with his hand at his nape, his eyes closing as he concentrated on searching every inch of the ship. His heart began to race.

Briana was gone.

Panicked, he leapt to his feet and flew through the corridors. Once he'd ascertained that the shuttle pod was gone, he returned to the bridge and replayed the security video, not surprised to see the damned sex bot/PA bashing him over the head with the blunt end of a synapse interrupter. Alex growled. He really hated droids and his inability to sense them or read them.

Dropping his head back against the headrest, he closed his eyes as pain lanced outward from his injury. Was it his love that had caused Bree to flee? He'd felt her surprise like a tangible thing and knew he'd frightened her. But they were almost to Tolan. The pressure had been on him to win her trust before they arrived at the planet and she tried to leave him behind.

He knew now that he should never have left the training room like he did. Had he been thinking clearly, he would have known she would be fragile after the brutal way he'd taken her. And a woman used to treading a difficult path alone would find the thought of relying on someone too scary. He should have set aside his own vulnerability to be there for her. Instead, he'd been equally distraught and arrogant fool that he was, he'd wanted her to come to him.

Because of his stupid pride, the woman he loved was now out there in danger without him. His worry was such that he was near mindless with it. He could barely sit still, barely keep from letting his beast free to tear apart anything that would threaten her safety. He wanted to howl out his frustration, but nothing would save her if he couldn't think clearly.

Alex reached over and hit the comm link. Due to the unusual time of his call, he waited long moments before Derek's face filled the screen.

"What is it?" the president asked without preamble.

He steeled himself before admitting, "Representative Michaels fled the ship with her droid an hour ago."

Derek took a deep breath. "Now she's Rep. Michaels again? You had a fight or lover's quarrel, right? *Goddamn it!*" the president roared, his fist hitting the table. "Where the hell are you?" He looked away to check the readout. "Tolan. I'll notify your backup to begin searching for her. Return to Thieves' Cove and await further instructions."

"I'm not leaving!" Alex protested. "Not while she's in danger."

"You've done quite enough. You transported her to Tolan. Leave the rest to the agents on the surface. Continue to shift through the information you downloaded from the droid and keep me posted."

"I'm not leaving," he said again, his voice softer than before, but no less determined.

Derek arched a brow. "You are if you want to continue working for the STF. Disobey a direct order, Night, and see what happens."

His hands clenching into fists under the console, Alex kept his face impassive. "As you wish, sir. Night out."

He turned off the comm and sat for a moment, considering what he should do next. One thing was certain—he wasn't leaving Tolan without making sure Briana was safe.

He reactivated the comm and a moment later the screen was filled with a blond man with laughing blue eyes. A longtime

STF agent, Christian Beaumont was one of his best friends and the only person he trusted to do what he was about to ask.

"Hey, Alex," Christian greeted with a wide smile that made most women melt. "How's it going?"

"Not good. Listen, I need you to do something for me and you can't let Derek find out what you're up to." Alex would lose his job for this, something that up until a week ago had been the most important thing in his life. But now he had something far more precious to lose.

"Aw shit." Christian groaned. "Are you in trouble again?"

"I'm going to send you some files I downloaded from a droid. Go through them and see if anything jumps out at you."

"Like what? What the hell am I looking for?"

"Recordings of ransom threats and anything at all pertaining to the Eastern Bill. It's a PA droid's database. It should contain your basic PA information. If anything doesn't fit, flag it and let me know. Oh…and you'll be looking these files over on a flight to Rashier 6."

"Rashier 6?" Christian cried. "I've got assignments of my own to do. What do you need on Rashier 6?"

"I'm going to send you some vid captures for visual reference. I want you to find the couple in the photos and guard them. But don't let them know what you're doing." Alex couldn't be two places at once and keeping Bree's family safe was as important to him as protecting Bree herself. He couldn't bear to see her injured, either physically or emotionally.

"Alex, you've got to be kidding. This isn't a favor. This is like 'you owe me your firstborn child' territory."

"I can't have kids, neither can you, but if you do this favor for me that could change."

The blond vamp stilled, his features changing from scowling frustration to alert awareness. "You're serious."

"Yeah. Can you help me?"

Christian nodded. "Send me what you have and I'll take care of it. Take a comm with you in case I have questions or find something you might want to know."

"Will do. I owe you, man. Huge."

"Yes. You do. Beaumont out."

The comm went dead.

Alex stood and left the bridge. He went to his room and breathed deeply as he entered, absorbing Bree's scent into his lungs. Inside him, the hunger stirred as it always did at the smell of her, clawing at his vitals with burning need, desperate for the feel of her beneath him and the taste of her upon his tongue. His mouth watered and his muscles rippled beneath his skin. Alex intended to use his endless craving for her to his advantage. He would track her with it and hunt her down. He'd find a way to keep her safe.

That way, when all was said and done, he could throttle her himself.

* * * * *

Briana stood outside the shuttle pod and gazed at the nearby forest. The brightness of the twin suns was slowly waning as the day lengthened into late afternoon. Tall, green grass grew to her hips. Swaying gently in the fragrant breeze it resembled the rippling waves of water in the lake just beyond the rise. Birds larger in size than she was flew in the air above her in swirling, dipping patterns she remembered fondly from her childhood. Despite the bleakness of her present task, it didn't detract from the knowledge that she was home. It had been a long time since her last visit. Too long.

Shortly the authorities would come to investigate the unauthorized landing, but that wasn't what worried her. The local police could be dismissed with a quick eye scan to verify her identity. It was Alexei Night that gave her the shivers. Vampires were predators. He would be able to track her easily if he wanted. And that was one thing she'd never doubted about him—he wanted. *Badly.*

"Let's get out of here," she said grimly, her fingers finding comfort in the grip of her blaster.

James stepped out of the shuttle and raised the ramp, sealing the craft. "I have everything we need."

They jogged quickly across the packed dirt of the clearing and slipped into the woods, heading toward the public transport hub just a few kilometers away.

As they moved silently through the golden trees, Bree felt occasional brushes of awareness along her spine. Alex couldn't be on her heels yet, there were still a few hours left before nightfall, but she was as cognizant of him as if he walked directly behind her. She quickened her pace.

Some type of tampering had happened to James, she didn't doubt her droid's claim. But why would Alex need to access her PA when her own thoughts were an open book? And who had he been communicating with the last week of their journey? She couldn't see any reason for him to have shared her information with anyone unless he'd meant to profit from it. Despite how well that fit in with his past record and his reputation as a criminal, she couldn't believe Alex would hurt her for credits. She was, however, starting to believe that he loved her. Or maybe she was just hoping he loved her. But if she was hoping for his love, wouldn't the implication be that her own feelings were stronger than she'd acknowledged?

What a fucking mess.

Don't say a word, James, she warned silently.

For once, her droid used his undeniable logic to keep his mouth shut.

* * * * *

Alex hit the catch on his boot and watched as his footwear sealed automatically. Straightening, he arched his neck, adjusting the fit of the scabbard that was slung across his back.

His laser sword clung to his thigh and his blaster hung fully charged in the holster at his side. Normally, he wouldn't need anything more than his own physical power, but he had no idea what he was walking into and he had Bree to worry about. He'd need the wooden sword at his back if he had to face off against his own kind, the blaster if he fought a droid and his laser sword — with a massive helping of good fortune — if he fought against a Shinite.

Growling with frustration and unbearable worry, he began to pace. He'd landed on the surface an hour ago, but he had to wait for the cursed twin suns of Tolan to set.

Bree was close despite her three-hour head start. He could sense her. His shuttlecraft's unique tracking signal had made it simple to find and he'd landed at the closest port. It was a public transport hub and they'd protested mightily at his request to land. His ship, the *Renegade*, was a deep-space Starwing, far too large for the design of the simple local hub. He'd had to beg, barter and plead for the clearance to land and in the end it had cost him a case of Anneri wine. The beverage wasn't illegal, but it was very hard to come by and very expensive.

The soft beeping from the bridge told him the suns had gone down far enough that it was safe for him to venture outside. The cargo ramp lowered with what Alex considered to be uncustomary leisure. His booted foot tapped out an impatient staccato as the landing bay slowly came into view.

Outside, beings of all nationalities scurried about their business. Flight information paged from the overhead speakers and various smells assaulted his senses. But the animal within him focused on just one scent — Bree's. She was close, very close.

With a shrug of his shoulders, Alex let the beast free. His fangs descended from their confinement, his nails lengthened into deadly claws, his muscles thickened and bulged. His sense of smell sharpened, his hearing and vision became acute and power visibly rippled beneath his taut skin. It was nearly orgasmic, the sensation of the hunger unleashed. He stepped out into the concourse and all eyes turned to him.

He licked his fangs and smiled.
The hunt was on.

Chapter Six

಄

Pacing in the darkness, Briana drummed her fingers against the hilt of her blaster and surveyed the transport hub in the wide valley below. She'd been waiting for hours for the instructions to come and her patience had long since run out.

"I want you to break into the comm room, James. Tap the lines going into the hub and trace the sender of the link when it comes in." At least with James working toward her cause she'd feel less helpless and more active.

"Of course, Mistress." James cut through the brush and made his way down the sloping hill toward the utility door visible from where they stood.

She watched him move, noting the way he detected the security vids and avoided them. For a sex bot, the variety of his skills impressed her. He was definitely one of the best investments she'd made.

What about me?

Her shoulders stiffened, the hairs on her nape tingling into a singular awareness, as did every cell in her body. She'd known he would come after her, she just hadn't expected it to happen so fast. "You shouldn't be here."

He growled.

"Don't growl at me. This isn't any of your business." Turning slowly, she faced Alexei Night and her mouth fell open at the sight of him. "Alex…?" she breathed, as the surface of her skin misted from a heretofore unknown level of desire. He looked larger, meaner and far more dangerous. The glint in his eyes was feral and voracious.

Damn, he was *hot*! Hard everywhere, he was the most gorgeous creature she'd ever seen. His thick, beautiful hair could have blended with the darkness, except for the loving caress of moonlight that caught the strands and made them gleam like starlight. His dark, liquid eyes glowed a brilliant red, burning through her clothing with a ravenous intensity. Dressed in his customary vest, his arms and chest rippled with lean power while skin-hugging pants showed off the beauty of his legs and luscious cock.

Her nipples pebbled into aching points and her pussy grew soft and damp, just from the sight of his dark skin burnished with the lunar glow. Fierce, painful arousal flooded her senses with a force so powerful she almost fell to her knees. She moved toward him, unable to do anything else. Delicious memories of their encounter in the workout room made her shiver and walk faster. She was desperate to have him that way again.

"Stay away," came the guttural order.

Glancing at the huge erection outlined by his trousers, Bree licked her lips. He was dressed to kill, literally, and it was so amazingly sexy.

She wanted him. And she would have him. Now.

Alex snarled. "Don't come closer."

The coiling tension radiating from him was a tangible thing. His fists clenched and unclenched rhythmically at his sides while the muscle in his jaw ticced with his effort at restraint.

He was barely in control, she could tell, and it was such a turn-on. Never in her life had she needed anything as badly as she needed him now. She ran the distance between them, determined to rip off the material that hid his body from her view. Her hands grabbed his pecs and squeezed, as she ground her aching pussy against the hard flesh of his thigh.

The next thing she knew, she was facedown on the ground, trussed up like a Tolan fowl.

"Hey!" she yelled, struggling against the bonds that held her. "Let me go!"

"No." His voice was nearly unrecognizable, deep and low and seductive as hell. He moved away and she heard him pacing like a caged beast, the fallen leaves rustling beneath his boots.

"Alexei, please," she begged, her entire body aching and burning for him. "Fuck me."

He came over her, hovering…needing…wanting…just as she was. She could feel the depth of his hunger. *I want to eat you up, lick your cream, drink from you.*

"Please!" she cried again, thrashing restlessly. "I need you."

A low rumbling growl filled the air and then he bounded away.

She couldn't believe it. He'd actually left her. Like this!

Her ears strained for a sound from him, but the forest was still and silent except for the soft nocturnal calls of the various insects and animals that made the woods their home.

Gradually the tightness of her flesh and muscles began to ease, the misty sweat on her skin drying in the cool night air. Only after her breathing returned to normal and her heart rate slowed to a more reasonable pace did Alexei return. She heard the steady, rhythmic crunching of his steps on dried leaves as he approached.

Crouching next to her, Alex brushed away the strands of hair that had fallen free from the tight coil at her nape. "Are you okay, sweetness?" he asked in a soothing whisper.

"I'm tied up on the ground. I wouldn't say I'm okay," she snapped. She glared up at him, noting that he looked like himself again. Just a man. An achingly beautiful man with a seductive smile and tightly leashed power beneath a flamboyant façade.

Alex laughed and made quick work of the ties that bound her. "Good. You sound like you're ready to kill me, which, sadly, is more appropriate at this moment than you raping me. However, please feel free to have your way with me at any another time."

Bree pulled her hands free and pushed up to a seated position. "What the hell *was* that?"

"My calling." He offered a sheepish smile that made her heart skip a beat. "I'm sorry. I can't contain it when I'm hunting. It's instinctive to subdue prey."

"Talk like that is why a lot of humans hate your kind." She wrinkled her nose. "Being called 'prey' isn't very endearing."

He chuckled and held out a hand to help her up. The moment they touched, a hot shiver ran through her. Calling or not, Alex had that effect on her.

"Hell," she grumbled as she was pulled to her feet. "I wanted to fuck you right here, right now, in the middle of waiting for an important comm." She shook her head and snorted in disgust. "I was acting like one of the *Too Stupid to Live* romance heroines in my e-books. You know, the ones that want to fuck right in the middle of the danger and the reader is sitting there going, 'What the hell is she doing?'."

"Um, no," Alex said dryly. "I don't know."

He began brushing the dead leaves off her with gentle hands, his fingers lingering in all the right places. "Sweetness, you really need to stop reading that stuff. If you want some entertainment, just see me. I'll keep you busy."

As if that were possible. She couldn't keep him bound to her and available for her pleasure like James was, although the thought was wickedly tempting. Alex had chosen his path a long time ago, just as she had. Their paths had converged briefly for this voyage, but in the long run there could never be anything lasting between them. She was mortal and he wasn't. He had friends and a life she could never fit into. Which reminded her...

"Alex. Who have you been talking to about me?"

Arching a brow, he asked, "What do you mean?"

"Don't play innocent." She slapped his wandering hands away. "Someone knew we were approaching Tolan and they knew I was with you. I certainly didn't tell anybody, so that leaves only you."

He caught her chin and studied her carefully. Not just her features, but in the deep recesses of her thoughts. "You trusted me." The pure pleasure on his face made her breath catch.

She sighed. It really should be illegal to be that yummy.

Thank you, sweetness. I think you're pretty tasty, too.

"While I'm sure reading minds is a neat trick if you're the one who has the ability," she mumbled, uncomfortable with how deeply he affected her. "On my end, it sucks."

"Whatever," he said dismissively. "All women want men to read their minds. You're damn lucky to have me. Eventually you'll realize that."

He made it sound like they had a future. Bree bit her lower lip to hide the giddy thrill his words gave her, but the glimmer in his eyes said he knew.

"Despite the suspicious evidence to the contrary you never once thought I'd sell you out." His smile was brilliant, the brush of his fingertips along her face reverent.

She was captured by the moment and his obvious relief, her mind twisting and turning in an effort to make sense of her riotous feelings. Crazy wild thoughts swirled through her head. There had to be a way for her to explore these emotions. How could she go on, wondering what could have been between them if she'd only given them a chance?

"You shouldn't be here." She crossed her arms over her chest. "I don't want you here."

"I know," he said agreeably, "and I love that you—a human—want to protect me, a vampire. Bashing me over the head and leaving me behind was actually a pretty romantic thing to do, Bree. In a fucked-up kind of way."

"Don't tease, Alex. This is not your fight."

"The hell it isn't. You're involved, that means I'm involved."

"I can't think when you're around," she complained, squelching the flare of pleasure his words gave her.

"You can't tell me that you don't feel better with me here." *You can't lie to me.*

A bright pinpoint beam of blue light cut through the trees.

"It's James," Bree whispered. "It's time."

"I know." Alex's thumb brushed across her bottom lip. "You're nervous. Don't be. Your family is safe."

"What?" She stared up into his beautiful face and knew without a doubt that the vamp was not only telling the truth, but he was also crazy about her. Something inside her melted.

Feel that?

"Yes." He was there, in her thoughts. A warm, loving, comforting presence.

I'll be with you the whole time. You let me handle the muscle, okay?

"I didn't hire you to go this far, Alexei. I don't want you hurt or injured. I-I couldn't bear it."

He lowered his head and took her mouth. The desperation in his kiss, the deep licks of his tongue, the shaking hands that cupped her face… It all broke her heart. She leaned into him, aligning her curves to his hardness, sharing her heat with his much cooler body.

I hate this, Bree. I can't bear to have you in danger. I wish there was another way. Any other way.

But there wasn't and they both knew it.

She pulled back reluctantly. Then following the urgings of her heart, she surged against him again and pressed a lingering kiss to his lips that said all the things she couldn't find the words for.

I love you, he replied, his voice husky and raw in her mind.

She left him, brushing tears from her lashes.

As Briana made her way through the brush to the hub below, she had the portentous feeling that something horrible was going to happen. And though Alex tried to reassure her, she knew he felt it too.

Chapter Seven

Alex watched Bree move with graceful efficiency down to the busy hub while the hunger within him howled at her loss. His fear for her caused his chest to heave with labored breaths and nearly destroyed his sanity. The woman he loved was walking straight into danger and he could only stand here, helpless.

Her thoughts and affection echoed in his mind, filling his heart with both joy and despair. She didn't love him, not like he loved her, but the possibility was there and he tucked that tiny promise close to his heart. If they could get through this mission, he'd find a way to be with her. Whatever the cost.

Closing his eyes, Alex sensed the other vamp corps agents around him, but the Shinite assassin, if he or she was down there, remained focused and therefore undetectable.

Briana was out in the open. Dressed in the trappings of her rank, she stood out and made an obvious target. There were built-in shields in her official garment, which would protect her from most indirect blaster fire, but it would never stave off the full assault of a laser sword and she had no protection from a direct shot to her head. His only comfort was the thought that she would be useless to them dead. Perhaps the attempt in Thieves' Cove had simply been a warning. He had to believe it was, because if he didn't, there was no way in hell he'd let her go down there.

Shaking off the foreboding that wouldn't leave him, he studied the buildings below. The transport hub was built in the universal design—four outlying concourses with an open-air center courtyard easily reached by any of four intersecting pathways. On planets with more dangerous atmospheres, the courtyard would be covered in UV-deflecting glass, but Tolan was known for its fresh air which was maintained by the abundance of golden-treed forests. It was a beautiful world and one he'd like to explore with Bree.

With that thought in mind, Alex slipped through the brush and leapt to the nearest rooftop. From his vantage in the darkness, he had an unhindered view of the brightly lit courtyard below. Crowds milled around Bree, who waited by the row of public comm links. He released the hunger to heighten his senses. He tuned out the steady paging of flight information and heard only the quickened rate of Bree's breathing and the rapid thudding of her heart.

His gaze raked restlessly over the people and he stiffened as several stopped to speak with Briana, whose public persona slipped over her with ease, despite the situation. Before his eyes, she changed from the passionate beauty he knew so intimately into a reserved politician, but whatever guise she wore he loved her just the same. What a fascinating woman she was, cut with so many facets, a person he admired more than any other being in the universe.

Despite his unwavering attention to Bree and the people conversing with her, in the back of his mind Alex maintained the awareness of the other agents assigned to back him up. They moved among the busy throng undetected. Like him, they didn't know what to expect. Because they were vamps, they were as cognizant of him as he was of them, and they queried him about why he was there and what he was doing. He brushed them off impatiently.

Pay attention to Michaels, he growled.

The comm closest to Bree began to beep and she excused herself from her admirers. Alex's muscles tensed so tightly with fear and apprehension they ached.

Something wasn't right. The tiny hairs on his nape stood on end and an icy sweat misted upon his skin.

As she picked up the phone, he caught a fleeting glimpse of a blue laser sight as it brushed over her golden chignon.

His heart nearly exploded in his chest.

Get down! he yelled as he drew his blaster and leapt from the roof.

His body stretched out and flew through the air, rapidly traversing the distance between them. In mindless horror he saw Bree turn toward him in surprise and the brilliant blue light settled directly over her heart.

The blood roaring through his ears made hearing impossible. Alex released an inhuman scream of agony as the light grew brighter and then flashed, leaving behind a gaping hole in her chest. The gap between them lessened with torturous slowness and he could only watch as she crumbled before him...

The moment before he was engulfed in a net.

Bound and helpless, he crashed to the ground. He howled, his claws ripping through the netting in his panic. Bree lay a few steps away, unmoving as her precious blood flowed freely from her wound to stain the stone floor of the courtyard.

"That's the vamp assassin! Tranq him before he escapes!"

Sharp stings pelted his thigh. Once. Twice. His pain and rage escaped in cries that rent the air while frightened travelers scattered madly, leaving him alone with the woman he loved so desperately. Unable to look away or reach her, Alex was arrested by the sight of Briana, her beautiful face still and pale in repose. Lost in anguish, he scarcely registered the local authorities who fired tranquilizer darts at him from several meters away.

While Bree lay dying with no one to care for her.

He fought the net like a man possessed, but the more he struggled the more entangled he became. His vision faded, his muscles grew weak. He reached for her mind and found nothing but darkness. Inside him the despair was killing him, his heart so shattered he wished he could die.

"He matches the description exactly..."

"…a known criminal and smuggler…"

"…tip came in about an assassination attempt…we'd hoped to prevent…"

"She's not going to make it…"

"We're losing her…"

Alex sank into hell with a vision of blue laser light burned in his mind.

Chapter Eight

೧

"How did you know?" Derek asked.

Alex stood at the window of the Council embassy on Tolan, and took in the view of the brightly lit city and the night sky above. The horror of the previous week's events would be forever burned onto his memory. He simply wanted to crawl between sheets still scented of Bree and sleep forever. An eternity without her was far too agonizing to consider.

"The blue laser," he replied in a choked voice. "The droid used it earlier to signal Briana in the woods. When I saw it again I realized James had to be responsible. I'm glad I got that thought across before I lost consciousness."

Derek spun his chair around to look at him. "Beaumont was able to track the droid programmer through the database files you forwarded to him. The woman responsible for corrupting the sex bot was apprehended last week, not long after the altercation in the transport hub."

Swallowing hard, Alex's hands clenched into fists. The authorities had shot him so full of tranquilizers he'd been asleep for a week, preventing him from personally seeing to the capture of the culprit responsible for Bree's death.

"The programmer is a member of a relatively small faction of vamp haters. Apparently, when she realized who she was preparing the droid for, she seized the opportunity of a lifetime. She programmed the sex bot to kill Michaels in a way guaranteed to shed no suspicion on herself. From there the droid took over. It chose a vamp to blame and picked a busy public venue—like Thieves' Cove and then the transport hub—so there could be no doubt that you were responsible. The plan would have worked if you'd been the criminal it thought you were."

"Can I go now?" Alex asked, his voice hoarse. Who the hell cared about the droid or the bitch who programmed it? Ever since he'd woken up, all he'd wanted was to be left alone to grieve. Instead he'd been ordered to see Derek immediately.

"I need to discuss your next assignment. I'm transferring you to—"

"I don't fucking care, Derek!" he shouted, turning away from the window. "She's dead. I don't care about assignments. I don't care about the corps. I don't give a shit about anything." He stalked toward the door.

"Night. Damn it! Wait a minute."

"Go to hell, Atkinson." Alex slammed the door behind him.

His vision blurred as he ran with inhuman speed and endurance from the embassy to his ship. His heart throbbed with a sharp, endless ache and he screamed out his agony as he flew through the golden-leafed woods. The beast within him howled and clawed to get out, and he released it with relief, eager to tear apart anything that got in his way. He leapt from tree to tree, his claws sinking easily into the solid bark, marking his trail with scars that mirrored the ones on his heart.

He wanted off this planet, this place that Bree had called home. He wanted to pick a fight with someone, anyone who had the skills to end his misery. And he knew just where to go to make that happen.

Reaching his ship, Alex leapt inside before the ramp finished lowering. He landed in a crouch and took a deep breath, his nostrils filling with the scent of his lost love. Surrounded by cold metal, the memories of Bree warmed the space—echoes of laughter and throaty cries of pleasure that drove him insane.

Bree! he cried, shuddering with the depth of his pain. He felt her so keenly here, in the place where he'd loved her.

Following his instincts, he flew down the corridor and into his room. He leapt onto the velvet-draped bed and paused, his senses bombarded with the lingering essence of Briana. Closing his eyes, he pictured her loveliness spread across his sheets — the wild blonde curls on red satin, the sweetly parted lips that knew just how to please him, the heavy-lidded eyes that begged for more...he could almost hear her giggling as he tickled her and her smart-ass comments when he teased her...he could feel her hands on his skin, caressing and kneading...

In such a short time, they'd shared so much. Lost in bittersweet memories, he was openly vulnerable and completely unprepared for the tackle that came from behind.

Astonished, he reacted without thought, rolling across the large bed and pinning his attacker. Fangs fully bared and eager for a fight, he snarled, ready to kill. Instead he froze in shock.

"Bree?"

The momentary hesitation was all she needed. Throwing her leg over his hip, she twisted, taking the advantage. Beautifully naked, she straddled him and smiled, her beloved face framed with riotous golden locks. Dumbfounded, Alex glanced at her chest and saw the healing, fist-sized scar above her left breast. He touched it hesitantly, consumed with guilt that he'd failed to protect her.

"Hi, baby," she said in a soft, breathy voice.

And then she bit him with her fangs.

Alex arched upward and hissed as the temporary discomfort melted into heated lust and endless relief. His cock swelled painfully, filling with his need for her.

Bree! He crushed her to him with pure, unadulterated joy while his stunned mind struggled to make sense of it all.

She was a vamp. Like him. Not gone. Not lost. But wonderfully, vibrantly, marvelously real.

Hush, she soothed, undulating her lithe body over his, rubbing the hard points of her nipples across his vest-covered chest.

How?

One of the other agents saved me. I'd lost so much blood, it was the only way.

No one told me.

President Atkinson commed me when you left his office. He thought you knew.

As she fed, she replayed the events of the past week in his mind while her soft silken hair brushed across his cheek. Awed by the feel of her, Alex arched his throat into her suckling mouth.

I love you, he moaned, intoxicated by the smell of her and the delight of finding she was not gone forever.

She lifted her head, licked her fangs and arched a wicked brow. "I trust you to protect me, Alexei. I want you to know that. You're assigned to me now, as my personal pilot and guard."

Alex swallowed hard and shook his head. "I failed you."

"No, you didn't. You defied a direct order and sent your friend to protect my sister. No one could have done any more than you did." She smoothed his brow. "I won't take 'No' for an answer."

"Oh, hell," he breathed, a single tear slipping down his temple. His hands ran restlessly up and down her thighs. "Tell me I haven't succumbed to grief-induced delirium."

"Nah, you're not crazy," she said, her fingertips drifting across his chest and teasing the flat points of his nipples through his vest. "But I wouldn't mind if you got a little wild. I'm a vamp now. I can take it."

He reached up and brushed her curls back. "How do you feel about that? You seem to have taken to feeding without any trouble."

"You're yummy, babe. I've always thought so."

"That's nice to know." Alex studied her features intently and searched her mind. She was putting on a brave face and trying to play it off, but she was still adjusting mentally and physically to the drastic change in her lifestyle. His love brushed across her jumbled thoughts soothingly.

Sighing, she sat back and settled over his aching cock. "Well, the way I see it is, I have this gorgeous vamp who just happens to have fallen in love with me."

"Lucky girl."

"Yes, I am. However, there was a slight caveat."

"Oh?"

"See, he was destined for an eternity of heart-stopping hotness and I... Well, I was going to turn into a wrinkled old hag. Sucking blood was the least I could do to keep him interested."

The tip of his finger slid down the valley between her breasts. "I bet he would love you anyway, no matter what you looked like."

Bree's eyes turned soft and liquid with adoration. "You know," she murmured in a husky voice. "I think he would have."

"Damn straight." He lifted her palm to his lips. "But I'm still not reassured. What about your career?"

She shrugged. "I was pretty solidly situated in my seat and being a vamp won't change that. PR-wise, it's not as newsworthy for a vamp to champion the vampire cause as it is for a human to do it, but oh well. I am what I am."

"And I love what you are," he promised her. "I lust for what you are. If you need to talk about it though, I'm here. Becoming a vamp is a big transition, sweetness."

"I know." Her nose wrinkled. "But let's talk about you right now. You were pretty upset when you came on board."

"I thought you were dead."

"You got it for me bad, don't you?"

"Really bad. Horribly bad."

Briana sighed. "You know for a guy with your reputation, you're awfully romantic."

"Shut up and kiss me, and then let me fuck you senseless. Is that better?"

She grinned. *First, you'll have to catch me!*

And the next instant she was gone.

Alex blinked at the spot where she'd just been. "What the hell?" he shouted, rising on his elbows. Damn it! She'd been naked in his bed and—

You'll have to hunt for me, Alexei.

Why? he grumbled. *Haven't I been through enough already?*

You should have told me you were STF.

But then the droid would have known, he said defensively.

Yes, yes, I know. But it was driving me mad trying to think of ways to keep you.

Awwww, Bree. That's so sweet.

I've got something sweet for you, baby. Right here.

He growled. *Are you sure you're ready? You've got to be a little weak.*

Are you scared? she taunted.

Are you kidding? He rolled from the bed, and shucked his trousers and vest. *I'm horny. And hungry.*

Come and get it then.

Leaping to the ceiling, Alex closed his eyes and let the hunger loose.

It burst free with a roar of triumph. Strong and powerful, it wanted its woman, wanted the taste of her on his tongue and the feel of her hot, tight cunt gripped like a fist around his cock. Crawling over the doorjamb, Alex moved down the corridor, following the scent of Bree's potent arousal. He took his time, silence being the key.

What's taking you so long? she complained.

Miss me?

I thought you'd be all over it.

Oh, trust me, sweetheart. I will be.

Undetected, he hovered over where she crouched in the padded training room. Bree chewed her lower lip and grumbled impatiently. He rolled his eyes. She had so much to learn about hunting and hiding.

Without warning, he dropped gracefully beside her.

She screeched in surprise. "How the hell…?"

"Gotcha!" he cried, triumphant.

Before he knew what hit him, she'd tossed him over her shoulder and was running down the corridor. "Nope. *I* got *you*."

"Hey!" he protested, laughing.

"You took too damn long. I'm horny." Bree threw him on the bed and pounced over him.

"Ah, back where we started."

"Yes, but now you're buck naked."

His mouth curved as his entire being filled with happiness. "What are you going to do about it?"

Her flashing red eyes revealed her hunger. "Finish what I started."

"Yum."

Briana bent her head and licked his nipple, her eyes closing as if she savored the taste of him. "Ummm… Definitely yum."

"Do that again," he urged.

She turned her head and her hot, lush lips enclosed his other nipple. Her tongue swirled and he gasped in pleasure, wishing desperately for her to perform the same service to rest of him.

Anything you want, she purred. Her taut, ripe breasts scraped across the ripples of his abdomen as she slid down the bed. *This mind-reading trick comes in handy, eh?*

The head of his shaft leaked its enjoyment as her breasts caressed the length of his cock. "Oh, man," he breathed. "I found a new favorite pleasure."

Her hot, wet tongue licked the drop of cum off the head of his shaft. He jerked and then shuddered as sharp needles of desire fired along his nerve endings.

"You're such a sensual creature," she murmured, her breath gusting across his skin in delicious torment. "It's one of the many things I love about you."

Alex closed his eyes at her words and sank farther into the pillows. His heart swelled as she took his cock deep into the haven of her mouth and suckled just the way he liked it. "Ah, sweetness." He groaned from deep in his throat. "You do that so well."

Humming, she caressed his length with her lips and then sucked him back inside. She repeated the movement, over and over, making him pant and clench the coverlet with grasping fists.

"Tell me you're wet," he gasped, on the verge of coming.

It wouldn't take much, she assured him.

Clutching her shoulders, he lifted her off him, her mouth leaving his cock with a wet popping sound.

"Oh," she cried as he flipped her and buried his face between her legs. "Oh *wow*."

Spreading her with his fingers, Alex dipped his tongue deep into her cunt. Her scent and flavor burst upon his senses in blinding brilliance, the added dimension of her vampirism appeasing the restless need of his hunger. She was hot and slick and quickly drenched, flooding his mouth until he groaned in desperation and ground his hips into the mattress.

"I-I'm wet now, Alex."

Are you ever.

"Uh…you can…you can stop now…and…oh hell, don't stop…" Bree arched her back. "Oh Alex…"

She came then, shivering beneath him, and he rose above her and thrust his cock deep into her grasping depths.

He shuddered at the silken feel of her and held himself still, gritting his teeth as she milked him in orgasm. Only when the tight tension of her tiny frame relaxed did he pull his cock out and then plunge in again.

Her nails scraped his sides and the quick stab of pain, combined with the heat of his lust and the depth of his love, broke the bonds that restrained his baser needs. He'd thought he'd lost her and now she was here, speared with his cock, mewling his name as he fucked her hard and deep. He growled and the rumbling warning had her eyes flying open in startled arousal.

"Yes," she encouraged, her voice raspy and low. "I can take it."

Alex pinned her hips, released his fangs and with all the hunger he possessed, claimed her body as his own to pleasure, his fangs sinking deep along with his cock.

The moment her blood flooded his mouth, he came. The taste of her life spilling down his throat spurred an orgasmic rush that threatened to kill him.

Screaming his name, writhing and scratching, Briana was more than enough for him, almost too much for him. What he'd thought would be a claiming was instead a matching. A joining of two beings destined one for the other.

Briana arched into his bite and wrapped long, lithe legs around his thrusting hips, meeting him stroke for stroke. He took her like an animal, his skin drenched in sweat, his aching erection unflagging despite the rapture of his release.

So much smaller than him, she was a damned tight fit, but she was built for his cock and took everything he gave her. Then begged for more. Sobbing and pleading, she demanded everything he was and he entered her mind with a rush of affection.

I love you, he cried with every cell in his body. He stiffened and roared, flooding her with his seed and his love until there was nothing more he could give her.

She fell with him into orgasm, hugging him close, and Alex felt that tiny promise within her flare into something far more powerful. A sentiment strong enough to take his fear and grief and her wary reticence, and banish them forever.

* * * * *

Later, tangled in the sheets and snuggled at his side, Briana turned her head and kissed his cooling skin.

Alex hummed, awash in contentment. He was exhausted and looked forward to sleeping with the love of his life in his arms.

"Awww..." She sniffled. "You are so romantic."

"I'll stop if you like."

"Don't you dare."

"If it bothers you—"

"It doesn't."

"I wouldn't want to—"

"If you quit, Alexei, I'll dump you. I swear."

"Well, we can't have that."

"No, we can't have that at all." She sighed and hugged him tight. "Promise me there won't be any more secrets between us."

He hugged her back hard. "I promise, sweetheart. There won't be anything between us. Ever."

It was silent for a while and then Alex said, "Bree?"

"Umm?"

"No more sex bots. Okay?"

"Could be interesting."

"No."

"Wouldn't you—"

"No. I wouldn't."

She laughed and his heart swelled at the sound. "I wouldn't either, you know. You're more than enough sex for me."

The compliment spoken in her well-sated voice stirred him again. "Does that mean you're done for now?"

"I thought you were sleepy."

"*I* am. But another part of me is not."

"Ooohh… I love that other part."

He gave a mock pout. "Just that other part?"

"Well, more than just that part," she conceded, tossing a leg over his hips.

"Don't keep me in suspense," he groaned. "What else do you love?"

"It would take me forever to name everything." She bent at the waist and kissed him, long and hard and wet and deep. He held her to him, her breasts to his chest, her hips to his, until she pulled far enough away to say with a smile, "Lucky for you, that's exactly how long we've got."

Enjoy An Excerpt From

ELLORA'S CAVEMEN: DREAMS OF THE OASIS II

TREASURE HUNTERS

Copyright © SYLVIA DAY, 2006

All Rights Reserved, Ellora's Cave Publishing, Inc.

∞

If the guy in her office weren't so damn gorgeous she might be able to think properly. But he was yummy. In fact, he was so unbelievably handsome Samantha was staring, something that was brought to her attention by the long, masculine fingers snapping in front of her face.

"Miss Tremain." His deep voice, though soft, was filled with exasperation. "Are you listening to me?"

"Beg your pardon?" She blinked rapidly.

He exhaled and took the seat in front of her desk. Crossing one ankle over the opposite knee, he bared to her view an impressive bulge behind the tightened lacings of his pants.

"Animal," she breathed. The bulge jerked in response.

"Huh?"

Sam coughed into her hand as her face heated. "A-animal skin."

"Yeah. It is." Bright blue eyes flashed briefly before narrowing. "I was told that you're the foremost expert on literary antiquities in this part of the galaxy, Miss Tremain. Is that right or should I be looking for help elsewhere?"

"Mr. Bronson—"

"Rick."

"Oh…" The way he said his own name, like it was a sensual threat, made her shiver. And the way he was dressed, in animal skin and some billowing material for a shirt, made her mouth dry. "Why aren't you wearing a bio-suit?"

A dark brow rose. "You want to talk about my clothes?" He shook his head. "You brainy types are always a little weird."

"Look who's talking," she retorted, stung by his comment, one which she'd heard a thousand times. "You are a twenty-third-century mercenary who dresses in nineteenth-century clothing while tracking down a legendary twenty-first-century treasure. Shouldn't you be doing something else? Killing for hire or something of that nature?"

Blowing a loose tendril of hair from her face, Sam stood and began to pace. As long as she didn't look at that breathtaking face, she could keep her wits about her. His dark hair, tan skin and eyes like the Laruvian Ocean were bad enough. When you added in the broad shoulders, tapered hips and animal skin-covered bulge, she had a living wet dream sitting right in her office.

Rick Bronson chuckled and the warm sound of amusement made her womb clench. "Whatever a mercenary does, he does for credits. Hunting treasure is a hunt for credits. Pretty easy to figure out."

"But why this particular treasure?"

"It's worth a fortune."

"It's *rumored* to be worth a fortune. Just as it's *rumored* to exist. You're most likely wasting your time." She hazarded a side glance and her heart skipped a beat at his soft smile. "It seems an odd treasure for a man to hunt for. Why not the Draken Cup? Or the Sarian Stone? Why the erotic e-books?"

"That's a silly question." The curve of his lips deepened. "You know how much those Romantica stories are worth. Ever since the Conservative Censorship Committee succeeded in banning erotica and erotic romance back in 2015 it's almost impossible to find. All the print books have long since turned into dust, but the remaining e-books that manage to make it to the black market bring in a small fortune. Can you imagine how much a database full of those stories would be worth?"

Sam sighed with longing. "Now that the ban has been revoked, finding those stories would not only return literary treasures to the people, but it would help lift this sexual repression that has stifled us all for so long."

"You sound like a woman who appreciates the erotic," Rick purred. He stood and came toward her, his gait slow and filled with seductive promise. The blaster strapped to one thigh and the laser sword strapped to the other only emphasized how dangerous he was. Against the backdrop of her small office, he was even more intimidating. And tantalizing.

Why an electronic book?

We live in the Information Age—an exciting time in the history of human civilization, in which technology rules supreme and continues to progress in leaps and bounds every minute of every day. For a multitude of reasons, more and more avid literary fans are opting to purchase e-books instead of paper books. The question from those not yet initiated into the world of electronic reading is simply: *Why?*

1. *Price.* An electronic title at Ellora's Cave Publishing and Cerridwen Press runs anywhere from 40% to 75% less than the cover price of the exact same title in paperback format. Why? Basic mathematics and cost. It is less expensive to publish an e-book (no paper and printing, no warehousing and shipping) than it is to publish a paperback, so the savings are passed along to the consumer.

2. *Space.* Running out of room in your house for your books? That is one worry you will never have with electronic books. For a low one-time cost, you can purchase a handheld device specifically designed for e-reading. Many e-readers have large, convenient screens for viewing. Better yet, hundreds of titles can be stored within your new library—on a single microchip. There are a variety of e-readers from different manufacturers. You can also read e-books on your PC or laptop computer. (Please note that Ellora's Cave does not endorse any specific brands. You can check our websites at www.ellorascave.com or

www.cerridwenpress.com for information we make available to new consumers.)

3. *Mobility*. Because your new e-library consists of only a microchip within a small, easily transportable e-reader, your entire cache of books can be taken with you wherever you go.

4. *Personal Viewing Preferences.* Are the words you are currently reading too small? Too large? Too… ANNOYING? Paperback books cannot be modified according to personal preferences, but e-books can.

5. *Instant Gratification.* Is it the middle of the night and all the bookstores near you are closed? Are you tired of waiting days, sometimes weeks, for bookstores to ship the novels you bought? Ellora's Cave Publishing sells instantaneous downloads twenty-four hours a day, seven days a week, every day of the year. Our webstore is never closed. Our e-book delivery system is 100% automated, meaning your order is filled as soon as you pay for it.

Those are a few of the top reasons why electronic books are replacing paperbacks for many avid readers.

As always, Ellora's Cave and Cerridwen Press welcome your questions and comments. We invite you to email us at Comments@ellorascave.com or write to us directly at Ellora's Cave Publishing Inc., 1056 Home Avenue, Akron, OH 44310-3502.

The
⚱ ELLORA'S CAVE ⚱
Library

Stay up to date with Ellora's Cave Titles in Print with our Quarterly Catalog.

To recieve a catalog,
send an email with your name
and mailing address to:

CATALOG@ELLORASCAVE.COM

or send a letter or postcard
with your mailing address to:

Catalog Request
c/o Ellora's Cave Publishing, Inc.
1056 Home Avenue
Akron, Ohio 44310-3502

Got Sex?

Share it with the world or just make a BOLD statement in the bedroom with an Ellora's Cave Got Sex? T-shirt.

$14.99

The world's largest e-publisher of Erotic Romance.

ELLORA'S CAVE PUBLISHING, INC.
WWW.ELLORASCAVE.COM

Cerridwen, the Celtic Goddess of wisdom, was the muse who brought inspiration to storytellers and those in the creative arts. Cerridwen Press encompasses the best and most innovative stories in all genres of today's fiction. Visit our site and discover the newest titles by talented authors who still get inspired - much like the ancient storytellers did, once upon a time.

Cerridwen Press
www.cerridwenpress.com

Discover for yourself why readers can't get enough of the multiple award-winning publisher

Ellora's Cave.

Whether you prefer e-books or paperbacks,

be sure to visit EC on the web at
www.ellorascave.com

for an erotic reading experience that will leave you breathless.